ACKNOWLEDGMENTS

No one ever writes a first novel without the help and cheerleading of friends and colleagues. I would like to thank the following experts who helped me with many factual questions about the jobs they do: Suzy Owens, Ames, Iowa, police detective; Bill Feithen, Monmouth Police Chief; John Cratty, former Monmouth Fire Chief; Bill Underwood, Warren County Coroner; and Becky Tracy Whitemore, graphic artist, for her invaluable technical help.

Also, I must thank the sharp eyes, ears, and brains of my "first-responder" readers: Susan, Lisa, and Hallie. Finally, I owe a debt of thanks to Lourdes Venard, my faithful first editor. She helped guide me through the intricacies of editing with expertise and professionalism.

PROLOGUE

Wednesday, November 26, 1975

She never saw her death coming.

Like a filmy silk scarf falling through the air in slow motion — gliding, twisting, turning — the whiff of smoke floated silently into her thoughts. Her unconscious mind struggled to remember where she was . . . a bonfire making s'mores with her Girl Scout friends . . . a fire on the lakeshore with Roger . . . a failed attempt at smoking in college . . . college . . .

She coughed abruptly and felt as if she were inhaling feathers. Or dust. Or — smoke. It was hard to get her breath in. Her nose smelled an acrid, heavy odor. She couldn't see, couldn't get her eyes open. Finally, her eyelashes fluttered, unstuck, and immediately her eyes stung. Darkness. Thickness. A feeling of suffocation. She tried to clear her throat, not to panic, to force some air in and out. Suffocating. No sound.

I have to get out. Adrenaline kicked in. She dragged herself to the edge of the bed and rolled off, falling hard onto a small rug. Her feet battered on college textbooks she'd abandoned on the floor. Her fall expelled more air from her lungs. She inched on her stomach across the floorboards, trying to take in tiny, rasping breaths. The throw rug slid along with her as she pressed her way under the thick, strangling smoke. Her legs were shaking. *Where was the door? Which way was her desk, her chair?* She tried to relax her throat, to swallow, to choke in some air. She couldn't scream or call for help because her voice wouldn't work. Her fingernails helped her inch across the bare floorboards until they touched a wall. *Or was it the door?* She squeezed her eyes and opened them a sliver, and saw a small opening between the wall and the floor — a door. She slid her hands into the space and tried to move it — a little sideways give. *The closet. It was the sliding door to her closet. Maybe inside. If she could get inside and breathe some air she could think, get her bearings.*

Another surge of smoke washed over her in the darkness and it felt like a layer of

8

smothering waves. *I can't do this. How am I ever . . . No. Find the bedroom door, the way out. It had to be to her left, past the desk and the chair and the lamp cord.* Her lungs panted in quick, short breaths. She twisted around, still trying to draw in what little oxygen was near the floor. A light through the darkness, a thin, grotesquely colored line. Red. She crawled toward the light — the door that must lead to the stairwell. She was gasping again and her eyes were slivers of pain. She pushed herself the last few inches and wrapped her fingers up through the slit of light under the door. It scorched her hands and she yanked them away, silently screaming. Her heart beat rapidly as she tried to take in short breaths.

Regroup. The window. She pressed her way to the left, toward the south side of her room. *Not to panic. Calm. Don't get flustered. Feel your way.* Blood was rushing to her head and she was covered in sweat. Her muscles were tense and her heart was pounding. *This is so hard. I can't. I can't.* She gasped again, her lungs on fire, and tried to take a breath but couldn't. She covered her mouth to ward off the smoke. Nothing came into her dry throat but a velvet coating. *I can't.*

9

And then she gave up. *Exhaled. Shut down.*
Silence. Darkness.

CHAPTER ONE:
GRACE

Wednesday, June 15, 2011

"Time to celebrate! Second retirement in our venerable and seasoned group. Here's to you, Grace," and Jill Cunningham raised her wine glass high and pointed toward the guest of honor. Grace, TJ, and Deb followed suit and clinked their glasses. "We oughta go out again tonight for margaritas. Anybody in?"

"Depends," Grace said, eyeing Jill. "By 'seasoned' do you mean 'spicy' or 'old'?"

She glanced at the women around the table — TJ Sweeney, Deb O'Hara, and Jill Cunningham. In this perfect summer setting with her friends, the dream that had kept her up half the night — the one about the terrible fire — seemed benign. She released her held-in breath and felt her muscles relax.

It was a perfect day in Endurance, Illinois, where Grace Kimball had lived among

11

15,000 souls since her arrival as a newlywed years ago. At noon on the Endurance Public Square, the sun was shining and the temperature was in the low 70s. The square, the center of town with surrounding businesses and shops, was more a circle than a square. No one knew the official rules for driving around it, so defensive driving was the local custom. This was particularly true since Danny Walker, after a few beers at Patsy's Pub, decided to cruise the square multiple times in the wrong direction and took out a fire hydrant and two signs for the Little People's Daycare Center and Bert's Collision Shop ("You Scratch It, We Patch It"). The only thing Danny missed was the neon "Open" sign for the Homestretch Funeral Home, but the hazy memory of seeing it go past several times undoubtedly contributed to his contrition once he sobered up.

The square was decked out for Flag Day with five huge flags billowing in the breeze. An ancient fountain, part of Endurance's history, gurgled in an endless stream of water that flowed from one platform to the next. Nearby, maple trees and ornamental bushes surrounded four wooden benches, and a plastic sign — stretched between two poles — announced the goal for the Red Cross fund and displayed a giant thermometer whose painted mercury rose toward its goal in shades of varying red increments.

Up and down the streets, summer had finally returned after the long, snowy, gray-skied Illinois winter. Even the air smelled clean and revived. The library windows were decked out with children's artwork and announcements about the summer reading program. Across the street Gimble's Paint and Wallpaper Store announced a 30% off Summer Extravaganza Sale, its sidewalk tables stacked with boxes of wallpaper borders and overstocked rolls. A deluge of summer annuals spilled out of huge pots that lined the walkways. Everyone breathed a sigh of relief that summer was finally here and school was out.

Off to the south of the square, on a small side alley, sat round umbrella tables with matching chairs for the first café of the summer. Nearby, a temporary wooden platform with a microphone and a row of chairs waited at attention. Artistically draped red, white, and blue bunting hung around the platform, and a city worker busily taped down the microphone cable, hoping to keep the town's liability insurance intact. Scattered throughout the alley, in smaller circles bordered by red bricks, were groups of white and yellow daisies. People milled around, quietly talked in small groups, and waited to hear the mayor's annual address.

"How'd the last few days go at school?" asked Deb. "Kids treat you well? Glad to be done with them? I know how they used to treat me in the junior high office. Better to retire to the Historical Society and volunteer than to keep dealing with the militant parents storming the front doors." She thought for a moment and then giggled. "By now they probably arrive in tanks."

Grace laughed too and then she looked away from her friends. "Actually, I still tear up a bit. Several teacher friends stopped by my room to say goodbye. Suddenly, it was the last day of school and I hugged the kids and the next day it was over. Twenty-five years at Endurance High School. Done. Just like that. Like I said, don't get me started or I'll cry again." She reached for some salsa, avoiding their eyes.

TJ glanced up at Grace. "Give yourself some time, Grace. After the same schedule for all those teacher years you need to take some time to get your act together."

Jill tried a tactical change of subject. "Grace, why don't you consider volunteering a few hours a week at the Historical Society like Deb?"

Grace's anxiety eased and she gave them

a playful grin. "Deb, Jill — and everyone else with plans for my life — I know you have the best intentions, keeping me busy and all, but —"

Before Grace could finish, a young waitress shuffled to their table and placed a salad in front of each of them. Grace noted her face as she leaned over, depositing dishes. *Another one she remembered. Lacey Lancing. Probably about twenty-three. Has two kids and is married to a guy who works for the Department of Transportation. Terrible speller. Did her research paper on whether the Loch Ness Monster — spelled "Lock Nest Monstir" — could be related to Big Foot.*

Shaking that cobweb out of her head, Grace recalled their retirement discussion. She asked casually, "TJ, you're a detective so you solve mysteries. Any job you want me to do at the police department? Everyone else is trying to put me to work."

"Let me give that some thought. I don't doubt you could pass the police exam, but I'd tremble in my boots to see a gun in your hand, Grace. Besides, you'd probably correct their grammar instead of reading them their rights before you cuffed them."

"Ladies, ladies, we're forgetting the subject." Jill, her squiggly red hair bouncing, along with her animated face, always drew them back into focus. "I think we need a little project for the summer, an entirely new plan so we can keep Grace from becoming bored. TJ, want to add any ideas? Maybe something without a gun involved?"

Grace quickly jumped in. "Stop talking about me as if I'm not here, please. Actually I'm going to write a novel. I won't have time for any of your schemes. And, by the way, Jill, I'm launching a preemptive strike: *You* may run two miles a morning, but before you get any ideas, don't figure I'm going to join in."

Deb put her hand up and whispered, "Shh. Mayor's starting to talk."

Fifteen minutes later Mayor Blandford wound down his usual rambling, patriotic speech about their noble history. His bald head was getting shinier and a faint trace of sweat ringed his shirt collar as he stretched his rotund, five-foot, five-inch frame to meet the microphone clutched in his pudgy hands.

"And so, my fellow citizens, after that first harrowing winter, when so many of our glorious ancestors died, the remaining band of hardy Scotch Presbyterians survived and named our illustrious town 'Endurance.' " He jabbed a finger in the air for emphasis.

Jill leaned toward her friends and whispered, "And to this day we have *endured* Mayor Blandford's blather as he babbles on for fifteen minutes at our Flag Day luncheon. By the way, I could use that Scotch he mentioned."

"Shh," cautioned Deb, but suppressing a giggle.

"And now it's on to our septaquintaques — ah — septequis — ah, okay, wait a minute while I stop and think about this darn word." The mayor glanced down at his notes, his glasses perched on the tip of his nose, his lips moving silently, and his demeanor impatient. "All right, folks. I think I got it. And now it's on to our septa-quinta-quin-que-centennial celebration." His face beamed.

"Is that a word, Grace?" asked Jill.

"Not a clue."

"On July 30, 1836," declared Mayor Blandford, his pace picking up with words he could actually pronounce, "our fair city was recognized by the territorial government exactly one hundred seventy-five years ago this summer. So we will soon be celebrating our town's septaquisicalquin — geez. Sesquecetinen —" He took a deep breath, removed his reading glasses, and put down his notes. Exasperated, he trudged on. "Anyway, folks, it's our anniversary and we're gonna do it up big. So we'll need some volunteers to be on the various committees to plan and execute this solemn endeavor. My administrative assistant, Tilly Thompson, is right over here." He pointed to his left at a matronly, silver-haired lady with an enormous red, white, and blue hat. She was holding a large clipboard and standing at attention next to a nearby table. "She'll come around and take your names and what you'd like to do. Let's make this work, people. And happy Flag Day!"

Applause sputtered, and Grace studied the expressions of her three friends who were giving her appraising glances.

Jill rubbed her hands together and blurted, "That's it! This project has landed in our laps. Come on, we can do this. It would be a great summer diversion. I'll sign us all up."

"Wait a minute. I protest! No volunteering me," Grace objected.

They were interrupted by the syrupy tones of Tilly Thompson, hat on head, clipboard in hand, patiently waiting and scanning the area for volunteers. "Ladies, would you like to help with the town's one hundred seventh-fifth? We have lots of committees — food, decorations, souvenir T-shirts, a parade, entertainment, flea circus, a real shootout and bank robbery, and period costumes. Any takers?"

"Sure," said Deb. "Put us all down for whatever you need."

"Especially Grace. She's retired."

"Just don't let her do the shootout."

Grace sputtered, "Now wait a —"

"That will be wonderful," chirped Tilly as if they had saved her life. "I'll get in touch with you when I'm all done and I can plug you into places we need help. Meanwhile, I'll scribble your names down." And she did just that with a pen made of a red, white, and blue feather. Then she stalked off in search of other prey.

"Thanks a lot!" Grace grumbled.

Jill countered, "What are friends for? It'll be fun. You'll see."

Suddenly, Deb touched Grace's arm, shuddered, and said in a shaky voice, "Oh, oh. Don't look now. Brenda Norris is heading straight toward our table. I hear she has a new editor at the newspaper."

The reporter's unmistakable, ear-splitting voice arrived far ahead of her physical presence. "Afternoon, girls," Brenda announced, and she stopped a foot from Grace and Jill. As Grace turned, she saw skinny-legged jeans and a threadbare, tight T-shirt that left little to the imagination. Glancing up, she noted Brenda's thin-lipped smile and calculating eyes. The reporter stuck a pencil back in her hair and looked up at Grace as if she'd suddenly remembered something. "Hey, I hear you've retired, Grace. Good for you! They'll have a hard time finding someone to take your place."

Grace wondered if she really meant that or if she was being sarcastic.

"Well, you know what I mean. They'll never be able to find someone as good as you. That old sleazebag, John Hardy. He's the worst principal I've ever tried to interview. Totally uncooperative, and when I mentioned 'Freedom of Information Act,' he had me escorted off the property by that goon who inhabits the office next to his. He really puts the 'ass' in assistant principal."

"I imagine they weren't anticipating a flattering story," Grace said, her voice quiet, and she became aware of a sudden hush from the tables nearby.

"I hear you have a new editor," TJ said.

Brenda looked up at the sky and rolled her eyes. "Oh, yeah, Mr.-New-York-City-I-know-everything guy. We'll see about that." She leaned toward Grace and TJ while looking around at the other tables. Then she lowered her voice and said in a tone both arrogant and snide, "I'm working on the biggest exposé ever. Huge secret. Blow the lid right off this town. I know things, and I figure it will win me a Pulitzer." She traced the headline in the air. "Brenda Norris, Pulitzer Prize for Investigative Journalism. I'll show this town. People won't laugh behind my back after this story."

Grace noticed that each time Brenda said something seemingly innocuous, her lips slid over her teeth into a narrow, calculating smile.

Jill stabbed at her salad without looking up. "Hope it all works out for you, Brenda."

"You'll see. Everyone will. They'll look at me with respect when this story breaks. And Deb, I'll see you at the historical place again this afternoon." Deb nodded — quick up and down movements — too afraid to say anything as Brenda turned and strode toward the square, grabbing the strap on her camera bag just before it slid down her shoulder.

A collective sigh broke the silence around the table.

Jill scowled. "You mark my words. That woman is trouble and she's going to find herself in legal hot water one of these days. News writer indeed! More like

unsubstantiated-rumors-and-gossip reporter."

Deb leaned in toward the table and whispered, "She's been spending days and weeks
looking up old articles from the newspapers
and journals at the Historical Society. Not
sure what she's researching. I just hate it
when I see her coming. It feels like the
temperature in the room drops ten degrees."
She shivered for effect.

TJ nodded. "Been to the jail too, going
through some cold cases that are so cold
they'll never be solved. She's pissed off —
excuse my French, Grace — an awful lot of
people in town."

Jill pressed her lips together and stared at
Brenda's retreating back. "After the story
where she implied Mike Sturgis's construction company used inferior materials, I
thought she'd ease off. But then she went
after police officers using their squad cars
during off-duty hours to do personal business and everyone is sure it was a total
fabrication. Who's next — the mayor?"

"You know," Grace began, "quite a few
years ago, before she worked at the newspaper, she used to teach with me. English.
Brenda was really good but a tough grader.
Kids gave her quite a time and so did the
parents. I always felt a little sorry for her

and tried to help her. But after some poor choices she made with terrible results — including her firing — she changed. It's as if she's on a crusade to get back at people she thinks have been responsible for her problems. But I'm afraid this mission she's on — digging up dirt on various people and their past history in the town — isn't going to solve those problems and sure isn't going to win her any friends."

"I'm not sure she's after friends," mumbled Deb. "I don't know where all this will end."

Jill took a sip of wine and set her glass decisively on the table. "She's a woman full of dark secrets and she's walking a fine line on the edge of disaster."

"You may be right — both of you," said Grace. "You know that old saying from Ben Franklin — 'Three may keep a secret — ' "

" ' — if two of them are dead,' " whispered Deb.

And then it was quiet.

Within seconds the calm was shattered as Grace's cell phone played the theme from *Jaws*.

"Ah, that's Lettie," announced Grace, and she touched the "answer" button.

Deb grabbed Jill's arm and whispered, "Her sister-in-law gets the theme from

Jaws?"

Jill raised both hands. "Ours is not to question why —"

"What? Who called?" Grace was silent again. "Sure. I'll be home soon," and she broke the connection.

"An emergency?" TJ questioned.

"Oh, that was Lettie. She's puttering around my kitchen making a pie. She declared it was an emergency because a man called me and wants me to call him back."

Deb, Jill, and TJ eyed each other.

"And this is a problem because — ?"

"When was the last time a man called me?"

"How long have I been alive?" TJ quipped. "Did she get the name by any chance?"

"Of course not. This is Lettie we're talking about."

"I'll have to check back with you later this afternoon," Deb surmised. "And then I'll call Jill."

TJ pointed to Jill. "And then you'll call me." She scraped her chair on the cement and dropped a few bills on the table.

Grace was quick to reply. "This sounds like that old telephone game. And with Lettie in the lead, the whole message will get so garbled that by the time it gets to TJ, I'll

be starring in a Jane Austen novel and elop-
ing by night to Gretna Green."

CHAPTER TWO

Grace took ten minutes to drive home instead of the usual five because she ended up behind Nub Swensen — license plate "Nub" — on the small-town streets doing fifteen mph. She considered how comforting it was to live in a small town where you knew people's license plates and even the identity of joggers by their running styles. But what gain she measured in familiarity was lost in miles per hour. "Can you drive any slower, Nub?" she bellowed at his flashing brake lights.

As she moved at a snail's pace and passed Endurance High School, her mind wandered to the empty school windows. Usually summer break was an opportunity to recharge her ambition so she could once again teach ninety high school students in the sweat-drenched, late summer days of August. She sighed and slid a little lower in the car seat. This fall would be different.

She pulled into her driveway and sat in her car, pensively staring at the house.

1036 Sweetbriar Court. She and Roger had bought the house right after they married, and although it had undergone various alterations over the years, it still reflected moments of their lives together. Roger's practice was thriving, their three children were born healthy, and Grace was into the nurturing phase of her life.

A Victorian house, it had white wooden siding and dark red brick masonry. Grace had planted Siberian iris and black-eyed Susans on the south end of the lot near a small, decorative corner of white wooden fencing. She could still picture her daughter Katherine in her sunbonnet and tiny shoe — one missing as usual — diligently helping her pat down the dirt with her tiny toddler hands.

She and Roger had both loved the wrap-around porch, protected from the rain by overhanging eaves. Beneath the bay window, Grace could see her red and pink rose bushes as they reached toward the morning sun on the east side of the house. Evenings, they had often sat on the floral cushioned chairs and discussed his day at the law office and their children.

Grace reached for the door handle of her

car but was stopped by a more somber memory. A heavy sigh escaped her lips. That idyllic, small-town life was suddenly shattered when Roger died at age thirty-five — too young — of a heart attack. She was lost for months after that. She walked around in a daze, her friends helping with the children and whispering in quiet tones. She remembered the day her sister-in-law, Lettie, gave her a verbal slap, telling Grace that the children needed her and she would have to decide whether to live her life or allow others to raise her family. So a year after her husband's death, Grace began teaching and the job healed her. It took her out of herself, and helping others learn gave her a life again.

She spent evenings sitting on this side porch alone, grading papers and occasionally drinking a glass of good wine. The cozy porch boasted a long wooden swing, several deep containers of geraniums, hanging pots with petunias clinging over the edges, and a tall basket that used to hold baseball bats and other sports equipment. From this spot — even now — she could see the children's tree house still sitting on the fork of an oak tree in the backyard. A rope swing had hung down from one of the widespread branches of a maple tree, but only a few shreds of rope still clung stubbornly from the branch. This yard had witnessed hundreds of croquet matches, T-ball games, kick-the-can sessions, and hide-and-seek contests. Sometimes Grace believed she could hear the familiar and loved voices of her children calling "All in free!" if she listened hard enough. *That was a long time ago,* she thought.

Squaring her shoulders, she unlocked her front door and passed through the rooms to her favorite, the library, where she had made thoughtful changes to the masculine milieu several years after Roger's death. Gone was the leather sofa, replaced by a soft blue and white plaid couch and matching chairs. She had pulled out the old carpet and replaced it with hardwood floors covered with a navy area rug. The bookshelves housed Hawthorne, Poe, Thoreau, Emerson, Fitzgerald, and other books of authors she had loved, marked up, and used over the years in her classroom. The rows of law books she gave to a young attorney who had just opened his practice in Endurance. She glanced around her space, a perfect refuge for a bibliophile. Single. Alone.

Well, not completely alone. She could hear Lettie in the kitchen at the back of the house, humming to herself as she polished

29

this and washed that. Lettie moved in with Grace after Roger died, but once the children reached high school age, she bought a small brick bungalow a couple of blocks away. That move was good since Grace loved her sister-in-law but needed her space. Lettie could be mildly irritating — scratch "mildly" and think "often" — but she still came over to help, fussing over Grace, and considering Grace's home within her purview. The two women tolerated each other's foibles, but agreed on their most valuable connection — the children.

"I'm home, Lettie," Grace called out, sitting at a huge antique desk and caressing the smooth walnut surface. She had kept this favorite piece of Roger's. "Had a nice lunch with the girls."

A lean, spare Lettisha Kimball sauntered into the office with a dishcloth in one hand and a slightly wet frying pan in the other. Lettie had the energy of a thirty-year-old and was constantly on the move, even though she was twelve years older than Grace. A few brown spots on her cheeks and arms revealed the only evidence of her real age, freckles earned during years of sunshine while she worked in her massive garden. She sniffed a couple of times and glanced at an end table looking for dust.

Grace fired the opening volley. "Let me have it. I can tell your curiosity is eating away at you."

Lettie reached into an apron pocket and handed Grace a piece of notepaper.

She checked out the paper, saying, "It's just a number. Did you get a name?"

"Nope. He was gone before I could sneeze. It's a local number."

"Thanks, Lettie."

"So. Aren't you going to call and see who it is?"

"In due time. I have bills to pay first."

"Gracie, I really think this is a good sign. It reflects your horoscope for today. Wait, I'll go get it." She turned and walked briskly to the kitchen, setting the towel and pan down on a counter and grabbing yesterday's newspaper. Returning, she opened several pages with great relish and folded them back. "See, here it is." She pointed at the crinkled paper. " 'Scorpio: A promising endeavor is likely to be put together through a chain of unique circumstances involving someone from a distant place. This opportunity won't linger long, so take it!' "

"A distant place, huh. This is a local number, Lettie."

"I know, I know, but I'm sure this is a sign."

"Oh, please, Lettie. Remember when you told me a tall, dark stranger would come into my life? Funny how the horoscope left out the part about him being a plumber who came to fix the clogged toilet. Or the time we had that argument, and the horoscope you took great pleasure in reading to me said I had done someone a terrible injustice and should apologize? Honestly, I think you make these up."

"You mark my words, Gracie Kimball. The stars don't lie." And Lettie turned and stalked out of the room to her kitchen domain.

Grace scowled a moment at the name "Gracie." She hated Lettie's habit of changing her name. She began organizing the bills on her desk and pushed the power button on her laptop, but before she could send a single payment, she stopped, looked out the bay window and thought about the heap of sheets and tangled bedspread upstairs. Her nightmare began shortly after Roger's death. She recalled the fog of those days, planning his funeral, arranging for the cemetery plot, walking around in an incomprehensible blur. And their three children — eight, seven, and five — couldn't understand that their father wasn't coming home. Ever.

She shook herself back to the present.

Lettie shouted from the kitchen, "I'm leaving. You can call me when you find out who that man is."

Grace chuckled. *Of course I will. You'll be my first call — not.* "Sure, Lettie."

She pushed herself up, crossed the room, and perused the CDs on her bookshelf. Grabbing several, she loaded them in the player, and adjusted the volume. Billy Joel's "Piano Man" came on and Grace settled back at the desk. She picked up a pen and then laid it down again. Somehow she just couldn't concentrate today.

Probably that nightmare. She hadn't mentioned it at lunch. Why would it suddenly show up now? She glanced down at the jagged, pale scar on the back of her right hand. Mostly her fire dream had receded to the Siberian closets of her memory, only to return during times when she lost her nerve or couldn't seem to trust her instincts. She shivered despite the June warmth and was reluctant to even think about going to bed tonight.

Restlessly she got up and walked to her bookshelves where she had an entire shelf of old photos. She picked up one of her favorites, a photograph of her, Deb, Jill, and TJ having lunch on a day trip to Springfield.

Jill's Andrea was in fourth grade and Grace's Katherine was in third when they first met and struck up a friendship over their PTA work and their concerns for their children. Next to Jill was Deb, her arm tentatively on Jill's shoulder. She was the secretarial presence at the junior high when Grace stopped in with her children's forgotten lunches or gym clothes. Retired, Deb volunteered for various good causes and kept an eye on her husband, John, now that their two daughters were grown up and gone. TJ came last, much younger than the rest of them, her beautiful olive skin a result of her biracial mix. In the photo she was holding a glass of wine at a jaunty angle.

Back in the present, Grace considered the history of "the four." They had shared shopping trips, plays in Woodbury, disasters with children and husbands, worries about aging parents, recipes, and plans to lose weight or keep it off. After Roger died, Grace had found herself alone in a world of couples. But these friends had pulled her into their lives and didn't seem to mind that she was a "single." Now they found themselves — with the exception of TJ — comparing their children's problems and considering how to tactfully make suggestions about discipline, toilet training, and child care when it came to their grandchildren.

The CD player switched discs, bringing her back to the present, and Paul Simon's "Slip Slidin' Away." Grace listened to the lyrics for a few minutes. Lately she found herself thinking often about Roger. Perhaps it was because she always assumed they would grow old together. Now she was alone.

She weighed her decision to retire. After all, she was only fifty-six. It was simple. She had grown tired of marking the same commas on the same papers, day in and day out. Two weeks earlier she had cleared out her file cabinets, erased the whiteboards for the last time, piled up the textbooks in neat rows, emptied her desk drawers, and carted home only a few precious mementoes from a lifetime of teaching. That hadn't been so hard. She glanced out the window. The bad part was turning in her room keys, keys that had jingled in her pockets for twenty-five years. That was when she realized she was done. *Stop feeling sorry for yourself.*

She sat down at her desk and looked at the pile of bills again. Retired. The nagging thought of writing a novel kept tugging at her but she wasn't sure she could do it. Oh, well. She would think about it later, like Scarlett, at Tara.

A man called. Grace glanced at the number on the slip of paper. It looked familiar. Should she call? She felt apprehensive and then said out loud, "This is silly. Call the number."

She stood up, cell phone in hand, and glanced in the mirror on the office wall, the one with the beveled glass edging. She fingered the collar of her light blue blouse thoughtfully. Her face was remarkably unlined for the life she'd lived, and her brown eyes still sparkled. She took an inventory. *Shoulders back. Slightly crooked smile. Good skin. No plastic surgery.* Grace grinned and then touched her hair. "Maybe I should do something about that gray," she mouthed to no one in particular.

She pulled up the number pad on her phone, glanced at the paper, and took a deep breath. Tapping the numbers, she heard it ring twice, three times, and, well, maybe she should hang up.

Then a deep male voice answered.

CHAPTER THREE

Grace walked through the darkly tinted doors of Tully's around 6:45 that evening. She hadn't been here since Bill Tully had extensively renovated his interior. She remembered when Tully had first come to Endurance in the early nineties. Over the next twenty-some years he had steadily built up a business that drew from the town and the area.

She checked out the new décor. Flat-screen televisions occupied every corner, and the middle of every wall, and each was tuned to different games or a sports center show. As her eyes grew accustomed to the dim lighting, she saw seven or eight booths built along the edge of the interior and a dozen tables scattered throughout the middle. On the north wall were two sets of photos. One grouping of framed photos had local sports teams from the high school and she walked over and perused the pictures that probably came from the local newspaper, the *Endurance Register*. Some were photos of old buildings that had since been destroyed or reused as needed for new businesses. There was the Historical Society where Deb worked, retrieved from its debilitated state as a failed grocery store. Other photos were from events where the mayor was cutting a ribbon, and other pictures were of the Pork Festival Five-K run. Grace noticed historical photos of parades and the college and buildings destroyed by fires and old trolley tracks downtown. Tully had created quite a display.

A steady music beat escaped from wall speakers and black boxes hanging from the ceiling pipes. The music — Rod Stewart singing "As Time Goes By" — wasn't overly loud, but it still competed with the hum of conversations. She focused on the tables and booths but didn't see anyone wave at her. Grace was meeting the new editor of the newspaper — that was the phone call — and he wouldn't be a familiar face. However, she was early, so she decided to go to the bar and talk with Bill Tully.

The hostess asked her, "How many, hon?" and Grace replied that she'd go back to the bar while she waited for a friend. She strolled beyond the heavy plastic partition and looked at all the changes Tully had made to the bar area. Gone were the booths with seats that had begun to show wear and gone was the poor lighting. She saw in their place neon signs that advertised Budweiser, Amber Bock, Blue Moon, Corona Extra, and Miller Lite, with race cars and faces of drivers Grace didn't recognize. As she moved toward a bar stool, Bill Tully saw her and walked over.

"Hey, Grace, I hear congratulations are in order. Finally hanging up the pencils and red pens, huh?"

Grace sat down on a bar stool and said, "Definitely no longer setting my alarm clock. It's good to see you, Bill."

"Lot of people are gonna miss you up at the high school. But now you can come here more often."

"And I'll miss a lot of the people. But it's time." She looked around at the bar. "Say, I really like what you've done to the place. Looks like you put your life's savings into all this redecoration."

"Yeah, well, people want sports bars these days, and it was worth the time and money to close up long enough to give 'em what they want. The scoreboard over the kitchen doors explodes if people ask me to hit the button. Makes a shitload of noise — oh, excuse the term, Grace — when it goes off so I don't do it very much." They both laughed.

Tully stretched his arms, his hands holding the edge of the bar. "What can I do you for?"

"Meeting someone for dinner but it looks like he isn't here yet. An amaretto sour?"

"On the rocks — see, I still remember. One amaretto sour coming up!"

She watched as he went over to the sink and grabbed some bottles, a glass, and ice. Grace didn't know exactly how old Bill was. In fact, when she thought about it, she didn't know much about him at all. He was a burly guy, probably an inch or two short of six feet, and he had a way of moving quietly for such a big man. He kept his black hair short, but it was thick and wiry like his beard and moustache and flecked with bits of gray. His blue eyes seemed tiny because of his bushy, black eyebrows.

He set down Grace's drink. "When your friend comes in we'll get you a table or you can eat in the bar if you'd like. And, Grace, it's on the house. Happy retirement!"

"Thanks, Bill."

He moved away to wait on another man who sported a baseball hat and a red T-shirt with a Cardinals logo on it. Grace glanced at his profile. *Jimmy Dolan. He must be in his forties by now. I remember he gave a speech on the history of condoms, hoping to shock me. I think he has six kids. What does that say for the old axiom that knowledge is power?*

Grace noticed the music switch from Rod Stewart to Lady Gaga. She checked the time: 7:10. Mr. Maitlin was definitely late. She was sure he had said seven on the phone. Maybe some unexpected problem had come up at the newspaper. Over Lady Gaga she heard the familiar strains of Bon Jovi's "Wanted, Dead or Alive" and realized she'd forgotten to turn off her phone. She grabbed it from her purse and hit the keypad to answer TJ's call.

"I can tell he's late because I just saw his car leave the parking lot at the newspaper." TJ never wasted time with "Hello."

"Do you have him under surveillance?"

"Definitely not. Happened to be going by on a routine drive and remembered you were meeting. Have a nice dinner, Grace."

"Thanks." She hit the "end" button. Exasperated, she realized how rapidly her phone conversation had spread among her friends. Lettie, of course.

An abrasive voice slashed through her thoughts. "Double Scotch on the rocks,

Bill," and Brenda Norris plopped down next to Grace. "It's been one hell of a day and I definitely deserve this!" Turning, she added, almost as an afterthought, "Hi, Grace."

Grace swallowed a sigh. "Hi, Brenda. Sorry to hear your job isn't going so well."

"Tracking some town history for the anniversary celebration. You know, there's a lot I didn't remember about this place."

"Is this a series of articles or are you writing some kind of special edition for the celebration?"

Before Brenda could answer, Bill Tully showed up, poured her drink, and casually joined the conversation. "Working hard, Brenda?"

"You can't imagine. Not only am I writing articles for the paper, as usual, but I'm still working on that special assignment for the town celebration. This was something the editor cooked up before Maitlin took over." Her eyes narrowed. "I was about to say 'May my former boss rest in peace,' but after this job he left me, I hope he's roasting." She pulled a cigarette out of her purse and Tully pointed to the "no smoking" sign over the bar. Resigned, she put the pack back. "I hate this new, healthier world," she announced. "It tramples on my right to kill myself."

"I'm curious about what kind of stuff you're researching," Bill said as he grabbed some glasses from a sink and began to wipe them with a dish towel.

"Besides the changes in buildings and various scandals, I've found some police cases I'm checking out too. Some are really old." She took several huge swallows of her drink and set it down. "Whew. That helps."

"Old? I've only been here since the early nineties. How old?" Bill asked.

"Oh, much older than that. A murder in the twenties, an embezzlement case in the thirties, and some fire deaths in the early seventies."

Bill set down a glass. "Ya don't say. Didn't realize the town had such a colorful history. The decorator put up some photos of local events, but she knew more about them than I do." Grace felt herself rocking and noticed Brenda's legs were crossed and her foot was rapidly moving back and forth.

Grace used her drink napkin to mop up a few drops of water that had condensed on her glass and dripped on the counter. "I've heard rumors flying around town. Is it true there may be a lawsuit against you about one of your stories?"

Brenda snickered. "Not officially, but I've heard Mike Sturgis is madder than hell and talking to a lawyer. Figures! I can't imagine he wants to drag it into court — what he does in his construction business. I said it all in that story, you know. I exposed his shoddy practices." She drained her glass and added, "Hit me with another one, Bill."

Grace took a sip of her drink and considered how to phrase her next sentence. Then, "Brenda, maybe you should worry about what people think of your reporting."

"Why the hell would I care? I'm just doin' my job. You wouldn't believe, Grace, the things I've had said to me. The phone calls, especially in the middle of the night. Dead stuff left in my front yard or my mailbox. But, you know, it all comes back to freedom of the press." Her eyes narrowed as she looked straight ahead at the mirror over the bar. "And, don't worry. I'm going to show them." She grabbed another drink from Bill Tully's hand and took a couple of swallows. Grace glanced at Bill and he raised his eyebrows.

"Sounds like an intellectual conversation about journalism," an unfamiliar voice boomed from behind Grace. "Sorry I'm late. Problems downtown. Hi, Brenda."

Without turning around, Brenda said, "Hi, Mr.-New-York-editor guy."

"And you must be Grace Kimball." Grace

turned and saw an attractive man, a little over six feet tall, slender, with thick, dark brown, silver-threaded hair that fell in a slight wave behind his ears. He was dressed in a light, cream-colored linen shirt with the top button open. *Kind of sophisticated for Endurance,* was her first thought. Grace shook his outstretched hand.

"I'm Jeff Maitlin. New editor at the paper. Well, at least part-time editor since it only comes out three times a week. Retirement job."

"Pleasure to meet you. And this is Bill Tully."

"Welcome," Tully shook his hand. "Hope you're enjoying the small-town atmosphere. Not exactly like New York City."

"True." He smiled and Grace took in a set of straight, white teeth and a look of pleasure. "I just noticed a couple of teenagers skateboarding down the middle of Endurance Avenue past the college, and there wasn't a car in sight. Don't see that much in the city."

"Hope your new job works out." Bill raised his hand to Ronda Burke, the floor manager, and made a sign that she should find them a table. "Ronda will take care of you two, and enjoy your dinner."

"Perfect." As she rose to follow Jeff, Grace

whispered, "Watch yourself, Brenda."

"Hey, Ms. Kimball. I can find you guys a nice booth right over here," said Ronda Burke, her face beaming. A bit over five feet tall, Ronda resembled a leprechaun who radiated efficiency.

"Don't you think you can call me Grace now?"

"Nope. You'll always be 'Ms. Kimball' who helped me overcome my speaking jitters."

"By the way, Ronda, this is Jeff Maitlin. He's the new editor at the *Register*. Jeff, Ronda usually knows everything going on in town. If you cross her palm with silver she'll spill her guts." Ronda laughed and strode back to the bar.

Once they sat down, Jeff opened his menu. "It seems like everyone knows everyone in this town. Sorry I was late. Not used to being a jack-of-all-trades at a small newspaper." He ran his fingers through his hair and turned off his cell phone. "There. Now we won't have any interruptions." He looked up at Grace and smiled.

"How did you happen to move to Endurance from the East Coast, Mr. Maitlin?"

"Please, call me Jeff. Friend of mine happened to see an ad through a website that focuses on journalism news. 'Part-time job in a small town' was on the list and I wanted to wind things down, you know, find something to keep me a little busy. Kind of a retirement job, I guess. I must say it has been quite a culture shock, but a pleasant one."

A waitress came up to the table and took their drink order. Grace recognized Tonsy Bellis, but it took her a moment since Tonsy had on more clothing than Grace remembered her wearing. *Must have been about five years ago. Every time Tonsy leaned over to get books out of her locker you could see her red satin thong and an elaborate tattoo on her lower back.* She shook her head slightly. *Will I ever stop remembering these dumb factoids?*

A few minutes later Tonsy brought their drinks and wrote down their order. Grace was about to ask Jeff about his first impressions, but her thoughts were interrupted by Brenda Norris laughing from the bar area, her shrill voice rupturing the pleasant calm.

"Don't suppose Brenda has a designated driver," Grace said and she looked at Jeff.

"Too much to hope for," Jeff shook his head. "I know she lives out in the country a few miles west of town. Not quite sure what I'm going to do with her at the paper."

"You think you might let her go?"

"I told myself I wouldn't make too many

changes right away. Need to see how the place shakes down. But she's made so many people angry. I've already received two calls from people last week and I just got here. One sounded threatening toward her. Some people take the paper, I think, because they love to read her latest unsubstantiated stories, and others cancel because they're so ticked off at her." He leaned over the table and said, "You know, I've heard only good things about you as I nosed around town, so I will quietly say that I wouldn't want this to get around, but it looks like Mike Sturgis is going to sue for libel."

"Guess that doesn't surprise me. She wrote some strongly worded allegations about the way he runs his construction business. He has a lot of city contracts, and she as much as said that he cut corners on materials and did shoddy workmanship. But he gets bids because he's the lowest."

"I don't know how much of that's true, but I know the owner, Torchlight Publications, is waiting to see if they get sued along with Brenda." Again they heard raucous laughter and Brenda's piercing voice over the music and conversations.

Grace waited a moment and said, "Mike Sturgis has a powerful temper and some anger control issues. Always has. He's been in a few very public scrapes with people around town."

Tonsy showed up with their salads and smiled at Jeff. "Hope everything's fine. Just let me know if there's, like, anything else I can do for you, Ms. Kimball and Handsome Man."

After she left, Grace raised one eyebrow at Jeff as if to say, "And now you know the type of students I've taught."

Jeff chuckled and jabbed his fork into a mound of lettuce. "I have a lot to get used to." Grace noticed a slight blush spread across his face. *It's been a while since I've seen a man blush,* she thought.

"And speaking of 'getting used to,' how's the first course?" Ronda said, appearing out of nowhere.

Grace looked up. "Great, Ronda."

"Mr. Maitlin, how we doing? Ms. Kimball here keeping you entertained?"

"Definitely, Ronda."

"Sorry. I haven't neglected you, but I've been in and out of the bar as I listened to Brenda and Tully talk about town history. Fascinating." She turned to Jeff, and in a conspirator's voice added, "I can fill you in on a lot you don't know about Ms. Kimball. I used to babysit her kids. Stop by and have lunch some time."

He smiled, glanced at Grace, set down his fork, and said, "Let's try a test of your powers. Impress me."

Grace looked up at the ceiling, wondering if she could change the topic.

"Let's see. Which story to tell?" Ronda pressed her fingers together and also glanced up at the ceiling. "So many to choose from. I know. How about the time she went on a wild rampage and totally TP-ed our house?"

"TP-ed?" Jeff asked.

Grace said dryly, "A tradition of small towns."

"My brother and a bunch of other guys went over to her house at night, you see, and threw toilet paper up in the trees. It was just because they liked her."

"Then they must have liked me a lot. Happened night after night for two weeks and the kids and I got unbelievably tired of cleaning it up."

"And it accelerated considerably, Mr. Maitlin. Began with ten rolls and eventually I think they were up to a hundred. Talk about escalation!" Ronda was in her element as she acted out her story.

"The grocery store was happy," Grace reminded her, a quiet Greek chorus of one.

"Finally, she figured out who was doing

50

it," Ronda lowered her voice, "and decided to get revenge."

"It was, oh, probably five years after my husband Roger died and the kids were the right age to teach them how to throw high."

Ronda was not to be deterred. "You know there's a law against that, Ms. Kimball. It's a misdemeanor — I think vandalism — and your kids could have ended up in jail with you." She crossed her arms and assumed her best indignant pose.

"Oh, I doubt it, Ronda. By then I'd had some of the policemen in class. A few owed me big time." Grace wiped her mouth quickly with her napkin.

"She drove the getaway car and her three kids had a heyday as they threw toilet paper all over the trees at about five houses, including ours. Can you imagine an English teacher doing such a thing?"

Jeff laughed and Grace rolled her eyes.

Ronda adjusted the bill pad in her apron pocket and prepared to leave. "Just thought you should know, Mr. Maitlin. Her youngest kid was only about nine or ten at the time. She encouraged them to become juvenile delinquents."

"Man, I'll have to keep that in mind, Ronda." He smiled at Grace and continued to look at her as he replied to Ronda. "I thought I would hire her to do a job for me, but maybe I should reconsider or do a background check." He was about to add another thought when his voice was drowned out by a huge disturbance that roared from the bar, and Brenda's voice, slurred and belligerent, rose in an ever-increasing crescendo.

Jeff folded his napkin and slid from the booth. "I'd better go check that out." He was a few steps behind Ronda with Grace following them. When they reached the bar Grace took in the scene quickly. She saw a lean, muscular Mike Sturgis towering over Brenda as he made threatening gestures — beer spilling out of his glass all over the floor — and shouted at her, "And wait till I see you in court, Norris. You're gonna wish you'd never been born. I'll sue you till you have nothing — no house, no car, no job, no money in the bank. You can't write them damned lies about me and expect to get away with it!" Brenda's unfocused eyes stared up at him.

Mike Sturgis had obviously come straight to the bar from work and had been drinking ever since. With a beer in one hand and his other hand pointing at Brenda, Sturgis was an intimidating figure who outweighed her by a hundred pounds. Grace watched uneasily and wondered how quickly this could dissolve into an explosive bar fight.

CHAPTER FOUR

For a big man, Bill Tully moved swiftly out from behind the bar. "Calm this down, Mike. Brenda here isn't bothering anyone at my bar. Keep the fireworks for somewhere else."

"Yeah," repeated Brenda, her voice slow and slurred. "Go 'way. Find some else one or else or someone else to har — har — harass," she sputtered and turned back to her drink.

Jeff walked up behind Sturgis and put a hand on his arm, and Sturgis spun around as his hand turned into a fist. Jeff ducked just in time.

"Who the hell are you? Get your hands off me!"

"Just trying to help, fella. Why don't we leave this lady alone and go about our business?"

Sturgis paused for a moment, hesitating as if he needed to consider Jeff's idea, and then turned his unfocused eyes toward Maitlin. "Who are you?"

Jeff stuck his hand out and introduced himself, all the while edging away from Sturgis, who followed him like a belligerent bull after a red flag, moving himself farther away from Brenda. "I'm Jeff Maitlin, the new editor of the *Endurance Register.* And who might you be?"

"Mike Sturgis, victim of your rag sheet of a paper. And, believe me, I'm gonna have my day in court." No handshake.

Jeff looked Sturgis in the eye. "I hope you do get a chance to do that. But in the meantime, it might be smart to calm down here where everyone is watching you and wondering if you'd hit a lady."

"Lady?" Sturgis's voice rose a few decibels, his arm flailing in frustration, his beer continuing to slop over the side of his glass and onto the floor. "Lady? She ain't no lady. She's a lying, sneaky bitch, and I'd have to stand in line behind all the people who'd like to show her how they feel about her trumped-up news stories." He stared at his now empty glass and set it down on the bar.

Grace could feel her heart pounding and took in the entire room where the bar patrons were hushed in an unnerving calm. She watched as Bill Tully stood on the other side of Sturgis, planting himself in front of Brenda, who was staring up at his back, her eyes blinking as if she wasn't sure who he was. Grace was close enough to see the tattoos on Sturgis's muscular shoulders, just beneath the cut-off sleeves of his T-shirt and the clenched fists.

"Hey, Mike," called a new voice, and everyone turned as two patrolmen from the Endurance Police Department walked into the tableau. Ted Collier patted Sturgis on the back and turned him around, all the while saying in a calm voice, "Now, Mike. We can't be disturbing people who are eating their dinner kind of quiet-like. It's time to head on home for now. I'll be glad to take you and you can pick up your truck tomorrow. I know your wife must be worried."

Sturgis smiled a drunken smile at Collier, put his arm over his shoulder, and Collier steered them toward the bar exit with Jim McGuire close behind. Grace felt her tense muscles relax while Bill Tully turned to Brenda and asked if she was all right.

"All right? Whadda ya mean? He can't say those things 'bout me. He called me a lying bitch. That can't be right. How can he say those things . . . ?" And her voice trailed off in a sigh.

"Why don't I give you a ride home, Brenda?" said Jeff.

"Home? Issit time to go home?" she murmured.

"Yes, it is. I'll be glad to run you out there," Jeff repeated, more insistent this time, and he put his hand under her arm and helped the drunken reporter off her barstool.

"Thanks," said Tully as he followed them to the door. "I have a buzzer that alerts the cops, and I hit it when I saw which way the wind was blowing Sturgis tonight. He always was a hothead and I don't want a brawl on my property. Appreciate it if you could get her home. Lots of nights I've called a cab. I'll make sure her car is locked up and it'll be safe here overnight. Won't be the first time, and probably won't be the last."

Jeff turned to Grace. "Can you wait for me to get back? We still have some unfinished business to discuss."

"Sure," she said, and she handed him Brenda's purse and gave Tully the car keys she'd fished out of it.

"No problem. I'll be back pronto." He steered Brenda toward the back exit and they were gone. Tully announced, "Excitement's over, folks. You all can go back to your drinks."

Five minutes later Grace drank her almost cold coffee and finished her salad as she waited for Jeff.

"Penny for your thoughts? Well, maybe adjusted for inflation, a nickel," and Bill Tully sat down across from Grace.

"I was listening to my heartbeat regain its steady tick tock. How do you do it?"

"Do what?" He glanced at her questioning eyes. "Oh, you mean keep the peace in the Wild West?"

"Yes." Grace looked into Tully's face and saw a darker look, one she hadn't seen before.

"Well, let me be clear. This is my place. I'm not about to let anyone — and especially not that idiot Sturgis — take it apart. Worked too many years to get to this point. No one's gonna tear it up."

Grace sat back a little deeper into the booth's back cushion, a reflex reaction to the surly look on Tully's face. Then, as quickly as it had come, his anger abated.

As if reading her body language, Tully sat back also, his facial features softening into a calmer place. "Sorry, Grace. Sometimes I just get so upset over things I can't control. Now that Jeff Maitlin, he has his work cut out for him. Just to keep Brenda corralled will be a full-time job. And, frankly, I hear plenty of gossip in my bar. Sometimes I think she's her own worst enemy."

Grace took a sip of her coffee. "I used to work with Brenda at the high school years ago."

"Really? I didn't know she'd ever done anything but work at the paper."

"Yes. We both taught English and she was an excellent teacher. Back then you had to be careful with your personal life. For example, I couldn't ever come here to your bar and sit and drink a beer. It would be all over town, and back then you had to be a pristine role model. Definitely no jokes that began 'A teacher walked into a bar.' " She paused for a moment. "And Brenda seemed to do it too often. Lost her the job, and that loss simply crushed her. Evidently she still has some problems in that area."

"True." He paused. "It'd be 'unprofessional' of me to tell you how often she's here. I feel sorry for her because she has too much on her plate. She seems pretty lonely even though she never lacks for male companionship."

Silence for a few moments. Then Grace picked up the conversation with, "So did you always live in a small town?"

"Yup. Tennessee before here. Elvis country. Worked in a bar for a number of years, so it seemed natural to open up my own."

"How did you happen to settle in Endurance? It's a long way from Tennessee."

"That's a complicated story. Maybe another time. But I've liked my place here and the folks are pretty well behaved, that is once they know I mean business about 'no funny business.' Oh, some nights we get a loud crowd that can get a little out of hand, but nothing I can't handle. I can get ahold of the cops pretty fast, as you saw. Other nights we have cleaning up to do after the college students, who sure throw up a lot. Fortunately, we're close enough to the college they can walk back."

Grace looked at Tully's smile and thought what a charming person he was. He always had a kind thing to say about people ever since she'd first met him. Then she changed the subject. "I laughed when I saw Ted Collier coming in with a uniform on. I knew he had joined the police department some time ago. Such a quiet kid in high school and one who blushed easily. Hard to believe he's a patrol cop." Grace's eyes brightened as she replayed the past. "But that Jim McGuire was a wild child. A specialist at drinking and parties. One time I remember he came to school on a Monday morning and I was his first class. Eight a.m. I swear he was still drunk or hung over. If I had lit a match near him, he would have exploded from the fumes. That was his senior year. Long time ago."

"Guess you've probably taught most of the people I see in town in your classroom, Grace. Do you remember 'em all?"

"I wish I did. No. Mostly I remember their faces. Some I remember because they were awesome students and others I remember because of the four-letter words they yelled at me as they walked out my door to the office." They both laughed. "My biggest fear is to have brain surgery and as they wheel me into the operating room, I notice that the surgeon is some kid who got a 'C' in my class. Hopefully, he did better in medical school."

Tully glanced toward the door. "Looks like Maitlin is back. I'd better get to work. I'll tell them to bring your main course now. Nice talking to ya, Grace. You should come around more often and grab your crazy friends. You know, Deb and the rest."

"That's a deal."

He went back to the bar just as Jeff walked toward them, threading his way through tables. "Now that was quite an experience."

61

He exhaled a huge breath as he slid into the booth across from Grace and let his head fall back momentarily.

"Only the beginning, Jeff."

"You're telling me. She slept most of the way to her house. Fortunately, I remembered where she lives since one of the guys at the paper gave me a tour of the town and the countryside when I first got here. Managed to wake her up to get her out of my car and in the door. And once she came to and was somewhat coherent, she kept saying your name and a word that sounded like 'Po.' Actually, she said a lot of things that made absolutely no sense. Then she rattled on about Sturgis and money and lawyers and threats." He shook his head. "I have to consider what to do about her." Silence for a few moments.

"Want some coffee?" offered Grace.

"Sure. I'll go up to the bar and order it from Bill." He scooted out of the booth and walked off toward the bar. Grace followed him with her eyes and couldn't help noticing the veins in his arms below the rolled-up sleeves and his broad shoulders, and she wondered why he wasn't married, or at least why he didn't wear a ring.

"There." He set his cup down on the table, along with a carafe of coffee. Tonsy followed him with their dinners and for a few minutes they ate in silence.

"Now, where were we?"

"Not sure we were anywhere, yet."

He hesitated, considering where to begin. "To go back to our earlier conversation, a friend of mine saw the ad for the editor job. I'd had enough of the city life. Grew up in a small town and have plenty of happy memories. I knew it would be a huge change and a welcome one. So far I think it's good. But obviously, I've already found a few bumps in the road that need to be fixed." He paused a moment, his fork in midair, and surveyed the scene in the restaurant. "It's so quiet here and it's away from all that goes with big towns — crime, rude people, hurriedness, cabbies to tip, and cold wind whistling around tall buildings. I could go on —"

"I think I get the picture. We complain about being bored and you complain about overstimulation!"

Jeff smiled. "Boredom isn't a bad thing, at least for a while."

"So, what exactly is this proposition you have for me? My friends are already chipping away at my spare time."

Jeff set his cup down. "I've thought about some of the content changes I want to make at the paper. Not big changes. I'd like you to write a column and it wouldn't take huge amounts of time."

"What kind of column?"

"A book review, say, every couple of weeks. You know, what's the latest book you'd recommend? I can make a deal with the local book store to buy books for you and after you're done reading them and writing the reviews, we could donate them to the library. I know you love to read. Have to. You are — or were — an English teacher. From what I hear, a darn good one."

Now it was Grace's turn to blush. "Thank you. Sure would beat grading term papers and essays." She took another sip of her coffee. "Let me sleep on it. I'll get back to you."

"Fair enough. You could choose the books. Since you've lived in this town a long time, you know your readers."

Again there was a pleasant silence and Grace considered how comfortable it felt.

He paused, folded his napkin, and looked up. "Well, I hate to end this pleasant evening, but maybe we should finish our coffee and call it a night. Early morning on the way. I wonder what time Brenda will come dragging in." Then he remembered. "Actually, someone will have to go get her."

Grace drained the last of her coffee. "I'll

get back to you tomorrow on the offer. Just need to sleep on it."

"I won't ask you — as part of the job — to keep an eye on Brenda."

"That's a deal."

They left Tully's and, despite all the coffee, Grace slept soundly that night, so soundly, in fact, that she didn't even stir when the Endurance fire engines, ambulance, and police cars raced through town at 2:54 a.m., emergency lights whirling and sirens blaring.

CHAPTER FIVE:
TJ

At 3:00 a.m., while Grace slept soundly across the street, TJ slipped out of her bed and reluctantly left the warm body beside her. After years of police work, she slept so lightly that she could put her phone on vibrate at night and still hear it. Now she grabbed her cell and moved smoothly out of the bedroom, closing the door.

"Sweeney here." The voice of the local dispatcher relayed the message, explained what TJ could expect, and added enough detail to cause a grimace.

"The old Quigley house on Route Six? Geez, that's —" and she remembered this wasn't a social call — "Got it. I'm leaving now." The detective tiptoed back into the bedroom, kissed her finger, and lightly touched the head of the sleeping body. She slipped into her uniform, buckled on her gun, and found her jacket. Seconds later, she glided silently out the kitchen door and into her car. Off in the distance she could hear sirens, their ominous message fading into the night.

The words of the emergency call played through her mind. They had made an agreement, one that would allow the dispatcher to quickly tell TJ enough detail to avoid surprises. A night janitor who was driving home from work in Woodbury glanced out the passenger window of his pickup truck and thought he saw flames in the distance. They were down a lane branching off the old highway. He immediately dialed 911 and the dispatcher said his voice was highly agitated. Now he was sure they were flames and he thought the universe was on fire.

In a town the size of Endurance, it only took TJ a few minutes to head west out of town. She could feel the adrenaline kick in, but it sure would be nice to have three cups of coffee straight down. Her fingers drummed a staccato melody on the steering wheel and every so often she glanced in her rearview mirror, but so far she was the lone car headed toward disaster, and she figured the emergency vehicles from the direction of Endurance were ahead of her. She rubbed the back of her neck and listened to the static and occasional voices on her radio.

The Endurance fire and police departments were already there. The radio crackled and she heard the dispatcher reel off the other fire departments from neighboring towns. More static. A body. A body had been pulled out. The coroner called. It *was* the Quigley house. The detective felt a fluttering in her stomach and checked her belt for her badge — anything to distract her.

Her red emergency light on top of her patrol car cast an eerie glow on the trees as she turned off onto the old highway. Now it was total blackness all around since the change in direction took her onto the crumbling asphalt of a road that used to be the main artery in and out of Endurance. It was no longer used much except for local farm traffic. The tree trunks along the side of the road were thick and their leafy branches so heavy that the darkness made TJ feel like she was in some subterranean world. Every so often she glanced out the side window and saw eyes that undoubtedly belonged to deer as her lights on the curves startled them.

Better slow down, she brooded. *Wouldn't do to have a collision with the wildlife before I get to the fire.* It was eerily still as if all the birds, insects, and anything else that made noise were silent or missing within a five-mile radius. In the quiet, she could hear the crunch of her tires as they hit gravel that had washed onto the road from the shoulder. She was almost there and now she could smell the unmistakable first whiffs of smoke.

The road changed direction and curved through a break in the trees that dipped down into a valley hidden from the highway by its depth and the tall timber all around it. Suddenly TJ's entire windshield was filled with a sky ignited in a panoramic picture so terrifying she felt her car skid a bit as she instinctively hit the brakes. Huge orange flames and heavy smoke rose into the night, obliterating the darkness and causing the detective to blink rapidly at the change in light. *They were lucky the janitor had seen the flames when it first started. The angle must have been just right,* she thought.

She pulled up in a clearing a good distance from the house. Two fire trucks, engines running and hooked up to water, toiled tirelessly near the inferno. The Endurance department was at work and she could now hear — ever closer — more sirens in the night as the fire departments from neighboring towns were on the way. Several patrol officers were setting up wooden barriers at a safe distance down the driveway to keep out anyone who might have heard about the fire on the police scanner.

Jim McGuire and Jake Williams were unrolling crime scene tape as an additional barrier. Ted Collier had a clipboard out so he could take names and their business. That way the emergency help would be on the scene but not any stray civilians. Collier let TJ through the tape and spoke through a radio to someone obviously closer to the fire.

TJ glanced at the endless activity and shook her head. The house was fully engulfed. She shielded her eyes and, looking up, saw flames blazing out of the downstairs windows and skyward to the second floor on the west side. Despite the widespread flames, the fire trucks must have gotten here in minutes. Two of the firemen were already inside pushing the fire out the lower windows with high-powered hoses and trying to save what was left of the property, but it appeared to be a losing battle. Chief Jim Bitterman was on his radio, keeping track of who was where. As TJ scanned the side yard, she could see a propane tank with several officers manning a line to protect it from the fire. The noise was deafening as the flames reached into the night, the air filled with the heaviness of smoke. Grit and sparks fell all around.

The heat was overpowering and TJ moved back toward the safety of the gravel driveway. It was virtually impossible for her to take in the entire scene at once: men pointing at various spots and moving from place to place, the fire chief barking directions into his radio, more fire engines pulling in and police waving them through, streams of water whooshing through the hoses and into the fire, and additional uniformed men jumping into the fray, loaded down with forty pounds of equipment. She wouldn't be needed yet, but it might be wise to keep back where she could have a view of everything and be able to stop any unauthorized people from coming closer.

Behind her a voice shouted to be heard over the fire. "Detective! I can see you're in for a long night." TJ turned and saw the newspaper editor — what was his name? — looking at the fire and balancing a camera and handheld recorder in his hands. In his eyes she saw the reflection of the flames behind her.

"Jeff Maitlin," he said, as if he could read the uncertainty on her face. He seemed overly agitated and concerned.

"Oh, yes, Mr. Maitlin."

"Call me Jeff, please, and —"

"Jeff. I guess you have a scanner and I

know you're looking for the story. But for now you'll have to stay back from the scene."

"Yes, I know." His voice was verging on desperate. "But what about Brenda? Is she in there? Did anyone get her out? I just brought her home a few hours ago. Please, you must be able to tell me something."

Instinctively, TJ went into detective mode. "What time was that?"

"What — ?" He seemed confused.

"What time did you bring her home last night?"

"Oh. Ah — it must have been eight, eight thirty, nine. Sometime around then. But is she all right?"

"So you were probably the last person to see her?"

"I assume so." And, a little calmer now, he quickly explained why he had driven her home. "She was in no condition to drive. Please, is she all right?"

"I know from the dispatcher's information that we have a body. Right now I can't stop anyone from what they're doing in order to ask, but the coroner is pulling up in his van and I have to wait for him. Not a good sign. I'll see what the story is. But please stick around, Mr. Maitlin. I'll need to hear some more about last night."

Ron Martinez, a short, slight man in shirtsleeves, jeans, and running shoes walked toward them. He was the local pediatrician but also doubled as the coroner when he was needed. His eyes looked as tired as everyone else's, and he walked slowly and carried a black, beat-up, leather medical bag. His jacket was just as worn, a button missing from the front.

"Hi, Doc," said TJ.

"Evening, Detective."

TJ introduced Jeff and remarked, "I take it we have a body."

Martinez nodded. "I'm headed over there now to take charge of it."

"I'll go with you," the detective said. "Jeff, I'll be back and let you know what I can." They left Maitlin standing in the driveway watching the uniformed army of ants scurrying around the fire, empowered now by more crews from Woodbury and Lexington. TJ could see another engine pulling up from the west. Could be from Cameron.

Several yards from the garage, which wasn't yet on fire, a dark green tarp lay on the ground near a stand of trees, and a fireman — totally motionless — waited nearby. *The silent fireman was obviously a newbie, just getting into the business,* TJ thought as she looked at his round, cherubic face and

73

his wide eyes watching the others go about their jobs. He was guarding the body the firemen pulled out of the house; they usually threw a tarp over it out of respect and to protect it for the police and coroner. Martinez took over the scene and told the fireman he could leave and get back to his company.

By six a.m. a weary TJ added up the death and destruction. They had examined the body and it was in surprisingly undamaged shape due to the quick actions of the first firemen on the scene. Martinez had transported the victim to Woodbury where the ME did autopsies for the area. TJ would have to drive over to the coroner's for the postmortem. The potentially deadly propane gas tank was safely out of harm's way since the fire was burned down to smoldering areas where men still kept an eye out for occasional secondary flare-ups. Parts of the house's frame and foundation were intact and most of the garage was simply smoke-damaged. The additional fire trucks had motored back to the neighboring towns with weary, exhausted crews, leaving the Endurance department to keep an eye on what was left of Brenda Norris's house.

TJ had spent a good part of the night

drinking coffee, keeping the media at a safe distance, and saying "no comment." Besides Maitlin, a number of townspeople — *why were scanners even put in the hands of the public?* — had come to watch the fire. During the night she saw several people she knew from town and a number of farmers who had fields in the area. People were curious. Bill Tully talked to Jeff and TJ while they waited for the rest of the crews to leave. Both of the men mentioned the threats of Mike Sturgis at the bar that night and TJ knew she would have a talk with Sturgis.

She moved away from the spectators when Chief Bitterman motioned her over to speak with him and Dan Wakeley, one of the senior firemen. Wakeley was in his late forties, with thinning hair and black eyebrows that matched the soot all over his face and uniform. A veteran on the force, he was a weightlifter who had a wrestler's build that supported with ease the heavy equipment he wore. TJ knew that Wakeley had been to special training at the state fire school, and with the years of experience in the department, he was an expert on fire origins. He was so good that often the state fire marshal's office called him in as a consultant. Right now, however, his face wore the fatigue of adrenaline drain, and he glanced at TJ and slowly moved his head back and forth.

"Suspicious?" asked TJ.

"It went up awfully fast," Wakeley muttered as he pulled off his gloves and began to dismantle some of his equipment.

TJ took another drink of coffee and mentioned, "I talked to Jeff Maitlin, the newspaper editor who took Brenda home last night, maybe around nine. He said she was pretty drunk and passed out on the sofa in the living room. He locked the front door on his way out and figured she'd sleep it off. But she is a smoker. Could be she woke up in the night and reached for a smoke."

"Possible," Bitterman concurred.

Wakeley set down his helmet on the ground next to him and pondered the idea. "Chief, one of the things we saw on the way into the house — early on — were those storm lamps that hold oil. Could be they had a part in it. Maybe she kept them around for decoration, possibly for power outages. But she could have tipped one over and she might have been smoking at the time. Maybe."

"The first responders and the guy who called it in mentioned orange flames. Not a good sign. An accelerant?" the chief replied.

TJ knew that it would be hours, maybe

days, before they could sift through the debris and try to figure out what started the fire and where it began.

"The body?" Bitterman turned to Wakeley.

"Found it on the floor curled up between a sofa and a small table."

TJ added, "As far as I can tell she had a nasty contusion on her forehead. Might have fallen and hit her head on a coffee table. Passed out. If she had been smoking, that could have done it. Didn't see any skin under her nails or defensive wounds. I have to wait for the medical examiner in Woodbury to tell me about the bruising. Otherwise she had a few secondary burns, only because they got her out so fast. The coroner should be able to tell me if she was dead before the fire started or if she died of the smoke. I should have more answers later today."

"All right, then," said Bitterman. He turned and issued orders for the finishing chores the firemen had to handle before the last engines pulled out. Police and a skeleton force from the fire department would stay on the scene until they were sure small flare-ups were out.

"If the autopsy says 'suspicious,' I'll call in the state boys too," said Police Chief Stephen Lomax. "Keep me in the loop, TJ."

"Will do."

They each separated and TJ's feet trudged wearily to her car for the ride back to Endurance. She wiped the sweat and soot from her face with the sleeve of her jacket. For a few seconds she simply sat in the patrol car and drank in the quiet, looking down at her filthy uniform.

She slumped down in the car seat and bent forward, laying her forehead on the steering wheel. After a few seconds she took in some deep breaths and felt the soreness in her throat and lungs. She straightened her back, shivered, and tried to lessen the heavy burden in her chest as she thought about Grace. TJ would have to deliver two messages that would leave her friend both grief-stricken and anxious: Brenda's death and the fire. Turning her car key, she heard the engine engage, and she slid the car into gear and began the long, dispiriting trek back to Endurance.

CHAPTER SIX:
GRACE

As TJ drove back to town at dawn, Grace opened her eyes a slit and looked slowly around her bedroom. It was early morning and she gradually became aware that no fire nightmare had tangled up her sheets and pillows during the night. Maybe the drinks at Tully's had helped.

Once the coffee cheerfully dripped into the pot and its enticing aroma filled the kitchen, she began a search for her newspaper. She looked through the lilac bushes near the porch and then she realized she didn't get a paper on Friday. *How am I ever going to remember what day it is?* Normally she would think of her first class of the day, but since she didn't teach in the summer, she decided this was no different than her usual confusion during summer break.

Her kitchen and family room were together in an open floor arrangement, and Grace switched on the family room television from the kitchen area and juggled the stations on the remote. Satisfied with the upcoming news station, she turned away and unlocked the back door, putting a container out for rainwater to feed her house plants. Then, coffee in hand, she sat down to watch the morning news on the sofa in the family room. Endurance wasn't big enough to have its own television station, but nearby Woodbury's WHOC usually covered the region.

The news anchor began in a somber voice. "In the news this morning we bring you coverage of a tragic event near Endurance. A farmhouse was the scene of a fire during the night and WHOC was there to bring you on-the-spot coverage. We turn now to Kelsey Karnes, who is on the scene where they are still putting out the fire. Kelsey?"

Grace sat up and watched the screen more closely at the mention of "Endurance" and "fire." Kelsey Karnes was a reporter who had just started at the station recently, and Grace had watched as she dropped her microphone on more than one occasion. Kelsey felt it was important to emphasize words by using her voice. Unfortunately, the novice reporter exaggerated the wrong words, leaving Grace scratching her head in bewilderment. Yesterday she began a story by saying, "*You* will need to *know* about the time of *the* event . . ." It was very disconcerting.

"Thank you, Dan. I have the Endurance fire chief, Jim Bitterman, on the scene with me. Chief Bitterman, can you give us an update on this fire?"

Chief Bitterman was a solid man, a safe port in any storm. He had been fire chief in Endurance for the past fifteen years, and his curly red hair and positive outlook inspired confidence in the hearts of most Endurance residents. Today he was covered in grime from hat to boot, and fatigue filled his face and his slack mouth, and matched the thickness in his throat.

"Sure, Kelsey. The house appears to be a total loss and we had one fatality. We're waiting on a family notification before we release the name of the victim. It's still too early to tell what caused the fire and where it started. Once it's safe to investigate we should have some answers. My men have been working since three a.m., but we'll stay here until we know it's entirely out and done smoldering. I'd like to thank all the fire personnel who answered the call from the neighboring fire departments as close as Woodbury and as far away as Charlotte."

"Thank you for that update, Chief Bitterman. The Endurance Police Department has announced that they will have a press conference once we have developments in the case." Grace watched as the camera swung past the newswoman toward the blackened and charred remains of what had once been Brenda Norris's house. She was lifting her cup to her mouth and, instead, dropped it on the coffee table where it shattered into pieces, coffee splattering over the table and onto the carpet. Her hand flew to her chest and her breath hitched in her lungs.

She realized she was holding her breath. The sight of a fire still tightened her breathing and quickened her pulse. As the camera panned the structure, she saw the remains of the familiar Norris garage.

"Oh, no!" she gasped aloud as she stood up and shuffled closer to the screen — barely missing pieces of her shattered cup on the floor — just in time to see Dan Wakeley, one of the Endurance firemen, spread water over the remains of the garage.

"This is Kelsey Karnes at WHOC-HD signing off."

Grace felt her legs get rubbery and, turning and moving in jerky strides, she plopped down on the sofa and reached for her tissue box. Her hands trembled. Then she found her balance again, got up, and started a slow, relentless pacing. "Why?" she gasped out loud. "This can't be happening. Last night I was with her and she was alive and breathing." She remembered their brief conversation at the bar and Jeff taking Brenda home. And all the while Grace slept, maybe Brenda fought for her life to get out of that fire. What happened? What caused it?

About that time Jill Cunningham — she always had great timing — sidled in through the kitchen door.

She called out as she looked up the staircase. "Grace? You up? Your door was open so I figured either you or —" She turned her head toward the family room. "Oh, Grace." As always when Jill had been out on her two-mile jog, her hair was plastered to her head, and her pink and white shorts and T-shirt stuck to her in soggy spots. She trod softly into the kitchen, looked at her friend's face, and added, "You heard, didn't you? I'd hoped I could get over here in time to break it to you gently." She took Grace into her arms and then Grace pulled back and scanned Jill's face.

"Jill. Why?"

Jill broke away, walked over and turned the television off, and guided Grace from the sofa to a chair at the kitchen table. "I've not a clue, but you know she was a smoker. Maybe it was accidental. Or maybe an electrical short."

Grace blew her nose and then shook her head slowly back and forth. "I saw her last night at Tully's."

Jill sat down across from her. "Really? I feel so bad for all the awful things I said about her at lunch." She paused and looked in earnest at Grace. "Do you think there's anything to the notion that Karma will come back to bite my butt?"

Grace shook her head, sniffed, and wiped her nose. "You only said those things to our group."

"Sure. You, Deb, and TJ. Oh, right. TJ's a police detective."

"I think you're safe. Do you think this wasn't an accident? The most crimes we have are a few burglaries. Oh, and sometimes mischievous pilfering by kids . . . usually ones I've taught."

"Grace, you are so naive. Plenty of people have been unhappy with Brenda because of stories she's put in the paper. She makes accusations that affect their lives, how people think of them, and their jobs. You don't know what crazy people walk around out there. Perhaps someone got desperate."

"But, murder?"

Jill was silent for a moment, looking down at her hands. "So how did she seem last night? You said you saw her last night."

"Yes, at Tully's. She was three sheets to the wind, so drunk that Jeff Maitlin gave her a ride home. I have the impression that happens often — the drinking, that is."

"Maybe she went in the house, lit a cigarette, and, in a stupor, passed out. That could explain it."

"I suppose. I can't stop thinking" — her voice cracked — "how awful that must have been. The fire."

"Stop, Grace. You mustn't get yourself all worked up about fires again. Besides, maybe she was unconscious when . . ." Jill paused. ". . . whatever happened, happened."

"That would be a blessing."

Jill walked over to the sofa, picked up the pieces of Grace's coffee cup, and deposited them in the kitchen trash can. She turned back, eyeing Grace's white knuckles grasping the edge of the table. Putting a hand on her friend's shoulder, she said, "If you need me any time today, call."

"Thanks." Grace regained some composure. "I imagine Lettie will show up soon and I need to go to the newspaper office." She paused and looked out the kitchen

85

window. "It will be weird not to see Brenda . . . there. At the office, I mean."

Jill turned, hand on the back door handle. "So how did that go? With Maitlin?"

"He wants me to do book reviews for the newspaper."

"And will you?"

"I think so. Won't take much of my time."

"Good deal. Between that and the quinta — oh, you know, the centennial thing, you'll have plenty to keep you busy. Bye."

Jill hadn't been gone five minutes when TJ walked across the yard to Grace's house. Her uniform had taken a beating, was covered with soot, and her face and hair were also smeared with black, soiled patches. She walked in Grace's back door and dropped into one of the kitchen chairs. The odor of smoke followed in her wake.

"Rough night. Please, TJ, tell me she died quickly."

TJ looked at Grace's tear-streaked face. "I imagine she did." She crossed her arms on the table and laid her head down. For a few moments both of them were quiet.

"Was the fire really horrible?" Grace asked quietly.

TJ's head rose. "Worst I've seen in all my time here. It was already raging by the time I got out there, but they had pulled Brenda out quickly. I don't think she suffered, Grace."

Grace wrinkled her nose and the anxiety began to build in her chest again. "That smell."

"Smell? Oh, yeah, it's probably the smoke from the fire."

"I'm trying not to smell it. I've made my mind stop thinking about it." She moved away from TJ toward the kitchen counter and picked up a coffee cup. "Want some coffee?"

"Don't think so, but thanks. I've had enough during the night to sink the *Titanic* over again. I'm sorry for the smoke smell. Probably makes you anxious."

Grace dropped into a chair across from TJ. "What happened? Does anyone know what caused it?"

"Don't know yet. From the color of the flames and how quickly it went up, an accelerant might have been involved. But we don't know that for sure. State guys are out there today."

"So what will happen?"

"The body — Brenda — has been sent on to the medical examiner in Woodbury since they can do a more thorough job. She'll be posted, ah, autopsied later this morning. We have a definite identification and they'll be able to tell if she died before or after the fire started."

"And the fire itself?"

"Well, Dan Wakeley's the local fireman with expertise on origin and cause. He's had several classes at the fire school. It's a bit early to be able to check that out because the fire's still smoldering and not the safest place. But once it burns down he'll be able to put a few pieces together. And they'll call in the state guys to examine the whole area."

"Has anyone said it was set?"

"Good question, Grace. So far the coroner has called Brenda's demise a 'suspicious death' because we won't know much until the autopsy. Takes time. Over the years they've gotten better at both victim identification and fire origins."

"No one else got hurt, right? The firemen?"

"No. Now don't start thinking about how this figures with your own life. No comparison. And that was years and years ago. I know it upsets you, but try to put it out of your mind." TJ yawned. "Think I'll go home, take a shower, and get a few hours' sleep before the postmortem. God, what a long night!" She plodded out the kitchen door.

Grace sat down and tried to ignore the

smoke fumes that trailed after TJ. She leaned back in the chair and thought about Brenda last night. Jeff said she was practically unconscious when he took her into the house and guided her to the sofa. Maybe she woke up and lit a cigarette and fell asleep again. *I wonder what family she has left,* Grace thought. *I know she has a brother somewhere, but her parents are gone.*

"Hey, Gracie, I brought you some blueberry muffins!" Lettie breezed in the kitchen door with arms full of bags.

"I suppose you heard about the fire."

"Sure did. Mildred at the bakery said Brenda Norris was at Tully's last night and some dark-haired guy took her home. Probably had his way with her and set the house on fire."

Grace smiled. Lettie could always make a dark day darker. Too much tabloid reading.

"And then I heard at the dry cleaners that Mike Sturgis was at the bar last night and threatened her. Evidently way drunk and the cops had to take him home, only they didn't. Took him to his office so he could sleep it off and the little lady, Janice, wouldn't find out. Of course, I'm not sure what she thought when he wasn't home this morning. I'd love to be a fly on the wall during that conversation. Anyway, he's the one people are putting money on."

"How do you hear all this stuff?"

Lettie took a cup and poured herself coffee. "Oh, I don't know. People just talk to me. I'm a listener, you know. Lots of theories floating around town. Gladys, my friend who works at the coffee shop, thinks Brenda was a lesbian and jilted her girlfriend, who set her house on fire outta revenge."

Grace, who was taking a sip of coffee, started choking and had to stand up, lean over the sink, and catch her breath. *I'm definitely having trouble with coffee this morning,* she thought.

Lettie, ignoring her, continued. "But I don't think so. I've heard that over the years she's played hanky-panky with a lot of guys in town, several of them married. She wasn't too selective." She paused a moment, thinking. "Actually, I guess they weren't either. And, of course, she's made no friends with some of the stories she's written. I'm surprised the fire department didn't just let it burn after what she wrote about them the other day."

"Lettie, I'd love to have the life of your imagination. How do you know the fire wasn't accidental?"

"Brenda Norris?" Lettie snorted. "She never did anything accidental in her life.

90

That woman was made for an unhappy ending. Sorry to say, but I think people could see something like this coming."

Grace shook her head gently and, in a quiet voice, replied, "I didn't." She took another sip of coffee and reflected for a moment. Then she put her cup on the counter and automatically reached for two plates from the cupboard next to the sink. "Let's eat, and then I have to shower and go to the newspaper office."

Lettie slid into a chair. "What's the new editor like? Is he good-looking? Funny? Smart?" She paused. "Your age, perhaps?"

"He seems quite congenial, although I don't know how he'll adjust to a small town compared to New York City. Everyone knows the newspaper's been on its last legs for some time, so he has his job cut out for him. He was the one who took Brenda home because she was so drunk, and he's worried about what to do with her at the newspaper." She was silent for a moment. "I guess that's no longer an issue. Perhaps Mike Sturgis's lawsuit will go away too." They ate in silence for several minutes.

"Is he married?"

Grace set her coffee down. "Don't know. Doesn't wear a wedding ring."

Lettie looked up over Grace's shoulder

and out the window. "Hmm . . . I wonder why some big-time New York editor would want to come to a small place like this," Lettie said. Then her voice turned ominous. "Mark my words. More goes on than meets the eye with that one."

He's definitely not hard on my eyes. "I haven't known him long enough to interrogate him on his dark and murky past, Lettie." Grace popped the last of the blueberry muffin in her mouth, scooped up the crumbs, ate them, and headed upstairs. "Time to get rolling."

Watching Grace climb the stairs, Lettie muttered, "Male, breathing. What more could she want?" Then she stood up, walked over, and yelled up the stairs, "You might want to wear something . . . attractive."

CHAPTER SEVEN

Grace pulled into the parking lot of the *Endurance Register,* somehow skillfully missing five potholes in the asphalt. The building should have had a cheerful exterior of red bricks, but over the years the red had faded and black soot and stains streamed down in several spots. It had all the signs of a small-town, hard-copy newspaper outlet struggling to compete. Scrubby grass, dirt, and straggly weeds occupied the space between the black, crusty edge of the parking lot and the bottom of the building. Near the entrance was a sign with the newspaper's name and the phrase "Founded in 1852." Below that the ownership announcement — "A Torchlight Publication" — completed the address.

She strolled in through the double doors and questioned if she should have made an appointment with Jeff Maitlin. It was Friday afternoon and an edition would be published tomorrow morning. The newspaper had changed from a six-day-a-week newspaper to three deliveries on Monday, Wednesday, and Saturday mornings, and the circulation had shrunk to 4,000.

Rick Enslow, the advertising and sales person, sat behind the counter. *Not a bad student in high school, eager to learn and deeply involved in the cross-country team and the track team. Maybe a long jumper?* Grace couldn't spit in Endurance without hitting former students. Cross country or track? She couldn't remember. But now — oh, twenty years later — his muscular, trim figure had rounded considerably and his belt size had definitely expanded. Maybe doubled. The once abundant blond hair that drove the girls wild in high school had receded to a shiny landing pad on the top with a few blades of grass on either side. To make up for her nitpicking thoughts, she added to herself, *He was a really kind person and had a lot of friends.*

He rose from his chair and came up to the counter.

"Hi, Rick. Do you suppose your new editor is in?"

"Sure, Ms. Kimball. He's working on the fire story for tomorrow. Pretty quiet around here today. Someone placed a wreath and a vase of flowers near Brenda's door. Unbelievable." He paused. "She was a presence to be reckoned with."

"You're so right."

"Hang on and I'll buzz Jeff — uh, Mr. Maitlin." He picked up the phone, announced Grace, listened momentarily, hung up, and said, "He has someone in his office but said to tell you to sit down and he'll be right with you." Rick pointed to a waiting area with a few stacks of the latest edition of the paper, and some sepia photographs from the paper's history on the wall. The phone resonated in the quiet room while Grace sat in the lobby, and she listened as Rick explained an advertising package.

It wasn't long before Jeff's door opened. Out came a woman Grace didn't know, about twenty-five, who scowled as she headed toward another office. Jeff followed her, picked up some messages from the front desk, and moved toward Grace with a smile on his face. His shirt and pants resembled TJ's soot-covered uniform and his eyes looked puffy from lack of sleep. Nevertheless, he smiled and extended his hand.

"Grace. Hope you've brought me good news."

"Yes. I'll write the column." She smiled

95

and then, remembering her morning, pursed her lips thoughtfully. "I'm terribly sorry about Brenda." She struggled to think of something else to say and decided to drop the attempt.

He nodded, let go of her hand, and added with his arms outspread, "Come on back to my office."

She followed him and settled into a chair in front of his desk. Behind him she saw shelves of books dealing with aspects of management, business, and newspapers. Her eyes wandered to his desk and noted an overflowing set of paper trays. The computer screen was over to the side of the desk and a half-empty bottle of water rested next to the wired mouse.

"Horrible night. Ghastly. I got the news on the scanner and headed out there. It seemed like I had just taken her home. But the house was totally up in flames when I arrived, and they had already brought her body out." He reached for his bottle of water and shook his head slowly. "Terrible." Grace noticed his hand tremble as he lifted the bottle.

"Did you get any sense of why this happened or how?"

"Not sure. Detective Sweeney is investigating. News conference to come. I don't know how long it will be before the state authorities figure out the reason for the fire. It sure went up fast. Police showed up here and pored over her files. Not sure they found anything useful and they've returned it all, including her laptop. I think Detective Sweeney told me they'd copied her hard drive."

"Did they say what they were looking for?"

"Any items that might implicate someone if it turns out her death is suspicious. Right now I don't know what they'll hit upon."

"I can't help but think, knowing the condition she was in, that she somehow caused it herself."

"Ah." He paused for a moment, his face pensive. "And I wonder if someone might have set it."

Grace shifted uneasily in her chair. "Why?"

"You see all kinds of things. When I was on another small paper, we had a fire-setter in town and I researched the kind of people who become enamored of fires. Their choice of accelerant is part of their crime because it causes a fire to catch quickly and travel rapidly. Last night I heard the firemen debate among themselves. Maybe kerosene or gasoline. I could just catch a word or two every so often."

She started to speak and found herself having to clear her throat. "You're kidding! Why would . . . would someone do that?"

"We don't really know yet if that's true. But if they did apply an accelerant, they didn't want her to escape alive."

Grace shivered as her heart pounded a little faster.

He noticed her pale face. "Grace? You all right?"

She looked up and whispered, "Yes. I've had a bad experience with a fire — long ago — and fires terrify me."

"I'm sorry. Let's change the subject. So you're all set to write and I've already opened an account at Harlow's Bookstore, since I hoped you'd say yes. You can come and go as you please and I'll have some keys cut for you. If you'd like, you can work from home and email your column in. Shannon can explain the address to use. Probably need a column every couple of weeks. How about for the Monday edition, say, two weeks from now?"

"Sure. Sounds perfect."

"Let me show you around. For now you can use Brenda's office, you know, in case you do want to come in and work here occasionally." They both rose and set off for the door when Jeff's cell phone chimed. He glanced at the number and said, "Excuse me for a moment."

Grace strolled out into the large, open area surrounded by several windowed offices. She thought she saw a brief glimpse of red moving around a corner down the hallway. Then Jeff returned.

After his impromptu tour they reached a hallway where Grace saw a wreath, some flowers, and a few candles on the floor in front of an office door. Jeff pointed out, "Of course, this is Brenda's. Oops. The door should be closed." He glanced inside the office and closed the door. "The police searched some of Brenda's belongings, but otherwise her office is as she left it. You know, some days I'd have a conversation with Brenda because someone had called in and cussed me out," he began. Then he sighed. "I guess I won't do that anymore." His hands fell to his sides and Grace waited as he drew in a couple of deep breaths.

"So you're working on tomorrow morning's edition?"

"Yes, and that's why I have to cut this short. I was up all last night, and once this edition is finished I'm going to crash. Monday they may have a press conference concerning the autopsy, so that's made a hell of a mess out of what I thought were my firm deadlines."

"I won't keep you then. Thanks for the tour. If it's all right, I think I'll go into Brenda's office, check out the computer, and think about my first book review. If you believe the police are done and you have a few cardboard cartons, I could pack her belongings for you. You know, personal stuff. Brenda and I were friends long ago, and I'd like to think that someone who knew her in a good light — at least in the past — would . . . touch her things." She stumbled through the last words, her voice wavering.

He seemed to compose himself. "Wonderful, Grace. I'll have Rick bring you some boxes. We have plenty. Welcome to the paper and I hope you'll decide to stay with us for a long time." He chuckled, turned, and plodded back toward his office.

Grace glanced into Shannon Shiveley's office and saw her sitting at her desk, her red dress a contrast with her chair. She stared at Grace with a smirk on her face. Grace was sure Shannon had come out of Brenda's office earlier. *Strange.*

Carefully stepping around the wreath and flowers on the floor, Grace reached up and gently stroked the letters on Brenda's door — "Brenda Norris" — and underneath,

"News Reporter." She remembered the determination, the set jaw, when she saw Brenda downtown as she said, "Some people are gonna wish they'd never done what they did." *Oh, Brenda. If you just hadn't pushed people so hard.* As she stood in the doorway, someone came up behind her and she panicked, jumped, and caught her breath.

"Jeff — uh, Mr. Maitlin — said you would need these. Sorry I scared you," and Rick handed her a cardboard box and set two more on the floor. "Wow, you're kind of jumpy, Ms. Kimball."

She let out her breath. "Thanks, Rick. Sorry. I didn't expect anyone. Just me — I'm, uh, skittish, I guess." Her breathing began to normalize. "And since I'm writing a column for the paper, you can call me Grace. And you don't have to call the boss Mr. Maitlin. He can be Jeff."

"I know you're Grace, but it's hard for me to say anything but Ms. Kimball. Jeff I can do. Let me know if I can help, Ms. Kimball." He left and strode back to the front.

Why am I so jumpy? Grace wondered. *Do I think Brenda's ghost haunts the place?* She glanced behind her quickly and moved all the boxes into the office. She pushed on the wall switch and the room filled with light.

That must be some of her research, Grace decided as her eyes first fell on several stacks of papers on a table near a loveseat. One whole wall held three shelves of books and lopsided piles of folders.

She moved in farther and examined the titles of the books. Some were college texts and others appeared to be books she'd used to teach. *The Great Gatsby, The Last of the Mohicans,* a few volumes of short stories, a well-worn handbook of literary terms, *The Devil's Dictionary,* some mysteries, a Poe short story collection, an anthology of American writing from the romantic period, several grammar textbooks, and a dictionary. Grace ran her hands over the titles and selected the Fitzgerald book about the ill-fated Gatsby. She opened it to the middle and saw Brenda's copious notes in the margins. On the inside cover she had scribbled Fitzgerald's quote, *There are no second acts in American lives.* "Or at least they're short second acts," Grace murmured.

On the shelf below Fitzgerald she looked at two different sets of Endurance High School yearbooks. One set included 1984–1988 and the other group covered 1968–1971. One set must comprise her teaching years and the other her high school years.

Grace recognized the 1987 and 1988 books. She had similar copies from the two years she'd worked with Brenda. She opened the 1971 book and was surprised at the huge graduating class: 150 students. "Well," she said out loud, "I guess that makes sense since the baby boomers had hit the high schools by then."

Thumbing through the senior section she saw Brenda's photo. Her black hair was stylishly flipped up and she wore dark-framed glasses, so she must have switched to contacts later. Slender and good-looking, she had been in the Future Teachers of America, the high school choir, and the journalism club. The hopeful caption announced she was "most likely to be the first woman journalist to anchor an evening news program."

I guess that didn't exactly come true, thought Grace. *What happened to you, Brenda? You had such promise.* Grace remembered meeting Brenda when she had first started teaching at the high school. Brenda had come back to Endurance to take care of her ailing father, who died shortly after her return. Her mother didn't live much longer, and Brenda stayed on in their house in the country. She had nursed them both and was getting over the strain when Grace showed up, newly widowed the year before. Perhaps misery loved company because they formed a bond that first year of Grace's job. At the end of the next year Brenda was fired, although the board allowed her to resign. But fired or resigned, everyone in town knew she'd lost her job because of drinking and sleeping around. That summer she got on at the newspaper in a clerical position and later became a reporter.

Grace broke off her trip through the past and looked at the family photos on the middle shelf. Brenda's parents stared back at her, standing in front of the farmhouse that Grace had seen in flames on the news. The house had deteriorated considerably since Brenda had inherited it. The picture must have been taken in the late sixties, because Grace saw Brenda's older brother, Doug, in uniform. He was later killed in a helicopter crash over the jungle in Vietnam. How terrible that must have been for her and her family. Brenda had idolized him. She had never completely gotten over his death. Her younger brother Dan looked to be in early junior high or late elementary school. And now only Dan and his family were left and they lived far away.

She turned to Brenda's desk and saw her

laptop peeking out from under a huge pile of papers. Several pencils, their erasers chewed down and their yellow cylinders filled with teeth marks, completed the picture. A well-thumbed thesaurus sat open. Above the desk were two framed diplomas on the wall: Endurance High School 1971 and McMichael College 1976.

Sitting down on the love seat, Grace looked through the papers on the small table. It appeared — as they'd mentioned at lunch — that Brenda was working on some cold-case files from the police department. TJ would know about those.

She rose and walked over to the bookshelves, pulling down several folders that were wedged into the bottom shelf between heavy reference books. Inside were lots of odds and ends: an advertisement for a sale at Binkle's Shoe Store that expired in 1990, a baby shower invitation, a bill for a tire rotation at Shreiber's, and several notes in Brenda's writing. Between the notes were some photos she had obviously stuck away and forgotten. As Grace thumbed through them she saw a photo of herself and Brenda as they talked in the hallway at the high school. It was a random shot, and she turned it over and saw an inscription on the back. "October 1986, with my friend,

Grace." She stared at the picture, remembering the dress she had worn and the locket around her neck. Brenda had a huge smile on her face. How young they were then! Brenda had kept the photo even though she had squirreled it away with other fragments of her past. Grace felt herself tearing up again. Brenda had given the rookie advice on more than one occasion that year, and Grace had been profoundly grateful.

She reached in her purse and pulled out a tissue. And then the flood came. She had managed to hold it off for most of the day. Grace stood up and closed the door so no one would hear her sobs. She didn't know if she cried for Brenda or for her own memories of another fire. *There but for the grace of God . . .*

Eventually the emotional wreckage subsided and she considered what a good friend Brenda had been that first year when Grace was in such need of support. She had lost her husband, was dealing with three small children and all the difficulties that went with raising them by herself, and she had this huge job that didn't stop at the classroom door. Brenda had been sympathetic when Grace rushed to her room after school, and tearfully asked what to do with the Hawkins boy who was making her life miserable.

Over the years they naturally drifted apart once Grace got her feet firmly planted on the classroom floor. She was busy with her children, and after Brenda lost her job Grace only saw her occasionally in passing. *I should have been a better friend to Brenda.*

The photo in her hand stared up at her. Brenda was laughing and pointing to someone outside the frame. Grace was cradling books in one arm, and had a squirt gun in her other hand, aiming it at Brenda. Grace laughed in spite of herself. Then she thought about the catastrophe after the photo. Everything went wrong for Brenda. She had no family support and had lost her job at the school in front of the entire town. Her newspaper job didn't pay well enough to keep up the house she'd inherited, and her drinking and affairs were just symptoms of a life out of control. She must have hated the town that witnessed her disgrace, and her newspaper articles were a way to get back at everyone.

Slipping the photo back in the folder, Grace sat down at Brenda's desk and thought about the last hour. Slowly it dawned on her. She would finish the job Brenda had started. She would research and write the centennial feature and it would be a kind of memorial. Despite what the town thought, Brenda deserved at least one friend to pay her back for her kindness in the past.

She'd leave Jeff a note in his mailbox and offer to do it. There. That was decided. Then she went to work and sorted through Brenda's belongings. As she placed the items in boxes, Grace wondered why Shannon had been surreptitiously sneaking out of Brenda's office. What was she searching for? And why did she give Grace such a nasty look?

CHAPTER EIGHT

Grace sat expectantly on the bleachers at the Endurance High School gymnasium on Monday morning and waited for the press conference to begin. Looking around, she watched the crowd of a couple hundred people, including ten or fifteen reporters from area newspapers and WHOC. They had positioned their equipment across from a long table where Chief Bitterman, TJ, and the police chief, Stephen Lomax, talked and drank coffee. Grace glanced at her phone to check the time. It was 9:58. Then, hoping not to be embarrassed if her son called and the theme from *Caddyshack* announced itself to the press conference, she set her cell phone on vibrate and stuffed it in her pocket.

She heard the hum of conversation and saw familiar faces all through the crowd. Grace turned her attention to people-watching at the main entrance to the gym and noticed Alex Reid walk in, dressed in jeans and a collared maroon shirt, its pocket sporting the Endurance Junior High logo. He was the principal there, and Grace surmised that he was a seasoned expert since he'd tried every trick he could think of when he was in her speech class. *He was suspended for three days after a going-away party for a teacher at the end of a first semester. He had spiked the punch with Boone's Farm strawberry wine combined with some homemade, high-proof alcohol. The principal had passed out.*

Lettie slipped in beside her and Grace figured her sister-in-law undoubtedly had concocted at least three theories about Brenda's death, culled from gossip around town.

Up at the table, TJ tapped the side of a microphone and announced, "One, two. Can everybody hear me?" Multiple "yes" answers went up from the crowd and the police chief took the microphone while TJ and Chief Bitterman, the fire chief, sat down. The crowd quieted, a few stragglers quickly taking some seats down in front.

Dan Wakeley silently slipped in and seated himself at the end of the table. Grace saw Wakeley here and there in town and always thought he was a handsome guy in a rugged sort of way. She broke off her thoughts about the people at the table when it appeared they were about to begin.

Stephen Lomax spoke into the microphone. "Thank you for coming today. I know there's been a lot of confusion concerning the recent fire and we thought a press conference would be the best way to disseminate facts. So I will try to tell you what I can, but I must remind everyone this is an ongoing investigation. Afterwards, if you have questions, we'll try to answer them with what we are able to discuss. The media can interview us separately after we finish," he said, turning and glancing at the pool of reporters. He shifted again to the crowd, shoulders back, holding the microphone with one hand and leaving his other arm loose at his side.

"Good morning, folks. As you know, we rarely have press conferences in Endurance, but due to all the inaccuracies floating around town, we felt it might be wise to at least give you the facts we can release at this time." He cleared his throat. "As many of you know, we had quite a fire on Friday night out at the old Quigley house that was owned by Brenda Norris. She has been positively identified as the victim our fire crew took from the house. Our prayers go out to her family and friends and her brother Dan, his wife Patty, and their children, who are all here with us today." He nodded toward a small group with three teenagers, a slightly younger boy, and their parents. Grace mainly knew Dan from photos. This morning Grace thought his face looked grim as he listened intently.

"Family and friends? She didn't have any friends that I could see," Lettie whispered.

"Shh," said Grace. "I want to hear this." Lettie snorted and a couple of people turned and gave her dirty looks, wanting her to shut up.

"I'd also like to thank all the fire departments that responded, the off-duty firemen, the police department, the ambulances, and the power company. All worked together in this effort to save both Brenda and her house. The Endurance trucks were on site in a matter of minutes but too late to prevent Ms. Norris's death." He hesitated for a moment before going on and looked down to consult his notes.

"We are still investigating the cause of the fire, and Dan Wakeley here is working with the state office to sift through the site for evidence. So at this point we believe it to be a suspicious fire based on witness accounts and what we have found so far."

A gasp went up from the crowd and people began murmuring in small groups.

Chief Lomax raised both of his hands and said, "Please, please, if I could get your attention. As I said, you can ask questions at the end." The crowd quieted once again and waited for more details.

"An autopsy was conducted on Saturday by the coroner in Woodbury with Detective Sweeney here attending. Ms. Norris died of smoke inhalation, but the autopsy has led us to believe her death is suspicious."

Another spate of talk erupted and this time it took longer to quiet the crowd.

Then, just as the noise died down, a voice directed toward the front yelled, "So what are you doing about it?" It was Tom Cogburn, a local grocer.

"Believe me, we have all the resources of the department at work on this as well as experts from the state fire and police offices. I don't want anyone to panic or worry. We have no proof that someone is planning any future attacks on anyone in town. And, folks, the last time we had a murder —"

Again a general rustling and talking increased after the word "murder," and the police chief tried to speak over the crowd. "As I was saying, we've rarely had suspicious deaths in Endurance. We had a murder in the 1920s. Since then we had a couple of domestic violence killings where the victim and shooter were married. And we had three fire deaths back in the sixties. Endurance, by and large, has always been a very safe town and citizens don't need to be worried."

Unless you're married, thought Grace.

"Just take the usual precautions of locking your doors at night and keeping your eyes open for unusual occurrences."

Oh great, Grace thought. *Now TJ will get all kinds of crank calls.*

Chiefs Bitterman and Lomax conferred briefly and then opened the conference up to questions. The first one came from Jeff Maitlin in the press pool.

"Chief Bitterman. Was there any suspicion or evidence of accelerants at this fire?"

"We're not sure yet, Mr. Maitlin. Eyewitness accounts would tend to point to the possibility, but we'll know more definitely in the next day or two."

A voice from the back yelled, "What about suspects?"

Mike Sturgis added, "Will you need to add more police to question that long line?"

Chief Bitterman glanced quickly over at Brenda's brother and family and answered, "Folks, please remember Brenda's family is here today. And yes, we are questioning some people of interest. But that's all I can say on that score right now."

Emily Dunworthy, retired postmistress, asked, "Is there any reason to think this might be the act of terrorists?" That brought some chuckles and lots of noisy reactions.

"Thank you, Ms. Dunworthy, for your question, but the answer is no. I don't see Endurance as a target for terrorists. No nuclear plants or weapons caches here."

Bill Tully rose and asked, "It seems to me that the first twenty-four hours are pretty important in catching the culprit. What are you doing? I've not heard any information about locking up suspects." He sat down and the audience turned back to the chief expectantly.

"Bill, we all know how difficult these things can be. TJ Sweeney is on the job and has already questioned a number of people. And police are canvassing for any possible witnesses that can help us with a timeline and with the events of that night."

"Well, that's not enough!" another belligerent voice shouted.

Then Tully rose again and hollered, "I, for one, want to see someone caught soon. I'm sick and tired of people in town" — and he looked around and added — "you know who you are — speculating it's my fault this death happened. Yes, Brenda had been drinking at my establishment, probably more than she should have. But I always made sure when that happened that she had a way to get home safely. And I took charge of her car until she came after it. I can't be responsible for what folks do after they're back in their houses. I sure didn't kill her." And now his voice rose in an angry bellow. "So I'm sick of talk that it's my fault, both to my face and undoubtedly behind my back. I repeat what I said before: What are you going to do about finding this murderer?" The buzz of conversation picked up again in the bleachers as well as some shouts in support of Tully.

"I'm afraid I can't comment on an ongoing investigation, Bill. I can simply assure you we will do all that we can. So if anyone has further questions, we'll be up here for a while and will try to answer your individual concerns. Thank you for coming and we'll call this to a close." He clicked off the microphone and everyone began to stand up and either move toward the doors or stand in small circles talking. Grace and Lettie left to go in different directions, Grace to the newspaper office and Lettie to her garden. Grace wondered what Jeff had found out in his interviews.

■ ■ ■ ■

When she got back to her office she noticed a desk drawer was slightly pulled out. *Had someone been here?* She figured she knew whom to ask.

She had talked with Shannon Shiveley on Saturday before she left in order to find out where to email reviews. Try as she might, she could tell Shannon would not be a helpful colleague or friend. But she was the person Jeff said to go to with questions. So this morning she marched straight down to Shannon's door.

"Shannon," she said, "have you been in my office?"

The reporter sat in her chair behind her desk filing her nails. Her dark hair was pulled back with a barrette today and she had on navy slacks and a T-shirt that had a photo of some band called The Day of Doom on the front. As always, her attitude and posture said, "I'm too busy to deal with you right now. Go away."

She looked up at Grace and scowled, "Why would you ask such a stupid question? What do I have to do with your office?"

Grace used her best "teacher" voice. "My

belongings have been moved and it's clear someone has gone through my desk drawers. I saw you in there on Friday when I got back from talking with Jeff, and I want to know what's so valuable in my office. Maybe I can help you find it and save you the trouble."

Shannon unfolded her legs and sat back in her chair, feigning nonchalance. "Well, as long as you put it that way, sure. I was in your office, although it's hardly 'your' office. You're just here to write some column no one will read. It's actually my office, or the one I should have since I'm the reporter. And the past occupant — who was hardly a writer — has something I need. Oops. That 'has' should have been 'had.' " Her voice dripped with disdain.

"I can't imagine what you're looking for," said Grace. "Describe it and I'll keep my eyes open."

Shannon laughed, an ugly, arrogant, contemptuous laugh. "It's a little book — a little black book. And in it she kept some information I need."

"Haven't seen any small black books but I'll keep a watch out for it. How big is it?"

"About four by six inches," said Shannon. "And if you find it, there might be something in it for you."

Grace turned and walked back to Brenda's — her — office. Her blood pressure was probably rocketing. This latest violation of Shannon's meant that anything she wrote or researched that was private would have to go home with her at night.

She sat down, calmed herself, and perused a copy of the morning newspaper. Obviously, the press conference and any other information didn't make the deadline. But Brenda's obituary was on the records page and Grace silently read:

ENDURANCE, Ill.–Brenda Anne Norris, 57, passed away June 17, 2011, in Endurance. She was born to Wilfred and Madeline Norris in Endurance on October 4, 1953.

She was preceded in death by her parents and one brother, Douglas.

Norris is survived by her brother, Dan (Penny) Norris, of Portland, Oregon, and four nieces and nephews, Allie Norris, Elizabeth Norris, Isabelle Norris, and Dan, Jr., also of Portland.

Brenda graduated from Endurance High School in 1971 and from McMichael College with her teaching certification in 1976. After graduation, she taught English in the Wamac, Illinois, consolidated district high school, from 1976 to 1980. She worked in several jobs until she returned to Endurance in 1984. Brenda taught English at Endurance High School from 1984 to 1988, and was sponsor of the yearbook and dance squad. After that she worked for the *Endurance Register* in several capacities, most recently as a news reporter.

Brenda was a loving aunt to her nieces and nephew and memorials may be taken to the First National Bank of Endurance to be placed in trust for their education. Please note that bequests should be made out to "The Norris Children's Educational Fund."

A private family graveside service will be held on Wednesday, June 22, with the Rev. Cynthia Andrews officiating. Internment will take place at the Shady Meadows Cemetery.

Online condolences may be sent to www.homestretchfuneralhome.com.

That makes it real, she thought. Sitting down at Brenda's — her — desk, Grace mulled over the press conference. What really surprised her were Bill Tully's comments. Rumor had it that he had quite a temper, but she hadn't heard or seen it before. He appeared almost paranoid about people's opinions of his part in Brenda's death. As he said, he couldn't help it if Brenda did something stupid after she left his place.

Swiveling around in her chair, she cupped her elbow with one hand and tapped her lips with her other hand. She surveyed her office in a slow, panoramic turn, and wondered where Brenda might have hidden that book Shannon wanted so badly. Folders of papers and pictures would be too obvious. She had moved most of Brenda's personal belongings, like her photographs and yearbooks, to boxes for her brother to pick up.

If she were going to hide something small and flat, where would she hide it? Turning back to her desk, she opened the desk drawers and felt around for false bottoms or a small booklet taped underneath the drawers. Nothing. Two containers of silk flowers occupied the bookshelves. She picked each of them up and looked inside and under them. She had already taken down the diplomas and there was nothing behind them.

She focused her eyes on the bookshelves again, raising her eyebrows and lingering on the titles. Brenda loved Poe. Maybe she hid that little black book inside or behind the

Poe anthology. Walking over to the bookshelves, Brenda pulled out the Poe book and thumbed through the pages. Nothing. She checked the binding and the endpapers glued onto the book's covers. Grace remembered a conversation with Brenda in which Grace had mentioned with amazement that a 1700s poet hid 900 pages of his poetry inside the endpapers of books in his library. When his personal library was sold in Nebraska in the twentieth century, the astonished buyer found the poems hidden in the bindings of his books. She returned to the Poe book. Well, nothing in here. Nothing loose and no places to slip in a small notebook.

Placing the book back on the shelf, Grace examined the other titles. *The Great Gatsby, The Last of the Mohicans, A Room of One's Own,* and *Moby Dick.* Then she spied Ambrose Bierce's *The Devil's Dictionary.* That was an acerbic volume if she ever saw one. It was also perfect for Brenda's sarcastic sense of what was humorous. She pulled it off the shelf and fanned the pages. Nothing. Then she inspected the binding in the front and the back. Inside the back cover was a small slit, so small that it might be overlooked unless someone were scrutinizing every inch with care. She slipped her baby finger under the edge of the backing page and could feel something inside, but the opening was too small and she didn't want to rip the paper. Walking over to the desk, she opened her purse, pulled out her cosmetic bag, and felt around for tweezers. Then she used her tweezers to pull out the object: a small, black-covered notebook. Turning it over, she recognized Brenda's handwriting on the front cover. She had written "Brenda's Retirement Fund."

CHAPTER NINE

Grace plopped down on the wooden bench at the edge of Endurance Park. She panted, coughed, and attempted to catch her breath. "Why . . . did I let you . . . talk me into this . . . TJ?"

TJ stopped jogging and sat down with a nonchalant air as she looked around the park and shrugged her shoulders. "I thought you invited me for a run because you said I needed to get some stress relief. You didn't tell me you hadn't run for a long time."

Grace could feel her pulse slow down. "And what about the fact . . . that you're still a youngster . . . and I'm . . . not?"

"You're the youngest fifty-six-year-old I know, and yes, I have seventeen years on you. But I don't think you need to trade yourself in for a new model yet."

"Two miles is enough . . . for a good start," Grace said as her breath returned. She opened the lid on her water bottle and drank deeply. "At least it's early so it isn't so hot and humid yet." She looked down at her sweat-drenched shorts and shirt. "You're right. I need to get back to this." She took another drink. "Feel any less stressed?"

TJ stretched her arms and replied, "Ah, this was a nice warm-up, Grace, and yes, I'm feeling better."

"And how is 'Mr. Construction Guy with the Chiseled Abs?' "

TJ smiled luxuriously. " 'Mr. Construction Guy' is just fine . . . and so are his abs."

Grace laughed and then broke into a fit of coughing. Once it stopped, she said, "I only ask because I have your best interests in mind. I can't help but see his battered brown truck when it's parked in your driveway. You know — neighborhood watch. The NRA sticker on the back is a dead giveaway that you're incompatible."

"Haven't had a great deal of time for my boy toy with this murder investigation. The chief got the report today that it definitely was arson that killed Brenda. Gasoline — multiple pours — no igniter. Whoever it was knew what he was doing."

"I suppose Mike Sturgis doesn't have much experience with burning down buildings."

"No." She shook her head. "I don't think

he has."

"What about Brenda's 'little black book'? Any luck?"

"Oh, crap! That was like throwing a stick of dynamite in the center of town. You wouldn't believe all the names and numbers with dollar signs in that book. We had to go back to square one. Some are reputable guys in town and others — well, reputable or not, I'd guess the male population of Endurance is sweating this out. Course they don't know we've found the book, but they will once we start questioning them today. Chief has called in reinforcements because we need more feet on the ground. I wonder if Brenda could be nominated for some book of world records for the most people who want to kill her."

"You must have some way to eliminate them."

"We do. And that's why I use you as a sounding board, Grace. You help me sort things through." She patted Grace on the shoulder. "And you don't divulge my secrets."

"Is that why we're sitting on a bench in the park at six-thirty in the morning?"

"Ah, you guessed my strategy."

Grace was silent for a moment. "How about alibis? If they have a strong alibi,

126

won't that eliminate them?"

"It would. And that's exactly where we'll start." TJ took a few swallows of water and looked off across the highway. "One of the key questions is, 'Where's the money?' Generally, we follow the money. We've checked her bank accounts and *nada.*"

"What about online accounts — you know — maybe a stock portfolio?"

"That's a possibility. I doubt that she has it stashed away in an offshore account in the Cayman Islands. I don't see her among corporate CEOs and millionaires who try to evade taxes." She pursed her lips and focused on the squirrels chasing each other around a small copse of trees. "I suppose we've missed something."

"I know people don't generally hide money under their mattresses these days, but could she have had it in her house? It would be long gone now."

"Possibility. On the other hand, where else might you stash cash that you don't want anyone to know about?"

Grace thought for a moment. "Lockbox at the bank? What about a friend who would put it in his or her account? I guess you'd have to trust them, wouldn't you?"

"Lockbox is a thought. I have that on my to-do list. The only possibility for a friend might be Shannon Shiveley. I don't trust that sniveling, little liar, but wasn't she close to Brenda?"

"She's the one who told me about the black book, so she's an obvious choice. I can't think of anyone else at the newspaper or at Tully's — she seems to have called the sports bar her home away from home."

"I'll check into both of those. Good thinking, Grace. Someday I may have to deputize you."

"To change the subject, I know you had Mike Sturgis in. It's all over town. He strikes me as too stupid to fit your description of 'knew what he was doing.'"

"Had him in for several hours and grilled him on a timeline the night of the fire. Fortunately for us, he was as naive as about eighty percent of the population — he talked, no lawyer. Unfortunately for me, I forgot to button a button on that cream-colored silk blouse and I saw him checking out my breasts throughout the interview."

"At least he has good taste."

"We do agree on something."

"Maybe no lawyer means he doesn't have anything to hide," Grace said as she took another drink from her water bottle. "Oops. Double negative."

"We got a search warrant based on witnesses to his threats. Actually, I guess you could be on that list, Grace, since you heard him at Tully's that night. His warehouse has plenty of gasoline — says he uses it all the time in his business and doesn't know if any is missing."

"Does it strike you that anyone at the bar that night could have seen Brenda drunk and taken advantage? You might want to consider the other people who were in the bar. Maybe one of them is someone she tried to blackmail." She yawned and then added, "Not me, of course."

TJ stood and began to do hamstring stretches. "Sturgis doesn't remember how many beers he drank or even who he talked to, not even Brenda. You were there. What was your take on his condition?"

"By the time I saw him he was wildly drunk and talked like a big shot. He threatened Brenda and might have assaulted her if Tully hadn't called for the police really fast. I thought he was scary, TJ."

"He said he'd never hurt her, but I believe he's lying about something. I think his exact words were, 'This is just great. Now that bitch is getting even with me from hell, since I'm sure that's where she is.' "

Grace gave TJ a point-blank look. "Do you

believe him — about the 'not hurting her' part?"

"Not sure. He definitely has a motive, but Jake and I both felt he lied about something — body language does it every time."

"By motive you mean —"

"Brenda. Tabloid stories. He says she made a serious impact on his business, not in a good way. If you remember, she accused him of taking shortcuts, overbilling, using poor-quality materials. He claims she took clients away from him and he has kids who will leave for college in the near future. Bingo: motive."

"Sure seems like you have quite a few motives. Is Sturgis at the top of the list?"

"He's hired an attorney to sue — for false arrest, only we didn't arrest him. All the time I questioned him he was quoting the Constitution, saying it puts reporters away for lying. Do you think he read the same document we studied back in high school?"

"Not sure he has a clue. You have to remember that Dave Cassandas taught him history and civics, and his classes probably consisted mostly of talk about the game plan for Friday night's basketball game."

"All right, you've got a point. I'll concede. So I tried to get Sturgis to reconstruct a timeline from that night. He was home the next morning but his truck was gone from Tully's parking lot by two a.m. He blacks out when he's had too much to drink, so he doesn't remember how his truck got from Tully's to his office or how he got home."

"An hour before Brenda died," Grace said. She paused thoughtfully and added, "Would he have had time to go to the warehouse, grab gasoline, and hightail it to Brenda's to have the fire up and going before three a.m.?"

"Plenty of time."

"How did he act when you questioned him?"

"I wish I could have knocked him off his chair. He was all sprawled out, cocky, and slammed his fist on the table at least twice. It's good that it was a simple crime because I can't see him planning anything elaborate."

Grace cleared her throat and sat up straighter. "You always talk about records. Does he have a record?"

"Nothing a little anger management training couldn't fix. He admits himself that he gets angry, drinks too much, and 'says crap.' His wife has threatened him with divorce if he comes home drunk once more. Three months ago he took care of some barn construction at Andrew Lawrence's farm.

Lawrence claimed the workmanship was shoddy — shades of Brenda, exposé writer — and, when he wouldn't pay, Sturgis got out of control and Andy called the police. Mike has, unfortunately, a very thick folder."

"Is he able to explain the bruise on Brenda's forehead?"

"No. Not a word. I can see various possibilities, but the one I explained to him was that he hated her and decided to give her a scare. He goes to her house and pours gasoline on the foundation. He's still drunk so that might excuse his lack of logic, but it doesn't excuse his stupidity. Figuring *she* isn't stupid and will smell smoke and get out, he lights the house. Of course, her car wasn't there, so he might have thought she was gone. But that still doesn't explain the bruise. He might have done that before he fired the house but he doesn't remember.

"We have a second scenario, too," TJ said.

"A second scenario?"

"Besides the line of people who have been blackmailed — and you have yet to find the money — we also have victims of her newspaper stories. Maybe Tully was right — we'd have a line around the block of possible murderers of opportunity. And then we have yet another possibility."

"Good grief! What else?"

"Sturgis claims Brenda was shacked up with a married man. Didn't get the name, of course. But he said he'd heard it from more than one person. I believe he ended that part of the conversation with, 'Enough people with motives to kill her but not enough cops to round them all up.' I have to admit he may be right on that one."

"Are you sure this wasn't smoke and mirrors to get himself off the hook?"

"It might be, but we will start on interviews with the blackmail-ees — I refuse to call them victims if they were dumb enough to get mixed up with Brenda — starting tomorrow morning."

"We?"

"Chief has sent for some help from the department in Woodbury."

"So, you have Mike Sturgis with means, opportunity, and motive. Standing behind him are, oh, twenty or thirty people with motives also. Sounds to me like you'll need an army on the ground."

TJ glanced at her phone. "Time to go, Grace. I've got to get to work. I swear I'll get this guy."

"Do we have time for a leisurely walk back to town?" she pleaded.

TJ smiled. "Not on your life," and she was up and jogging in place.

Grace sighed, gave a half-hearted shrug, and stowed away her water bottle. "Guess that was too much to ask. You go on. I think I'll take a more leisurely pace and call it a nature walk."

"And I'm going to catch a killer."

Grace watched TJ head down the path out toward the highway. Once across that barrier, the sidewalks would take her to town. *I have to get back to this running,* Grace thought. *It makes me feel better and gives me a chance to talk to TJ. She has so much on her hands right now. In some ways she isn't any different than she was in high school — well, maybe a little less stubborn, but still she loved to explore possibilities and was curious about everything.*

She laughed out loud when she thought of TJ, the contentious teenager. She had moved the future detective into her Honors English class during her freshman year at Endurance High School. TJ had dropped her head on her desk and refused to do anything. Grace smiled at the memory of her indignant demands. *Too much work, too many white kids, no one that looks like me. You placed me in this class against my will and I'm not gonna do it.*

Not to be outmaneuvered, Grace had shown up at TJ's rundown, ramshackle house. She remembered that visit vividly. Ms. Sweeney hesitantly let her in the door after Grace explained who she was and her mission. Inside, every doily, photograph, pillow, and knickknack was in place and squeaky clean. Grace sat down as if she visited the house of an African American lady every day, and Ms. Sweeney brought out fresh lemonade and cookies as if she entertained white ladies in her home every day. Ms. Kimball assured her that TJ should be in her Honors class. Laughing, Grace remembered TJ's remark: "So whadda ya want with a skinny-ass black girl in your white-bread class?"

Her mother had scolded her with "that look" and called her "Teresa Johanna." After that TJ was quiet.

Grace remembered she stayed calm and composed and told Ms. Sweeney that TJ could write her ticket to college if she took the Honors class and other hard classes. She was extremely bright.

"And who's gonna pay for that ticket?" asked Mama Sweeney in her quiet, polite voice.

"She'll get a scholarship," Grace had said.

"We ain't takin' no charity," Ms. Sweeney had sniffed and mumbled.

"This wouldn't be charity. Colleges give

scholarships because they recognize academic promise. This could be her chance."

"We've been promised to before," her mama said. Grace could see the hurt in her eyes but also the ramrod-straight back as she sat on the edge of her chair.

"This time is different. She'll have to work hard and it will pay off. I promise. Just let her try it for a year and see what happens," Grace had said.

Mama Sweeney said "yes" and Grace had TJ trapped in her net. After that, TJ's world changed. She read books she'd never heard of before — Richard Wright's *Black Boy* and *Native Son* — and books about worlds she'd never imagined: *Jane Eyre* and *Things Fall Apart*. Grace steered her toward books about strong women who struggled and overcame adversity, especially when the world was younger and belonged to men. She got a full ride to the state university, took a law enforcement class because nothing else fit in her schedule, and found her niche.

Her mama and brother Tyrone were so proud of her the day she graduated from college. And then — in an utterly surprise move — she announced that she would come back to Endurance and take the police exam. Everyone said it would never happen

— not a woman, and especially not a woman who was biracial. But she made it happen when she scored the highest total in the history of anyone who'd applied for the department — ever. And, laughing, she said she planned to come home to keep an eye on her mama. It was only a matter of time before she became the first Endurance female detective. *She worked hard at calling me "Grace,"* she thought, *and she fit into our group right away. She teased us about our concerns when it came to children and grandchildren, and we teased her about the men in her life.*

Storing her thoughts away so she could concentrate on getting across the highway, Grace jogged across the asphalt, slowed to a leisurely walk, and vowed that she would do whatever she could to help TJ get through this tough time and solve this murder.

CHAPTER TEN

Grace leaned back in her chair at the *Endurance Register* and tapped a pencil over and over against her lower lip. She stared at her three children in the photo on her desk but didn't see their faces. Her two-year-old granddaughter, Natalie, stared back from a second frame. But Grace's mind was not on her family. Her thoughts were back at the Shady Meadows Cemetery, contemplating a story Brenda had researched. Pictures Grace had taken of three graves — one set a little off from the other two — were etched in her brain. And now, back at her office, she examined Brenda's story about the graves as well as the town's history leading to those three deaths. It was almost as if the story of the fire that had killed these three people was a story that had also consumed Brenda.

And if I remember correctly, Grace thought, *she said she was working on an exposé, something that would blow the lid off this town. Could it have something to do with this story of a fire that happened out in the country back in the late 1960s?*

Fingering the pages of Brenda's first draft, which lay on her desk, Grace had found it unique and enthralling. As she read Brenda's words, she could see her sharp mind, pulling out entertaining and little-known facts about the town's history. In the margins where Brenda had written questions and notes to herself, each pencil stroke was perfectly connected and beautifully scripted, as if Brenda had taken her time. Every so often Grace felt as if she could read Brenda's thoughts — her points of indecision and her points of certainty. This writing was nothing like her stories in the newspaper that had angered half the town. Brenda had pondered the details — way too many details. This would take considerable condensing. But Brenda hadn't finished so Grace wasn't sure what her huge surprise was.

The first part of the draft about the town's history didn't have an overabundance of margin notes. When Grace got to the three cold-case files that Brenda had selected, she saw very few notes about the first two cases. They had happened long ago. But when she read about the third cold case — the fire story — Grace observed a multitude of notes, questions, and thoughts Brenda had written in her clear, concise hand.

Her cell phone broke the silence — "I Wanna Dance with Somebody" — it was Deb. She hit the "ignore" button and figured she'd call her later.

Before quitting for the day, Grace decided to reexamine her last few hours of work concerning the town's early days. The village of Endurance was originally a tract of land created by Congress after the War of 1812. The first settlers had arrived from Ohio and erected some simple cabins, a church, a military stockade — and later — a dry goods store. During those early years, families journeyed to the town, fording rivers and streams, and plodding down footpaths to reach a place where they could establish new lives. The soil was rich, black loam, perfect for growing wheat, and the plain was still a vast sea of open land with prairie grass that shimmered in the wind, unchecked to the horizon. As time passed, farms became visible on the landscape, followed by a post office. *I'll bet they delivered no junk mail,* Grace mused. She skipped over information about surveying and the public auction of lots.

More charming were some of the early settlers' adventures and the archaic laws the city council enacted. She read with alarm about one or two Indian scares and some horrific winters when the snow and ice made life lonely, impossible, and isolated since they had no modern machinery to remove it. They used oxen to break the snow drifts. Many settlers' surnames were identical to some of the modern-day townspeople, but then some other names she'd never heard. She examined the rolls of early voters — all men, of course — and she saw Blair, Morgan, Atwell, Woolsey, and Hargraw. Once the town of Endurance incorporated, the town council passed laws regarding public intoxication, tavern licenses, gambling, and curfews. No citizen was allowed to let "horses gallop or cows wander down the public streets." No stores or taverns could be open on the Lord's Day.

The mid-1800s also brought the railroad dashing across the land. More settlers followed, and the expanding town of Endurance was granted a state charter and was named the county seat. The tiny village of huddled houses and diminutive stores, perched on the edge of the wilderness, gradually evolved into an industrial town sustained by the produce of the agriculture industry. Besides agriculture, these businesses and factories revealed the needs of various decades: candle and wax works, a telegraph office, hardware stores, shoe makers and shoe menders, tailors and haberdashers, and barber shops. As time passed and new inventions altered the landscape of prairie life, some stores disappeared and others took their places.

Endurance built a school to accommodate the influx of women and the growth of families. Its first teachers were "the godly Misses Emma and Elizabeth Farley, daughters of the local Presbyterian minister."

Grace sighed. She had so much more to work on in her story about the history of the town. She glanced at the calendar. It was only the twenty-third of June and she still had plenty of time to finish the background piece. Putting her pencil down, she rubbed her eyes, stood up, and gently flexed her legs. *Did she eat lunch?* She couldn't remember. She had been going at this since ten a.m. and it was now almost three.

Glancing through Brenda's notes brought back a sharp reminder of how smart her friend had been. Brenda had condensed lesser facts and bundled periods of time that were sure to intrigue her readers. Grace would shape them a bit more.

After a break and a cup of yogurt, Grace considered the three sets of cold-case files that Brenda had chosen. Apparently she had planned a piece on each of them. These were the stories that had led Grace on a fact-finding, photograph-generating tour of the burial ground south of town yesterday.

Shady Meadows Cemetery yielded some clear images of graves that held the remains of several residents in the three cold cases. The first cold case concerned a man named Swensen. Grace located his grave and took a snapshot. He had died "a lawbreaker" in 1926. Gustav Swensen sat in on a card game at Samuel Davies's home, and the players indulged in "overflowing beer mugs — manufactured at the illegal still of one Boone Whitemore." It was Prohibition, with laws that would have been applauded by the stern Presbyterian founders of the town.

Leaving the house two hours after midnight, Swensen was "gunned down by a single shot, rudely administered," and his stash of $1,500 poker winnings disappeared into the night. Neither the killer nor the loot was ever found. Grace looked long and hard to find Swensen's grave in one of the older parts of the cemetery among other Swensens, Ahlstroms, Engbergs, and Olofssons. *My,* Grace had thought as she positioned her camera to take several photos of Gustav Swensen's grave, *I didn't realize we had such a Scandinavian presence in the early town. I'm sure he must be an ancestor of Nub — his horse couldn't have been much slower than Nub's car.* Despite his sins, Gustav was ultimately allowed burial near his upstanding neighbors. *I'll bet that ruffled a few feathers.*

Brenda's second story was a case of embezzlement at a shaky local bank. In the 1930s when financial institutions hung on by their fingertips, one Dooley O'Hara, an accountant at the First Bank of Endurance, embezzled most of the bank's reserves, pulling them right out of the vault, once again "in the dead of night." *Just goes to prove what my mother always told my rebellious teenage self — that nothing good happens after eleven at night.* Dooley was caught, tried, and convicted in ten minutes by disgruntled bank clients and neighbors. He was sent to the penitentiary in Lexington and the stolen money was never recovered. A few months later the bank crumbled under the economic weight of the times and the town had even more reason to despise him. O'Hara died in the penitentiary the following year, a stabbing victim. According to the local historian, Alfred Peters, "Numerous of the prison's inmates were blood relatives to recently-made-penurious people in the town of Endurance." O'Hara was buried in a grave at the prison since the town wasn't interested in having him back, dead or alive.

Brenda had spent most of her time on the third cold case, perhaps because she had been alive when it occurred. These were the three graves Grace had found and photographed — two together and one a few feet away. A fire killed a husband, wife, and a young teenager they had taken into their home. Prior to that fatal fire, the town experienced a number of damaging fires, too many, Grace surmised, to be accidental. During 1964–1968, several fires were attributed to arson. The fire chief's theory was that a pyromaniac was loose in Endurance. They never caught him. A whole block of the town burned down in 1964, destroying a bank, a clothing store, a doctor's office, a pharmacy, and a shoe store. In 1966, two more houses went up in flames and the cause appeared to be electrical. The year 1967 brought two barn fires in the country that were total losses in both property and livestock, but so far Grace read of no human fatalities. Each of the fires happened at night.

That all changed in January 1968, when William and Terry Kessler were killed in a farmhouse fire, along with Nick Lawler, a teenage friend of the family. The three bodies were severely burned and they did not find the body of Ted Kessler, the teenage son of the family. It was widely believed that he had set the fire.

The fire chief's theory at the time was that Ted Kessler was also responsible for the earlier fires. Whether his family discovered his role or he argued with them concerning something else, no one knew. The Kesslers had taken the Lawler kid into their home because their son Ted had befriended him at school. Nick came from a transient family whose parents were habitual drug and alcohol abusers, and Nick spent most of his time at the Kesslers'. Witnesses claimed the Kesslers felt sorry for him because the family was dirt poor and he was allegedly the favorite target of his parents' abuse. The graves Grace photographed at the cemetery belonged to the Kessler parents and Lawler. Grace read in Brenda's notes that the high school football coach had collected money from townspeople to erect a small stone over Nick Lawler's grave.

I bet there are still people around who'd remember that fire, Grace thought. *Let me think.* She glanced back at Brenda's dates from the obituary. *Brenda would have been fourteen or fifteen at the time. Maybe she knew some of the principal players. With all of these margin notes perhaps she had formed a theory about this fire. It was never really cleared up since the Kessler boy disappeared.*

Suddenly, Grace's shoulders hurt and her eyes burned. She yawned, stretched her arms, and moved her head in circles to loosen her neck. She'd been at this paper-sorting all day. She collected Brenda's pages scattered here and there across the table and the floor of the office. She hadn't managed to read everything, but she had made good progress. Her focus was drawn to a piece of paper near the bottom of the Kessler stack. She hadn't reached that pile yet. Brenda had sketched a face in black ink and written "E. A. Poe" next to it. *It was a good likeness,* thought Grace. Next to the face were several numbers and a huge question mark. *What could she have meant by that?*

Grace surveyed the two cardboard cartons on the floor near the filing cabinet, cold-case files about the fire at the Kessler house. While Brenda's account was based on the newspaper stories at the time, she had also studied the contents of these boxes. Grace would need to look through them also to add more details to the story. The date of the fire was listed on the outside. *Do I have enough energy left to look through those boxes?* she wondered. *Well, maybe I'll sneak a peek inside.*

She tore open the packing tape that Brenda or the police had resealed. Before that the boxes had stayed pristine for forty-some years. Pulling back the flaps, she still caught the suggestion of mustiness from the police department's basement.

Inside each box was a diverse collection of objects and papers, along with a list of contents. Piled in no certain order were papers pertaining to the fire at the Kessler house. Many were sheer onionskin paper and some were carbon copies hunt-and-pecked on police typewriters long ago. Grace thumbed through them quickly, reminding herself that the 1960s did things differently compared to 2011. She saw the medical examiner's reports, lab reports, witness interviews, meetings of a task force, detective reports — *Oh, Sean Helmsley was the lead detective and he's been gone quite a while* — newspaper articles, some handwritten notes, more interviews, and some black-and-white photographs. Some were long-ago Polaroids that were simply decomposed gray blurs. Evidently they had set up a task force with detectives, state police, and crime scene investigators, but eventually it was disbanded. *Hmm. Where had she seen those photos of the house burning and the fire department valiantly trying to save it? She couldn't remember. Maybe it would come to her later. The deputy fire chief was Richard White. I must remember to check if he's still around or deceased like Helmsley.*

She reached down to the bottom of one of the boxes and found a few scraps of dark material and several small objects. Other objects were still in paper evidence bags with writing on the outside. Maybe these had come from the house after they had put out the last of the sparks and smoldering boards. Grace put the papers and objects back in the boxes, figuring she would study them more tomorrow. She didn't feel up to the medical examiner's reports or the old photos of the bodies yet.

She folded the flaps back together and pushed the boxes in the corner, determined to do battle with them tomorrow. Standing up, she suddenly realized that she had gone through all this evidence and it was about a fire. *And I'm fine,* she thought. *My heart is not beating rapidly, and sweat is not pouring off my face, and I'm feeling no anxiety.*

Grace heard a noise behind her. She

turned and saw TJ Sweeney standing in the doorway.

" 'Bout ready to end your day, I hope," TJ said. "Guess retirement is rougher than I thought."

"Yes. I'm bone-tired. Ready for a drink and some quiet conversation, or perhaps no conversation but instead the office sofa at home for a nap."

"I'm on my way back to the police department, but thought I'd stop by and treat you to a little surprise."

"Surprise?" She raised one eyebrow. "Please don't tell me you've brought photos from the morgue or something else macabre."

"Nah. Couldn't actually bring the surprise. Had to drop it off at the department with a witness and have it videotaped. You know, all the typical routine police stuff. I'll have to describe it. Remember the black book you left for me that the Shiveley woman who works here was trying to find? Well, it had a number of interesting initials and even a few names in it, along with abundant dollar signs. I questioned one of the people named and it was enough to give me a search warrant for Brenda's lockbox, which was sealed when she died. No one's been in it. Her brother figured he'd have to come back and settle her estate after probate and once we'd finished the investigation. Among other objects, you will not believe what we found." She unfolded a piece of paper and laid it down on Grace's desk.

Grace walked closer to her desk next to TJ, and she stared at the paper.

"Oh, my God! You have to be kidding!"

"Nope."

On the paper in large, black marker letters, TJ had written:

"Evidence seized from Brenda Norris's lockbox with a search warrant: $270,000 in hundred-dollar bundles."

CHAPTER ELEVEN:
RONDA

Ronda Burke slouched over her kitchen table, as snores came from her nose and saliva dried in a pool below her mouth. The only sound that competed with her nasal symphony was the slurping and teeth-grinding of her twenty-six-pound Bordeaux bulldog as he devoured the remains of a three-day-old pizza spoiling in the delivery box on the kitchen floor. It was next to the overflowing wastebasket. Spilling onto the table near Ronda's head was a limitless pile of cigarette butts, both in and near an ashtray. These accompanied the seven empty Keystone cans lying on their sides on the Formica surface, three of them with large dents.

Her back door, which opened onto a long flight of stairs, contained a mail slot. A pile of junk mail and envelopes covered the floor under the mail slot, a few white envelopes peeking from underneath catalogues, brochures, and credit card applications. Next to the mail pile was the edge of a kitchen counter whose top was filled with dirty dishes, half-eaten pieces of food that were quickly acquiring mold, and an occasional fly that feasted on the remains of several meals. This was not the home Grace would have pictured while thinking of the woman who had watched her children so long ago.

The metallic sound of the mail slot opening and closing caused a stir in Ronda and an alteration in her snores. Slowly she opened her eyes, moaned, and closed them. She licked her dry lips, tasting the remains of last night's nicotine. A few seconds later she opened them again, groaned, sat up cautiously, placed one hand on her throbbing head, and attempted to read her kitchen clock on the wall across the room.

"Oh God, oh God, oh God, what a night," she said to no one but the bulldog. "Why does something that tastes so smooth going down have to make me feel so rotten?" Briefly, she wondered what day it was. She pushed herself up carefully from the chair, put her hand on the place where her head hurt, and lurched over closer to the clock. "Four-thirty. Can't be night 'cause the sun's still out." Then she picked up her cell phone, pushed the button at the bottom, and watched it light up. "Oh, Jesus, Mary, and Joseph, it's Thursday and I'm due at work in twenty minutes. Can't call in sick again. Tully'd kill me."

The dog trotted over, carrying the remains of a slice of pepperoni in his massive teeth. "You shouldn't have that," Ronda muttered and, groaning, reached over and pulled hard on it, willing him to open his mouth. "Ahhh, even that hurts." Winning the battle, she patted him on the head and promised, "I'll get you some nice doggie food in a minute, Adonis," and started into the bedroom.

Once she had showered, pulled out her hair with a pick, and put on a uniform — she smelled the armpits first and made a face — she shuffled into the kitchen and, noticing the pile of mail, leaned over and carefully picked it up. She threw it on the table in a revised mound of shapes and colors. A dark green postcard slid from the stack and she tried to remember where she had seen the logo. *Oh, yeah.* It was from a comedy club on the river where she had done some standup routines a couple of months ago. She turned it over and read the handwritten note from Jimmy Millard, the owner. "When are we gonna see you again? People are askin'." *Hmm. I'll have to think about that,* she brooded, too tired to figure it out at the moment. She laid it back on the table, isolating it from the pile.

Ronda shambled over to the kitchen sink, selected a glass heavily ringed with sour milk, drew some water, and planted it on one of the few empty spaces left on the counter. Reaching in a cupboard, she pulled out a canister marked "sugar." She inspected the inside and noticed she was low on her joy pills, her black beauties. She palmed a couple, threw them in her mouth, and guzzled down the entire glass of water. *I've got a few more minutes,* she thought. *I'll let those lovelies do their job.*

She plopped down at the table, stared at the pile of bills, and pondered how she had ended up in this mess. *You know, Mom, you were right. I could have made something of myself, but I always seemed to make the wrong choices. By the time I was in high school I earned my own money in waitressing jobs and fast-food restaurants. My grades were decent and I was pretty confident. But, you know, I came last, after the other four, and by then without a decent-paying job you were sliding steadily downward. You were so tired and overworked that you didn't have much time for your youngest daughter. No clue who my father was. Gone. Missing.* Ronda began to stack the bills in piles: pay, leave, throw out. *But I'm not complaining, Mom. You got me used to taking care of myself, paying for my own clothes, and often for the grocery bill. But you were right that I'd follow in your footsteps, especially with men.*

His name had been Jim Burke. By then she was out of school and working as a bartender in a dive on South Main called Dirty Dave's. Jamie, as she liked to call him then, was a truck driver, a hard drinker and smoker, who straggled his way into the bar during a massive downpour on a jet-black night. She should have seen that as an omen. *You always said I was the foolish one, Mom,* she sighed. Ronda had never met someone like Jamie, who had seen the entire country from highways that crisscrossed every state. He had the gift of gab and the charm to go with it. Two hasty months later they were married.

And that's when the fun began, thought Ronda. He had not used her well. Between booze, womanizing, and long jobs away for weeks, he'd come home and she was the one he'd pounded on. They were married five years. *Well,* she thought, *it might have been five years, but in bruises, aches, broken bones, and pain, it was more like twenty-five.* She thought about leaving town, just disappearing. But why should she let him chase her away from the only home she'd ever known? She just wanted out but couldn't afford a lawyer.

The first couple of years she always worried that he'd show up. She signed an order of protection with the Endurance Police Department but knew it would be a worthless piece of paper when he turned up unexpectedly. But one blissful day she heard he'd been knifed and had died in a bar in Waco, Texas. She could breathe easy again.

Tully hired her five years ago and paid her a decent salary. He was a very demanding boss, a management style that she was used to, and it didn't bother her at first. But Bill was moody and she finally reached a point where she could tell as soon as she got to work if he was listening to his demons or playing the clever and charming host. She made herself indispensable, and he left her in charge whenever he had to be gone. Ronda was an efficient manager and had a huge and loyal following among customers. Tully knew she brought in business.

Often Ronda was aware of what happened in town before the police knew. And she listened and watched people's body language. *Damn, I could have made a good psychologist,* she thought.

Her head had stopped hurting and she felt

157

a little energy pick-me-up. She put a cigarette in her mouth, lit it, and drew in the smoke deeply, coughing a couple of times.

She picked up the green postcard. She made some extra money — when she could get a night off — by playing in dives along the river. She had a funny — albeit raunchy — act that had built up a fair following. But as soon as she made a little cash, the brakes went out on her car or a pipe broke under her kitchen sink. She managed to scrape along. But never again would she depend on a man for her living. She was fine, safe, and sometimes lonely. She occasionally brought a man home and they used each other to stave off the emptiness. *That was enough,* she thought.

If only I could get a stake together, I'd go to California. Everyone had told Ronda that she had a natural gift for comedy and she loved to make people laugh. She didn't have the means to get out of town. Well, maybe she could change that. Tired of living from paycheck to paycheck, holding off the collection agencies that called on her phone — and her phone was always a few payments from being turned off — she knew she had to do something soon. She was smart, heard things, and could find an edge, a way to use what she knew to get a stake. *But how?* she thought.

Then, just as she gathered her keys and purse and started for the door, her cell went off. It was her friend, Shannon, who worked at the *Endurance Register.*

"Yeah, what?" she said. "I gotta be at work and I'm headed out the door."

Listening to her phone as she pulled the door open and trudged down the stairs in the lowering sunlight, she thought she finally had a way to get that stake. Shannon Shiveley had been working with Brenda Norris on a very profitable blackmail scheme. Shannon had spilled her guts one night when she was drunk at one of Ronda's parties. According to Shannon, Brenda had been sleeping with somebody — some married somebody — and Ronda needed to figure out who that was. Listening to Shannon, she knew she had to nail down a name before Shannon did. She thought she had an idea already. This could be her ticket to ride.

Chapter Twelve:
Grace

Grace glanced at the clock on her desk at the *Endurance Register*. 11:30. *I've been at this for the last three hours.* She arched her back and raised her arms behind her stiff neck. She was sitting on the sofa with myriad piles of papers stacked in every which direction. Two cold-case boxes for the 1968 fire were the center of Brenda's investigation. She had made a timeline with gaps and inconsistencies about the case, and Grace began looking at that timeline after reading and rereading nearly every paper in the box. So far she had a solid grounding in the facts of the case. Time to sit back and review it in her head.

The fire had erupted in the home of William and Terry Kessler, who lived on a farm outside of Endurance, on the night of January 25, 1968. A massive blaze broke out before anyone discovered it. The fire marshal estimated that it began around 2:00 to

2:30 a.m. The two-story house sat among a few trees on a ten-acre farm that was in an isolated setting. It had a barn nearby filled with hay, as well as a few horses and cows. None of the livestock was injured nor was the barn destroyed since it was fifty yards from the house. Fire crews from nearby towns answered the call but they were not able to save the Kesslers' home.

Onlookers reported that massive orange flames escaped from the upstairs windows and the heavy, black smoke could be seen for several miles. Winds of fifteen mph sent the smoke hurling into the night and hampered the firefighters' efforts. The house and its contents were a total loss.

"By the time we arrived," Deputy Fire Chief Richard White reported, "the house was fully engulfed and we realized it would not be a salvage operation. The best we could do was to keep the fire from spreading to other structures."

Grace sifted through the papers and lifted up another newspaper story published several days after the fire. State examiners on the scene the day of the fire stayed to study the debris for several days. The *Endurance Register* carried a story about their work and explained that they sorted through the rubble to determine the point of origin and the cause, one layer at a time, and they placed objects in evidence bags for the police. Grace glanced at some of the piles she had set aside on the floor. *Those must have been some of the items they found,* she thought.

The paper, wood, and plastics in the house ignited quickly and some bottles of linseed oil, liquid solvents, and cleaners in the downstairs kitchen exploded. *Even the furniture back then was probably toxic, I'd bet.* Examiners looked for an igniter — a pile of rags or an electric heater — but didn't find one. Everything was blackened and charred and the coroner estimated that two or three breaths of the carbon monoxide would have put people to sleep in a fire of that magnitude.

Two weeks later the state fire marshal's office issued a report that the fire was incendiary and undoubtedly set. Their determination came from eyewitness reports of the flame and smoke colors, evidence of multiple pours of gasoline in various parts of the house, and an absence of any other possible cause. They continued to work the case, but no perpetrator was ever caught.

"Hi, Grace." Jeff Maitlin stuck his head in the frame of her open office door.

His sudden voice broke her concentration

and made her jump.

"Oh. You startled me. I'm going over the fire story Brenda was checking out." She noticed that the light blue dress shirt he wore brought out the blue of his eyes.

"Find anything interesting?" He leaned on the door frame. *My, that man is a dresser,* she thought. *Hard to believe I only met him a week or two ago.*

"Right now it's just a mass of facts and jumbled ideas, but I think I'll have it under control sometime today. Get my book review?"

"Yes, and thanks for getting it in early." He walked over to the sofa and looked into the cold-case boxes. "Looks like you have plenty to do." He smiled.

Grace held up a huge pile of papers. "I really find this fire story interesting. I can see why Brenda did too. I imagine she knew some of these poor people."

Jeff nodded and turned to go. He stopped at the door as if trying to figure out something else to say. Then he added, "Well, I'll leave you to your research."

Watching his departing back, Grace felt a flush spread over her face. *Well,* she thought, *he didn't have to walk back here to thank me. He could have sent an email.* A heavy sigh escaped her mouth. *Grace, you are too old for this silliness.*

She turned back to the family information and within seconds she was totally absorbed in the details. William and Terry Kessler had lived in the house on their farm since shortly after World War II. Their son, Ted, was born in 1952 and went to the local schools. His body was never found, and speculation was that he had fled town after the fire. *Hmmm . . . he would have been fifteen or sixteen when that fire took place.* From all reports of witnesses and people who knew him, he was a quiet kid. But a store owner in town came forward and said he thought Kessler was devious. Perhaps he was a quiet kid, but the store owner had caught him shoplifting small items several times in the previous year. He didn't turn him in to the police, but he did talk to the parents, who assured him they would punish the boy and paid him for the stolen items.

She examined the detectives' notes from their conversations with people at the high school. They interviewed several teachers and their impression of Ted Kessler ranged from "wonderful kid" to "moody and disinterested." *Evidently he loved science and hated math,* Grace thought, from the interview notes of those teachers. He had gone out for football but didn't get much playing time. The football coach kept him on the team and put him in occasionally when they were far ahead. He reported that Kessler was a quiet boy, kept to himself, and didn't have more than a friend or two. One of his friends was a kid named Nick Lawler.

The third body in the house was identified as Nick Lawler. The Kessler parents were found in their upstairs bedroom, burned beyond recognition. Lawler's body was found, also burned beyond recognition, on the floor beside the bed in the third bedroom. The Kessler kid's bedroom was empty. The coroner determined that all three had died of smoke inhalation.

Numerous witnesses came forward to tell of how the Kesslers had "taken in" Nick Lawler. His parents were transients, often in trouble with the law, and certainly into various drugs. The Lawler boy had struck up a friendship with Ted Kessler over football practices and had taken on the role of "guardian" of the younger boy. *Well,* thought Grace. *I suppose bullying happened even back then.* Lawler spent weeks at a time with the Kesslers and roamed the fields with Ted Kessler, fishing and hunting.

Detectives questioned the Lawler parents. They knew the Lawlers well since the family had drifted in and out of trouble. They were careless people, careless with their drugs and booze and careless with their son and his four siblings. Both parents had extensive police records for theft and drug possession, and they had lost their children a couple of times to Child Services. Mr. Lawler managed to make a little money with odd jobs for people who felt sorry for him, but mostly they lived off the government dole. The children were dirty, ragged, and neglected, and lived in a tiny house south of the tracks on Myrtle Avenue. Nick had an inconsistent record of attendance at the high school and, according to his parents, had never been to a doctor or hospital because he'd never been sick. *If he'd had bruises, scrapes, and injuries in that house,* thought Grace, *he'd never have seen a doctor. Free dental clinics didn't exist then either.*

During high school Lawler played football but never really distinguished himself. He was good-sized for a high school player but didn't always make practice. The coach, like many others, felt sorry for him and bought him shoes for football his sophomore year when Lawler couldn't go out for the season because he needed cleats.

Grace yawned and rolled her shoulders a couple of times. *This Lawler kid might have*

*come from a horrible background, but he must
have been a charmer to get so many people
to be kind to him or take him in.*

Gazing at the brutal coroner's photos,
Grace thought again about how lucky she
had been to escape the fire in her off-
campus house in college. Her hands began
to shake slightly as she held the photos.
Don't think any deeper. But her mind kept
spinning. *These people didn't stand a chance.
The fire started in the middle of the night and
was widespread before they even woke up —
just like her college roommates, Gail and
Robin. And the fire marshal said it was set.
What possible motive could the Kessler kid
have for burning up his family and friend in
such a merciless, barbaric act? I wonder
where he is today,* thought Grace.

Brenda had organized all the information
in the cold-case files. She had also kept a
timeline and running set of notes and questions of her own. Near the notes on the
Kessler boy she had written, "Poe?" and
next to it "279." Then she had scribbled
"what if?" *What did this pertain to — the fire,
the parents, the house, or the Kessler boy?*
Grace couldn't decide what Brenda meant
and decided to look at some of the objects.
Maybe they'd give her some ideas.

They must have originally been in evidence bags. But now several items had fallen to the bottom of the box and Grace pulled them out and set them on the table. She examined them: several bottle caps, worn and dirty, sat on the table, along with some shards of pottery or dishes. A small knife, perhaps a Swiss army knife, lay on the table beside what looked like frames or part of a frame for old glasses. A number of coins — someone had cleaned them off — sat in a small pile in the bottom of the box, and Grace could see that not one had a date on it later than the mid-1960s. *Well, that makes sense.* Another coin — it looked like a good-luck piece of some kind — sat among the other coins. Grace picked up each of them and scrutinized them, along with the glasses frame. The coins weren't unusual and the good-luck piece — if that is what it was — had a bird on it and a small hole through the middle. *It looks like a Raven. Poe again?*

It's like a puzzle, she thought. She turned the good-luck piece over in her fingers, and wondered whose pocket it might have occupied. Or perhaps someone found it on the floor of the house after the fire. *Maybe Nick Lawler carried it because it gave him some hope in the ugly surroundings of his own home. Oh, shut up. You're being a romantic now.* She didn't see anything else unique or unusual in the bottom of the box or among the items she had already examined. *What could you have meant by your notes, Brenda? Why Poe?* She suddenly remembered that she had heard the author's name somewhere else recently. *Where?*

She figured the math. If Ted Kessler were fifteen at the beginning of 1968, how old was Brenda? She walked over to her desk and slipped the copy of Brenda's obituary out of a pile of papers. Brenda had been born in 1953. So when the fire occurred she was fourteen, just a year behind the Kessler boy. How old was Nick Lawler? She checked with the detective files of his record and found he was seventeen when the fire happened. Did Brenda know either of these guys? Grace looked over at the bookshelf and realized she had sent Brenda's yearbooks home to her brother. Deb would have the same books at the Historical Society. Grace could check them and see if they had any photos of the three.

She sat at her desk and looked at the medical examiner's reports. *Such a young age for Nick Lawler to die, and after such a crushing, heartbreaking life among a family that neither cared for him nor gave him any life. No wonder he spent time at the Kesslers'.*

What happened that night? Did Ted get angry with his parents? Nick? Did they discover Ted was setting fires? Grace was determined to sift through the rest of the boxes and try to figure out what Brenda was telling her, and she'd make a trip over to Deb's Historical Society and investigate those yearbooks.

She glanced at the scar on her hand and thought of her two college roommates who hadn't been as lucky as she had. They had died in that fire. Their parents — and they were getting up in age now — and their brothers and sisters had to learn to spend the rest of their lives without their precious daughters or sisters. Every birthday, every Christmas, for thirty-six years, they relived that pain, as did Grace. She still got cards at Christmas from both Gail's and Robin's families. She still sent their parents a note on their daughters' birthdays. Over those years, Grace had spent inexhaustible time questioning why she had lived and they had died at the age of twenty. *And what of Nick Lawler's family? Did they, too, experience the uncertainties, questions, and sadness of their son's death way too early?*

CHAPTER THIRTEEN

"So, we have everything under control. Big septaquintaquinquecentennial is only two weeks away. See, I can say it. I've been practicing," Jill said. She looked at Deb and Grace with a smirk, as if she had done something wonderful.

"Works for me," Deb countered. "The planning hasn't been without its glitches, however."

Lettie walked into Grace's living room with some more ice and lemonade as well as another plate of gingerbread cookies. Putting them on the coffee table, she said, "I hear the mayor's wife, Polly, will be in the lead car, standing up with a torch and dressed like the Statue of Liberty. Humph! It would be better if they put her at the end of the parade with a microphone so she'd remind people of the fat lady." Grabbing one cookie for herself, she made a smooth exit.

"Glad to see Lettie is that same old paragon of tolerance," Deb whispered, reaching for a cookie.

"The college is letting us use the football field for fireworks on Friday night and their athletic center for the huge dinner and dance on Saturday night. So this means Grace has the music for the dance to arrange, Deb has the line-up for the parade on Saturday morning, and I have the job of working on the decorations for the dance. See, Grace, we did manage to keep you off the shootout at the bank on Saturday."

Grace frowned for a moment. "My dad did teach me to shoot, you know, but it's been decades since I went with him to the firing range back home."

Jill chimed in, "Did I hear we had some confusion with the parade route, Deb?"

"Not exactly confusion, just decisions. Amos Tuckner is supposed to deal with the horses and the cleanup, and some people wanted the horses near the front of the parade. But horses being horses, I think they are now scheduled for the end of the parade with the street cleaner following. I am pleased to announce, however, that we have bands from both Cameron and Woodbury to supplement our own little high school and junior high bands. And we also have the winner and runners-up for Miss Pork Queen on a float. After her float come the politicians. Hmmm." She put her hands up as if she were weighing two items. "Politicians. Pork. Seems to be a connection there. And after the politicians we'll have at least a block of farm equipment ahead of the horses."

Grace looked at Jill, and they both burst into laughter.

"What's so funny?" Deb asked.

"I'm thinking about what a proud parent I'd be if my daughter won the Miss Pork Queen title. Surely they can come up with something less . . . descriptive." Grace giggled. She reached for her glass of lemonade and held it up. "Here's to the new Miss Pork Queen, whoever she is." And the three friends clicked their glasses together.

"Grace, where's your watch? You never go anywhere without it," Deb asked.

Grace looked down at the white mark that circled her wrist. "That's my celebration of retirement. I shouldn't have to wear a watch anymore. Besides, I always have my cell phone."

"Makes sense to me."

Jill looked up and her face became animated at the mention of "cell phone."

"Oh, do I have a great story for you," she began.

"How come you always hear these things? I never hear anything about anything going on around town," said Deb.

"Your cell phone remark reminded me. You know Judy Winkler," Jill began.

"Sure," Grace said. "She works for some company out of her home. Some kind of place where she does writing about directions for their products — you know, puts them in 'real people language.'"

"Right. So she walks to the library pretty regularly — about a mile — and she always sticks her cell phone in her pocket — only this time she got halfway there and had to kneel down to tie her tennis shoe. The phone falls out of her pocket and she doesn't realize it. She gets home and no phone. But she has a message on her answering machine from Jim Allison. He'd found a phone in the street and checked to see which number had been called last. He called the number and it was Suzanne Edwards's number, a friend of Judy's. Jim knew Suzanne so he asked her whose phone had called her with this number and, of course, it was Judy. Presto! He called Judy's house phone and left a message that he had her phone and would give it back to her if she brought a ransom in unmarked hundred-dollar bills. And all this before she even got home."

"Amazing," said Grace. "No one stole it and it wasn't smashed to smithereens by all the traffic in Endurance."

"Exactly," said Deb. "I guess we do have some honest people — and very little traffic."

"Somebody should send that story into one of those morning talk shows on TV," said Deb. "You know, the ones that are billed as 'news shows' but mostly spend hours on some guy who has a hatchet through his head and survived, or the fifteenth rendition of a story about how someone's pet dog was accidently left in their old house and miraculously travelled thousands of miles to find them again."

Jill nodded at Deb. "Great idea. Send it in." She glanced at Grace. "So, to change the subject, what are the float themes?"

"The committee came to the Historical Society a couple of weeks ago and made a list of scenes from the town's history to reenact," Deb said. "I think they decided that one would be the suffragettes breaking kegs of liquor, like Carrie Nation, and carrying axes and Bibles. They are going to have one woman carrying a sign that says,

'Lips that Touch Liquor Shall Not Touch Ours.' "

"That would eliminate the entire male population of the town," Jill quipped.

"Then there's the float about the Underground Railroad. It will have Emmeline Folger standing up on the footboard of her carriage with a whip aimed toward a slave hunter. And in the back of the carriage you'll see the famous secret door and someone dressed as Zacharias Butler, his wife Rebecca, and their two small children, who will look out the opened door. You know the story about ole Emmeline hiding slaves on the Underground Railroad."

"That's a great idea," said Grace. "I also heard a rumor they plan to use Charlie Sims's Model T Ford."

"Yes, that's for the story of Emmeline Folger's son, Nathaniel, who had the first Model T Ford in town, and before he learned how to run it well, he drove it through the window of Silas Rountree's hardware store. I think the title of that one is Silas's quote, 'Never Happened with Horses.' "

"The last one they chose was the rescue of little Sally Aberdine from the river back in 1905 when she fell through the ice while skating. They tried to figure out how they could do ice when it's eighty-seven degrees in July. I think they decided to eliminate that one."

"We about done here?" asked Grace.

Jill glanced through her papers and looked for any last-minute details. "Just a minute. Let me double-check." She straightened the papers and examined each quickly. "Yes. Finished and everything looks to be in good shape." She turned to Grace. "So, what's happening with the murder investigation, Grace?"

Before she could answer, each of them noticed as Lettie tiptoed in and sat down to listen. But Lettie couldn't resist. "So, will you put Polly Blandford ahead of or behind the horses? I know where I'd put her."

"I think the parade order has already been determined," Deb said, "and she'll be kicking things off. If she has her way she'll sing 'God Bless America' like Ethel Merman." Audible groans filled the room.

"A great reason to arrive fifteen minutes late," said Lettie.

"Back to my original question," said Jill. She turned to Grace. "Murder investigation?"

"TJ keeps that to herself." Grace worked hard to keep a straight face on that statement. "Mostly what I know is what the town knows. Mike Sturgis was taken in for questioning and released, but he is being called 'a person of interest.' The state fire marshal ruled the fire at Brenda's as 'a suspicious fire, humanly induced,' so they're looking for the person who set it. Evidently Brenda's life was filled with multiple possibilities for suspects, so I think TJ has her work cut out for her. I've boxed Brenda's stuff and sent it on to her brother."

"Hmm." Lettie sniffed. "If some homicidal maniac is still out there, we'd better keep a sharp eye out, especially you, Grace. Who knows what Brenda knew that might have gotten her killed?"

"I don't think it has anything to do with her research of the town's history. It seems rather innocuous at this point. My guess is she was killed for something she saw or did or knew in recent days," Grace reasoned.

"And what about your historical research? How's that going?" asked Deb.

"It's awesome. I've learned so many things about what happened before we lived here," Grace said. "I've researched stories on three cold cases, too. The police department let me borrow the evidence, probably because it's really old."

Jill grabbed her papers. "Sounds interesting, Grace. I, for one, need to go. Errands call. It is Saturday," Jill said as she stood up and headed for the door. Deb followed her. "Thanks, everyone." Grace followed them out the front door and watched as they went their separate ways.

"Yeah, Sturgis is lawyered up," TJ said quietly, sitting on the swing on Grace's front porch that evening. She took another swig from her bottle of beer. "Right now I've got plenty of leads and not a lot of connections between them. Darned if I can figure out some of the relationships."

"What do you mean?" asked Grace.

"Well, although Sturgis is lawyered up, it's obvious he's hiding something. He doesn't have an alibi for part of the night when Brenda was killed, and since he's usually in trouble with Janice, I figure what he's hiding has something to do with information he doesn't want her to know. It might not have anything to do with the murder. On the other hand, he sure had one heck of a motive, and he had the means and the opportunity with no alibi for the time just before her death. Add to that the fact that he does stupid stuff when he's drunk and then he forgets what he did."

"I know he had a really good reason to be angry with Brenda, but I find it hard to believe he'd set her house on fire."

"That's exactly what he might have done. He had plenty of gasoline on his trucks. We've arrested him at times when he was out of his mind with anger. You have no idea, Grace."

Grace was silent since she knew TJ was right.

"Then we have Shannon Shiveley. Something funny's going on there. She knew about Brenda's blackmail book, and when I questioned her about it she was her devious, evasive self. She did mention that guys are really stupid with letters, emails, and phone messages, leading me to believe that she may be involved somehow in Brenda's blackmail schemes. Did she and Brenda have a falling out?"

"Does she have an alibi for that night?"

TJ laughed. "She thinks she does. But supposedly she was with her boyfriend, a thirty-five-year-old loser who mows lawns for a living. We checked his gasoline buys and he must have quite a stockpile but can't account for it now. Shannon is uncooperative and the boyfriend went for a lawyer immediately since he has a cousin who's a lawyer and won't bill him."

"Shannon uncooperative? Can't imagine that. But if she were in on some of Brenda's schemes, wouldn't someone have come after her too?"

"Good question."

"And then we have the 'unsub,' the suspect out there who had a beef with Brenda and we don't have him on our radar. What if Sturgis and Shiveley, or her boyfriend, have nothing to do with any of this? So I'm also checking Brenda's newspaper stories and making a list of who else she might have pissed off." She shook her head. "So how are your centennial stories going?"

"Really well. I read about the fires we had back in 1965 through 1968. It's fascinating stuff. The deputy fire marshal was someone named Richard White. Ever heard of him?"

"Sure, he's still around. He lives over in the newer subdivision with his wife."

"I think I'll talk with him about the fire that killed three people in 'sixty-eight. They never solved it. Of course, it was before your time."

"I've read the details of those fires and heard people talk from time to time. Never caught the kid who did it. I'm curious, though. How come you can read those when you have this thing about fires?"

Grace sat quietly, biting her lip before she spoke. "That's a good question. Maybe it's because it's more of an intellectual study and I didn't know any of those people."

TJ nodded. "Could be."

"Actually, I have a way to find out. Tomorrow I plan to look back through the clippings from my college fire and see if I'm ready to deal with them."

"Grace, just remember you are a strong woman. They're just clippings and if they start to bother you, grade the grammar."

CHAPTER FOURTEEN

After changing out of her church clothes and eating lunch, Grace grabbed a kitchen step stool and trudged to her office. She pulled open the door handle of a closet she seldom used. Tugging on an overhead light chain, she scanned multiple boxes on the upper shelf, labeled and neatly stacked. A handful of these boxes came from her childhood home after the deaths of her parents.

She climbed on the step stool and pushed several cartons around until she saw the one she sought. It was marked "Grace's Fire — 1975" in her mother's spidery handwriting. *She must have used a fine black marker. Interesting that she wrote the label as if the fire belonged to me. It's more like I have been possessed by it — for years,* she thought.

Her heart raced a little and she told herself, *Stop it. You're being silly. It was all so long ago. Think of something happy. Think of Roger.* The year before the fire Grace had met a young attorney, Roger Kimball, when he came to speak at her college. She was assigned to escort him around the campus, and after that they began a long-distance courtship, with Roger visiting when he could and taking her to Endurance occasionally over holidays. By the time she was a senior they were engaged.

Then came the fire. After the disaster, Roger took her back to Illinois to his parents' home because he thought she would heal better if she were not in Indianapolis, the location of the fire. Her parents had visited — her mother staying for several weeks — and both mothers had nursed her back to health, but it wasn't her body that needed nurturing. For weeks she was a zombie, her emotions fragile, her tears always close.

Guilt.

Eventually she was able to function normally, but the feeling that she too should have died in that fire never left her. Nor did she forget that she gave up, and only the actions of the fire department saved her. *So much for being strong, Mother.*

The box. It was a nightmare she'd never opened. But it was also a part of her past and she had been reluctant to destroy it. She'd brought it back from her parents' house, tied with twine — her mother seemed to save vast amounts of twine.

She considered the best place to examine it and decided to take the dreaded object out to the porch, a place of happy memories with both Roger and their children. Out here the sun was shining and the sky was blue with clouds that slowly swept past as if on their way to a pleasant destination, a rendezvous. She would do it today. She had a full stomach, plenty of sleep, and this sunshine. The sunny porch was a perfect place to pry open something dark and loathsome. She was stronger now and could deal with this.

Sitting down on the rattan loveseat, she untied the twine and laid it aside on the table. Her hands still shook a little but she grasped the lid and pulled it off, laying it upside down on top of the twine. All she could see in the box was white tissue paper. *Well, this isn't so bad.* She carefully pulled it aside, revealing an envelope with her name on it addressed in her mother's familiar handwriting. Grace looked at it for a moment and brushed her fingers across the letters. Instantly, tears welled up in her eyes. *Oh, Mother, I wish you were still here. But if you were, you'd want me to be strong. You would remind me again to put this awful mess aside once and for all.*

She opened the envelope and began reading. The world seemed to slow down, and tears ran down her cheeks at the sight of the familiar handwriting. Her mother's note explained that she had saved these clippings so that someday Grace could read them when she wasn't "so debilitated." She admonished Grace to read the last couple of sentences of the inquest article. "You must understand, my lovely but fragile daughter, that none of this was your fault. And someday when you face this disaster as the strong woman I know you are, you will finally put it behind you."

Grace wiped her tears away before they fell on the spidery ink. Her mother was a believer in "facing things." Grace looked up at the robin's-egg sky and heard the buzzing of bees in the flowers near the porch. She could do anything on such a day. *You were right, Mother, as always. I need to do this.* She folded the letter and placed it carefully on the box lid and began hesitantly fingering her way through the tissue paper.

In the bottom of the box was a handful of clippings. First her fingers touched a thin, yellowed news story and she carefully unfolded it, lest the fragile edges fall to pieces. It was a story from the *Indianapolis*

Gazette dated November 26, 1975. *As if she needed to be reminded of the date.* She glanced at the bold, black headline: "Two BHC Students Die, One Injured in House Fire." *The fire had happened in the wee hours of the morning so it still made the evening newspaper.* Grace read silently, unfolding the paper as she went.

"A fast-moving fire on the second floor of a two-story frame house at 4587 East Wayne Avenue claimed the lives of two college women and injured a third. All three roommates were students at Benjamin Harrison College and lived in the off-campus house. Robin Ellis, 20, of Vincennes, Ind., and Gail Prestrella, 21, of Effingham, Ill., were pronounced dead at the scene, and a third victim, Grace Eklund of Indianapolis, was taken to Our Lady of Hope Hospital, where she is listed in fair condition."

Grace was startled by squealing voices and looked across the street at the Pratskis' two shrieking children. She watched them a few moments and smiled wistfully. *To be so young and fearless.* Then she looked back at the clipping, which was practically falling apart at the seams, willing herself to read more. A neighbor had called in the fire when he was out with his dog at two a.m. And she, Grace Eklund, had survived. *Yes,*

I did. I lived. I lived to marry a loving man and have three beautiful children and a grandchild and I guess that was how it was supposed to be.

Gingerly placing the clipping next to her on the chair, she dug into the box again and pulled out two small funeral programs. *Gail and Robin.* (G and R as she called them.) This was a direct blow to her gut. She looked up and took in a deep breath. *I couldn't go to their funerals because I was still recovering.* The three of them had met during their freshman year and had been inseparable throughout college. She remembered their joy at snagging an off-campus house. Their senior year was going to be amazing. *Oh, such fun we had that year, knowing that we were living off campus and could do whatever we wanted. The house was perfect and it was ours.* She had never considered G and R's funerals. It was as if those events hadn't happened since she, Grace, hadn't been there.

She glanced across the street as Ms. Pratski sprayed her screaming children with the garden hose and their screeches rose in a crescendo. She set the box on the floor and got up for a few minutes, wandering around on the porch and stretching her legs. Silently she watched the water babies across the street. Gail's and Robin's parents exchanged Christmas cards with her every year, and she always sent them a card on G and R's birthdays. *Well, we used to call ourselves GGR. How young and silly we were back then.* Their parents were well into their seventies now, and Robin's father was into his eighties. *So many years to exist without their daughters.* Sadly, she shook her head and her chest tightened with that familiar feeling of anxiety. She sat down to finish opening the articles. It seemed so strange that she had never seen these clippings before. But then, why would she have seen them?

Setting the box back on her lap, she reached in and pulled out still another *Gazette* clipping. This time it was about the autopsies. *I hope they never woke up in that fire. Everyone kept telling me they didn't.* After reading the report of a Dr. Lambert C. Brown, Marion County coroner, she gazed out to the corner of Sweetbriar, absently staring at the street sign.

Wayne Avenue. In the years since the disaster, Grace had visited her parents in Indianapolis, first with Roger and later with the children. But they had always scrupulously avoided Wayne Avenue. The only exception was when they went back for her five-year college reunion and drove past the off-campus house. She had expected a blackened, charred dwelling looming up over the landscape. Instead, she saw a somewhat familiar house that had been renovated after the tragedy. A woman sat on the front steps watching two children draw chalk pictures on the sidewalk. It should have been an ordinary house where people lived now. But one glance at it and the dread that had hounded Grace came right back, and she closed her eyes and looked away. Even that was years ago.

Now she looked down at the scar on her hand and rubbed her fingers across it. *Such a little spot to remind me — always there, always causing me to remember that I lived.*

She sat deeper in her chair and took in a long breath. Glancing at the clippings on the seat beside her, she shook her head. *A small set of words to describe such an enormous event.* Then she reached into the box and pulled out the last item. It was a clipping about the inquest a week or so after the fire.

"Despite the best efforts of the Indianapolis Fire Department, electrical malfunctions cost the lives of two Benjamin Harrison

College coeds and injured a third. Ironically, the students would have left the house to go home for Thanksgiving later the day of the fire."

That's right. How could I have forgotten the next day was Thanksgiving? She glanced back down at the fragile piece of newsprint and read that Robin and Gail died as a result of carbon monoxide poisoning and asphyxiation from the smoke and fumes. The pathologist, Dr. Francis Willis, concluded that they had a carbon dioxide level of thirty-five percent in their bloodstream and a body can usually absorb three percent or less "with no deleterious effect." *So they did die without regaining consciousness, right?*
She vaguely remembered sitting in the courthouse listening to the inquest witnesses. Their testimony had vanished like the first wisps of smoke, signaling fear and then escaping from her memory — as if lingering might make it all too real. And she hadn't wanted that.
In the next paragraph the fire chief, William Ancel, talked about the fire itself. An extension cord in Robin's room shorted, sending out deadly sparks that caught the bed coverings and adjacent curtains on fire, spreading through the upstairs very quickly.

All three women were asleep in separate bedrooms on the second floor. Out loud she said, "And I was the only one to survive because I happened to be in the farthest bedroom and woke up." Her throat felt scratchy and her voice broke. She bit her lip but read on, determined to finish.

Reading the electrical inspector's words, she thought, *I know I was there that day, but I don't remember any of this testimony. I know I was there because I testified too.* She looked back down at the fragile paper.

"Grace Eklund, a third roommate who survived the fire, said that she woke up in the middle of the night, smelled smoke, and realized the house was on fire. Before she could check on her roommates or find a way out of the bedroom, she was overcome by fumes and heat and passed out. She expressed her gratitude to the fire department whose quick arrival saved her life. Miss Eklund's appearance was brief since she still appeared to be shaken. She had a bandage on one of her hands. Her testimony was very slow and halting and she had to stop occasionally to regain her composure."

And now Grace's hands were shaking, and

she dropped the clipping into the tissue paper, set the box aside, and stood up. A gentle breeze touched her cheeks as she stood next to the column supporting the porch roof and then she leaned against it. *Yes, I was there. I said all the right things. But I couldn't save R and G and I couldn't even save myself.* A single tear crept down her face from each eye and she wiped them away. That was all.

She realized she was looking back through a distant expanse of time and she was stronger. Her mother was right. She laughed as she heard what her mother would have said: *Of course, I'm right. What did you think?* She walked back to the chair, picked up the inquest article, and read the very end, as her mother had suggested.

"The fire chief theorized about the events of that night. He finished by saying, 'Miss Eklund's room had a window, and she could have knocked out the window and climbed out on a flat roof from the attached garage. She attempted to crawl to a place of safety even though she was probably suffering from shock. She was unconscious when my men rescued her. She was fortunate that they were able to get to her in a matter of minutes. Fires kill very quickly, and because she dropped to the floor beneath the smoke, they were able to save her.' "

So you were right — I did do something right, Mother. It was a combination of luck, amazingly brave firemen, and my decision to drop to the floor. Grace sat in the chair, totally still, for several minutes. Her eyes shining, she reread the last sentence. *How many years had it been?* She added it up in her head. *Thirty-six years and I have never been able to face this Pandora's box. But now it feels as if I've released its hold on me and diffused some bits and pieces of the darkness.* Her facial features softened and her clenched fists loosened into a calm stillness on her lap.

And I have years of life ahead to keep getting stronger.

CHAPTER FIFTEEN

The following night Grace worked late at the newspaper, going over Brenda's papers once again, trying to figure out her cryptic notes. After her description of the Kessler fire investigation back in 1968, Brenda had scribbled some question marks on the right side of the page and written "Poe" and "279." No matter how many times she looked at those notes, Grace could not figure out their message. *I've been trying and trying, Brenda, to figure out what you meant by that. Help me.* She decided to sleep on it. Maybe her subconscious would kick in with an answer.

A couple of pages later, Brenda had written more question marks, "Lawler," and another number: "32." Try as she might, Grace was at a standstill on those numbers. Sitting forward, she arched her back, stretched her arms, and let out a long breath. She understood most of Brenda's notes, but these little details still weighed on her mind. She put down her pencil, wandered out of her office, and got a drink at the hallway fountain. Glancing out into the newsroom, she saw light under Jeff Maitlin's door, so she walked over and knocked lightly.

"Come in," his voice said absent-mindedly.

"I didn't realize you were working late."

"I've got some figures here I have to deal with, you know, the business end of the paper." He leaned back, pointed to a chair, and put his hands behind his head. "I don't think we're paying you enough to be working late."

She sat down across from him. "I don't mind. I've been trying to make heads or tails out of some puzzling notes Brenda left about the Kessler fire so long ago. She was alive then too — back in 1968 — and probably not much younger than the Kessler boy or that Lawler kid. Maybe she knew something. At least she must have had a theory."

"She didn't say anything to me about that story. It was as if she were waiting to spring the unexpected on everyone. You know Brenda — master of surprises."

"Very true," Grace said. She glanced at Jeff. "You mentioned that you worked at a paper before with a fire-setter incident. What do you remember about that?"

"Oh, that was in a little town in North Carolina. Went there to write news stories and it was only my second job. Before I moved to town they had experienced several fires, mainly at night, all of them set. So I spoke with several experts in the area about fire-setters and their motives. I believe some are psychopaths."

"Really? Did they ever catch this person?"

"Yes. A teenage boy, fifteen or sixteen, who used a slow fuse and kerosene. Most of the houses he lit were empty, but the last one wasn't." He stopped and rubbed a hand over his chin, remembering something terrible. "Unfortunately, the family was home at the time and the mother and two kids were killed. The father and another kid survived."

"That's horrible. Why did he do it?"

"Well . . ." He paused and glanced thoughtfully into the newsroom. "It was a combination of things. He came from a family that had — I guess you'd call it 'impulse control problems.' From what I learned back then, such a characteristic can be somewhat genetic. Father was an alcoholic and mother was a far-right religious nut. She probably should have been hospitalized in a mental ward or program. They had several kids and he was the youngest. And then, you know, the usual: abuse, neglect. He, in particular, was the most neglected one, being the youngest. Failure at school and the suggestion that he had been bullied. And he was a loner, didn't have any friends. So one day he decided to set an old, empty house on fire. He did a thorough job, too. Then, when the fire department attempted to put out the fire, this kid was there on the front lines, watching."

"What satisfaction can there be in destroying property like that?"

"I think the satisfaction comes from eluding the police, doing a great deal of damage, and getting people's attention." He raised his eyebrows and sat back in his chair. "Now, at least, he was getting attention, more so than he was getting at home."

"Did you ever talk to him, I mean, as a reporter?"

"Yes. At the jail. I was allowed to interview him after the trial was over — he'd been found guilty. I don't think I'll forget that interview till the day I die. He just sat there and smiled at me as he admitted to killing those people." He shook his head. "A demented whack job, a lot like his crazy mother. Sat right across from me and smiled as he talked about how he set the fires. No remorse — no compassion — as if that family, those children, meant nothing. He was consumed by his cleverness and how long it had taken the police to figure out he was the fire-setter. That's mostly what he came back to. Every time I asked him about why he did it or how, he always came back to how clever he was. All the while he had watched those fires from the civilian lines and reveled in his brilliance while firefighters were putting their lives in danger. I'll never forget his eyes — just blank — or his smile." He shook his head and rearranged some items on his desk — a stapler, a couple of pencils.

Grace was silent for a moment. Then she cleared her voice and said, "I keep reading the notes from the Kessler fire and the newspaper clippings. Seems as if the Kessler boy could have had some of the qualities you describe. He was a loner — well, except for befriending this Lawler boy — and he had been in some trouble at school. I keep wondering where he is now. And since he did get away, I keep wondering if he's set fires elsewhere."

"Good question. Of course he's living under an alias. And I seem to recall that often pyromaniacs can have a period of remission. But I think it's like many other compulsions. At some point the gratification and the arousal of setting fires would become too much for him."

"Do authorities have any way to verify his identity now?"

"Not if his prints had never been taken. What about dental records?"

Grace raked her hand through her hair. "I gather from the news coverage back then he hadn't been to a dentist, so those wouldn't exist either."

Jeff leaned forward again and put his hands on the desk. "So he could just have escaped into the night and, even if his fingerprints had been put in the system since then, he would be living under an assumed name. Or possibly in prison by now. He's one of those shadow people who fall through the cracks."

"Yes. And no current DNA testing would work because his relatives — his parents — are long gone, and, as far as we know, he had no other relatives. So, dead end."

"That does sometimes happen, even for the most intrepid reporter," Jeff smiled. His eyes held hers for a moment before she looked away.

"I'd better get back to work," Grace said,

and rose to go back to her office. She walked toward the door, then turned and added, "I keep thinking I've seen some of those Kessler fire photos before somewhere, but I just can't remember where."

"Perhaps." He rose from his seat and picked up some books to put back on the shelf behind him. "Say, I haven't had much to eat today. Are you at a stopping place where you could use a little food at Tully's?"

Grace considered. Dinner with Jeff — well, kind of like a date, and she'd been sitting for quite a long time and hadn't had anything to eat since noon. "Now that you mention it, I'm hungry, too. Sure. I'll just go close up my office."

"Might as well take both cars. Meet you at Tully's in ten minutes."

"I know the police are feeling tremendous pressure to come up with a suspect in Brenda's death. Talked to TJ yesterday and she said she's 'dancing as fast as she can,' " Jeff said as he spread mustard on the bun of a huge tenderloin. "I feel kind of bad for her. She's such a professional, and I know she's had a lot of state help on all this, but how often do you have a murder in this town? I think I read that it's been quite some time."

"Could be whoever it was is long gone," Tully chimed in, standing behind the bar and monitoring the room. "I don't think the town's had as bad a fire as Brenda's in years. Leastways I can't remember one and I've been here about twenty years or so. And I suppose they'll never know if anything was missing with all the destruction. Her house was isolated. Could have been a burglar thinking no one was home. Maybe set a fire to cover the crime."

"I don't know what TJ's theory is just now, but I have a feeling she has no lack of suspects. Between the newspaper stories and some creative blackmail on Brenda's part, sinister possibilities abound," Grace said.

Another voice came into their circle with a querulous remark. "Blackmail?" Ronda Burke asked, leaning closer over the edge of the bar. "Brenda?"

"Rumors are flying around town about Brenda blackmailing people," Tully said. "Not sure where they started. Don't know if they're true. But if she blackmailed the wrong person, well . . ."

"Wow," Ronda said. "Really? Brenda blackmailing people. Well, guess I wouldn't have put it past her, now that I think about it." She picked up some napkins from the counter and walked toward the other end of the bar.

"How's your story-writing coming along, Grace?" Tully picked up another glass from an unseen sink behind the bar and started wiping it dry.

"I have an amusing piece done on the town history and I'm finishing off some stories on old cold cases. I didn't realize we had so many Swedish settlers until I read about Gustav Swensen's death."

Tully set down the glass and grabbed another one. "I thought you were working on something about fires."

"Oh, I am." She picked up another French fry and popped it in her mouth.

"So what's going on with that story?" Jeff asked.

"I still have more research to do on that one. It's about a fire that killed some people around here in the late sixties."

Ronda returned after sending off some drinks with a waitress. "Would have been before my time since I was born in 'seventy-four. But I remember my mom talking about that one."

"I wasn't here yet so I have not a clue. Bad fire?" Tully looked at Grace quizzically and continued drying glasses.

"A husband and wife killed and a kid who

stayed with them sometimes. Kessler was the name of the family. The Kessler teenager was the main suspect, and he took off. Never was caught. I'm still working on it, and I think I'm going to interview the deputy fire chief from back then on Wednesday."

"How come that story? I'd imagine you could have your pick of a lot of interesting stories that are unsolved," Jeff remarked.

"I think I'm drawn to it because Brenda added a lot of thoughts, comments, and notes to the research she'd done. I think she must have been alive then and old enough to remember the fire. Maybe she even knew some of the people involved. She was intrigued and so am I."

"Had she figured anything out or drawn any conclusions?" Jeff asked.

Grace took a swallow of her beer. "Still working on that. I'm on to a clue if I can just wrap my mind around it."

"Sounds like kind of a dead end to me," said Tully.

"Sturgis was in the other night," said Ronda. "He keeps swearing he didn't have anything to do with that fire. I know he's been questioned by the cops."

"He's probably on a short list that Sweeney's composing," Jeff said.

Suddenly a light went on in Grace's head. "Oh," she turned to Jeff. "I just thought of something I've been trying to figure out for days."

Tully leaned forward. "What's that, Grace?"

"Brenda left a lot of research notes. Police went through them and returned them. But she wrote questions throughout the notes and the word 'Poe' with a number."

Jeff turned toward her on the bar stool. "Poe? That's the word she said to me the night I took her home. I had no idea what she was talking about."

"I think I do. She taught English — like me — and so I think I get her note. The number must refer to a page in a book of Poe stories and I believe she has a book like that — although I don't remember for sure — in her office. But what that fire has to do with a Poe story, I have no clue. I don't remember old Edgar writing about fires. Maybe the number refers to something she wanted to remember. It's like a code that no one else would understand."

"Maybe a street number?" Jeff suggested.

"Or a page number," answered Grace.

"Codes! Symbols! No one except English teachers," Ronda inserted.

"I'm not sure what Edgar Allan Poe could

have to do with Brenda's death," Jeff said.

Grace hesitated for a moment and then said very quietly, "I wonder if we are going in the wrong direction, TJ included. What if Brenda was killed for something she knew, not for her stories in the paper?"

"You mean like someone she was blackmailing?" Tully said.

"Perhaps. Of course, I could be all wrong, too. We'll see," Grace wiped off her mouth with her napkin, and looked up at Ronda. "All this talk about work makes me famished. Pie?"

CHAPTER SIXTEEN

Grace recognized Richard White, the former deputy fire chief, as soon as she walked into Tully's on Wednesday afternoon. TJ had described him perfectly. He rose from his chair, a tall, slightly stoop-shouldered man with a military buzz cut to his gray hair and what looked like a bill to mail in his shirt pocket.

"Mr. White?"

"Call me Richard, and you must be Grace Kimball. Knew your husband. Went to his funeral so long ago. He was a good man."

"Thank you. Please, sit back down," Grace said, warming at his mention of Roger. She waved to a waitress and gestured for a cup of coffee.

White looked earnestly into her eyes. "You intrigued me when you asked on the phone about that particular fire. The Kessler fire."

A waitress stopped with coffee for Grace

and also refilled the elderly fireman's cup, too.

"Thanks," he glanced up at her. Then he went on without missing a beat. "That was January 25, 1968. Remember it well because it's always stayed with me." He stirred some cream into his coffee, laid down the spoon, and went on with his explanation. "You know, you talk to cops and firemen and teachers and there's always something — a murder, a fire, a student — that stays in their minds long after they hang up their job. This Kessler fire was one of those."

"I'm really curious now. Why this fire in particular?"

"First, it was a horrendous fire, one of the worst I ever fought in my whole career. We'd been having some fires prior to the Kessler one, and I was positive we had a firebug in the area. Those fires were set. They all happened at night with the same mode of operation. Multiple pours. Gasoline. No igniter left at the scene. Whoever did it vanished into the night, just like the smoke. Police put out extra patrols and everyone in town was worried." He took a sip of coffee. "Ever seen what it's like in a scared town? People afraid to go out or go to sleep? But there were no victims in any of the earlier fires. Vacant houses. Garages. That kind of thing." He leaned in and spoke softly, tapping a finger on the table for emphasis. "Like a teenager out to destroy property and getting better at it each time."

Grace set down her pen next to her notebook and thought for a moment. Then she asked, "Was it your theory that the earlier fires were set by the same person who set the Kessler fire?"

"I thought so at the time. Of course, we never caught him."

"You say 'him' as if you know it was a male."

"Well, Mrs. Kimball —"

"Grace."

"Well, Grace, I've watched training videos of arsonist interviews, and they are most interesting and usually male. They don't feel any guilt about what they do." He shook his head gently. "Darnedest thing. No remorse at all. About eighty percent of 'em are white, male, and not very well educated. At least half have mental health problems and that includes sociopaths."

"But the other half that aren't mentally ill are good at planning?"

"Very. Lots of times they set things on fire to destroy the evidence of another crime, say a murder. But I don't think that was the case here."

"Why do you say that?"

"The earlier fires didn't have a crime involved — no insurance, so they weren't expecting to collect money. No one was killed so they weren't trying to murder someone to keep a secret."

"So what was this Kessler firebug's motive?"

"Darned if I know. And I've thought about it over and over through the years. Hard to get it out of my head. It was very frustrating at the time. A third of those fire-setters just do it for excitement. They get a thrill out of fires — setting them, watching them, and getting away with it. Sometimes they even show up at the fire to watch the fire engines and the firemen struggling with what they started. It gives them a lot of attention and pleasure, even if no one knows they set it."

"You said —" and Grace hesitated as the waitress came back with a carafe of coffee and filled their cups again. "Thanks."

Grace poured a little more cream in her coffee and noticed a man just leaving the bar. *Seems awfully early in the morning to be drinking,* but then she saw his face. *Austin Pettet. She had him in school, maybe ten years ago, and he had brought in a raw fish to demonstrate how to skin and fillet it. The entire lower floor in the school reeked for days of dead fish.* Grace smiled at the thought.

She settled back in her chair and resumed her thought. "You said that the arsonist you were after back then might have been a teenager. How did you come up with that theory?"

"I noticed some things about the non-fatal fires that seemed to be the work of an amateur — some rags left here or there, the obvious clue that there were multiple pours. That's a dead giveaway that it's a set fire. And, frankly, a great many arsonists who aren't in it for profit or to hide a crime are teenagers. Often they're in trouble somewhere else and they're sorry only if they get caught." He took another sip of coffee and seemed to consider what he should say next.

"Well . . ." He paused. "As I said before, the Kessler fire bothered me. The one kid — his name was Lawler — was kind of taken in by the Kesslers, as I remember. He died in the fire, and it seemed like he was turning his life around. His parents were no good — always in trouble with the police, and this kid was abused, neglected."

"Did you know this Lawler kid?"

"Not really, but I'd heard of him and I'd seen him once or twice. You know, small towns. He played football at the high school and was decent. People seemed to think he was pleasant despite his awful home situation."

"I get the impression that the son — Ted — was the one who set the fire and then took off. Was he jealous of the attention this Lawler kid was getting from his parents?"

"That I can't tell you. But Ted Kessler wasn't a saint. He had some problems at school and was suspended a few times. Lots of stories around town about his 'extracurricular activities.' He could have set those earlier fires, too. I had the impression the parents were just holding on. And he took off after that fire."

"So I guess no one has heard from him in all these years?"

"Not that I know of. You could ask Detective Sweeney if they have anything else on him, I s'pose. We didn't have DNA testing back then — guess that's how he got away."

"That's a good thought." She closed her notebook and took a sip of coffee. "Well, I think that answers my questions. I thank you for your time, Richard."

He rose. "I hope that helps with your story. It would be great if we could find the Kessler kid, get Sweeney to grill him, and close the books on that one. If you think of any more questions, you can always call me." He rose, dropped some money on the table, and shook her hand.

"Here, keep your money," she put it in his hand. "Call it a payment for excellent information — I'm on a tight budget at the paper but I can manage coffee." She laughed.

"Thanks, Grace. It's been nice." He sauntered out of the sports bar and left Grace to consider her story. *That's two things I have to check on,* she thought. *First, the Poe reference and I'll have to do that at the office. Second, I need to go to the Historical Society and check the old high school yearbooks. I sent Brenda's back to her brother. Lawler, Kessler, Brenda. They were all of an age.*

CHAPTER SEVENTEEN: RONDA

While Grace was at Tully's interviewing Deputy Chief White, across town Ronda Burke shuffled from her kitchen sink to the table, tying her bathrobe belt a little tighter. She placed a pencil on the table and turned back to the counter, grabbing a spoon to stir her coffee.

"Well, Adonis, I'm actually getting a few things done today. Cleaned the apartment, took out the garbage, two loads of laundry, and now it's time to balance the checkbook."

Adonis turned his head sideways quizzically as he dribbled saliva around the floor near his food dish. He padded over to Ronda and rubbed his head against her leg, leaving a wet streak.

"I know, I know, you want attention. Right now, however, I need to get this done so I can figure out how to bring that sucker down with a huge charitable donation to the Ronda Burke/Adonis-Go-to-California-and-Become-a-Star fund." She turned back to her checkbook. Sensing his owner's disinterest, Adonis padded over to a spot on the floor where the sun came through the window.

"This is it, baby. This will be our lucky day." Her FM country radio station shifted to a new song, "Four Wives, Four Divorces, and No Place to Lay My Head Tonight."

"Ah, great song." She opened her checkbook, picked up her pencil, and began jotting down numbers. Her head bobbed back and forth from checkbook to bank statement. Adonis, watching her, followed suit, his head bobbing back and forth from her to his food bowl. "Great music, stuff to do, and my doggie by my side." Adonis glanced up from his comfortable spot on the floor and put his head down on his paws, feeling the warmth of the sun from the south window.

Ronda took a long drink of her coffee and pulled her phone closer so she could use its calculator. "All right . . . a few numbers here . . . add this up to that . . . round this off . . . subtract . . . a few checks still out . . . and bippity, boppity, bingo! All balanced." She looked over at her napping dog and said in a quiet voice, "Well, it's official, baby. We have a whole twenty-seven dollars and sixty-two cents in the bank. That won't even keep you in dog food this week." Adonis opened his eyes and raised his head at the mention of food and then, looking at Ronda's expression, lowered it again, his eyelids closing.

She shut the checkbook, pushed the unpaid bills to the side of the table, and pulled a coffee-stained sheet of paper out of a pile. "Okay. Now to figure out our traveling expenses. You're going to love, love, love California. Lots of palm trees to pee on and beautiful weather. Not like the snow and cold here. And I'll bet there's a bevy of beauties out there just waiting for a handsome stud like you, Adonis. You'll never run low on food or a nice place to sleep once I get us bankrolled."

At the mention of food, Adonis padded back over to the table, rubbing Ronda's leg as if to remind her to fill his bowl.

She shifted her vocal inflections to baby talk. "Yes, yes. I'll put some doggie food in your little bowl." Then she straightened up. "At this time tomorrow we'll be packed and on our way. Don't need to take much of this junk," she said as she scrunched up her nose and glanced around the kitchen and into the small living room. "I'll just throw a few things together after my meeting tonight, and tomorrow it's off to the sunshine state. Have to figure out a few of the expenses, but we won't have to worry about money now, will we?"

The dog sauntered over to Ronda and stood close by. She reached out and patted his back and rubbed his stomach. "Oh, such a good, good baby. I have to go take care of some last-minute business, and then I have a date with a target. When I get back I'll have a fistful of money. No, make that a bag full. And then we won't be on the bottom anymore, Adonis, honey. We'll be at the top of the food chain, and I'll have enough to keep us in clover until that first big comedy gig. And I'll buy you a beautiful, jeweled collar. I'll go to Rodeo Drive just like in that movie. Only, unlike that Julia chick, they'll want my money. You'll be the posh pooch then." She stopped and considered a different subject. She put her finger in front of her mouth to let Adonis know he'd better not tell anyone. "Shannon thinks this is gonna be a joint venture, but by the time she figures things out we'll be on our way to the big C."

Adonis didn't know what she was saying, but he liked the stomach rub. He pushed up against her leg and closed his eyes.

"I have a little appointment tonight and

we're meeting out on Shady Meadows Cemetery Road. That way we won't be disturbed as we do our business. I have a feeling Brenda — wherever she's now residing — is sorry she ticked him off. But ole Ronda keeps her eyes and ears open and she knows who's who in this little drama." She finished writing figures on the paper, looked at it with a satisfied air, and put her pencil down. Staring out the kitchen window, she added, "He sure knows how to set a fire." Then she said with a laugh, "But then, after all, he should."

Adonis began to whine softly, saliva congealing on Ronda's leg.

"Oh, don't worry. I won't be as stupid as Brenda." She walked over to the desk she had so carefully refinished years ago, opened a drawer, and pulled out a small, dark object. Holding it up to the dog, she said, "I have this sweet gun. He won't try anything with me. And this time tomorrow we'll be rolling in the dough and off to the land of milk and honey. Just wait, Adonis, baby." She checked the chambers and then dropped the gun in the bottom of her purse and stuffed some tissues on top of it. Walking over to a kitchen cupboard, she pulled out a dog food bag that was almost empty.

"This should hold you till I return." She

dumped the food into the bowl on the floor, filled the water bowl up from the sink, and set it down. "Now you be a good boy while Mommy is gone today. I'm getting dressed, running some errands since I have some last things to do before we go, and then I'll be home after my big appointment. Never you worry."

She left the dog happily lapping up water and crunching dog food and went to her bedroom to get dressed, muttering, "Just wait . . ."

CHAPTER EIGHTEEN:
TJ

TJ listened for the satisfying "thud" as she sent a third dart flying into her wall calendar. All three had stuck in the small square that was Thursday, June 30. Darts helped her think. She walked over to the wall and pulled them out, laying them on her desk. She sat down and propped her feet on one of the opened desk drawers. In front of her on the wall was a whiteboard with multiple lists. The left column had possible suspects followed by two more columns with motives and alibis. She had used this technique for years and found that it helped her mull over the cases she was trying to solve. Talking to Grace helped too, but today she needed to be alone.

She had already drawn a line through various suspects Brenda had blackmailed. They were crossed off if they had an alibi that was ironclad. That took out, for example, Jim Vance on Tanglefoot Road, who had an affair with Brenda and paid her four thousand dollars. But the night she died he was in an all-night poker game with a bunch of his cronies, all of whom vouched for him, especially since he had lost a lot of money to them. What a stupid thing to do. Married men. Why did they sleep with people who had less to lose than they had? Vance was in the lower echelons of city government at the courthouse. TJ had already crossed him off. He didn't have the guts to kill anyone.

After Vance, she had written down Tom Mendez, a construction worker who definitely had the physical build to attract Brenda. Another married guy. Family. Relieved of several thousand dollars by Brenda. He also undoubtedly had the means since he worked with construction equipment and that included plenty of gasoline. But Mendez had been on a job in Wisconsin for a week prior to, and a week following, Brenda's murder. Again, he had plenty of witnesses as to his whereabouts the night of the murder. So, cross him off too.

Dennis Weidemann, an "outsider" who'd moved to Endurance from Chicago, owned a computer software company and was doing quite well. He'd built a beautiful home up on the hill that overlooked a rolling meadow full of wildflowers and prairie grass on one side and the town on the other. His wife could have been a fashion model with her good looks, and she was involved in a lot of local charitable organizations. They had two kids, both in elementary school. What the hell was he doing playing around with Brenda? Weidemann was probably the richest of her marks. He didn't say how much he had paid her, but he'd been on a vacation with his wife and kids at the time Brenda was killed. Her little black book indicated that he had made quite a charitable contribution. Another cross-off.

The list was long, and TJ had covered a lot of territory in the thirteen days since Brenda's death. Corey Rafferty, a state cop, was lent out to her, and they had investigated at least twenty-five people on Brenda's list. Corey agreed with TJ that many of the victims of Brenda's little plan were not really viable suspects. She still felt that Sturgis and Shiveley were live possibilities. Neither had strong alibis. Sturgis was still fuming about the death blow Brenda had struck to his business, and he still couldn't account for his whereabouts on the night of the crime. Where had he been? And was he capable of setting a fire like that? He certainly had a supply of gasoline and he wasn't stupid . . . well, relatively speaking.

Judging from his uncontrolled anger and his physical strength, he was definitely a possibility. But how to tie him directly to the crime?

Shannon Shiveley was a shifty little piece, and TJ didn't for a minute believe that she had been with her grass-mowing, gasoline-buying boyfriend the night of the fire. She too was angry that she was supposed to have been in on the take from Brenda's "business." TJ had questioned Shannon a couple of days earlier. Brenda was too slick for Shannon and kept making her promises she hadn't intended to keep. Finally, Shannon blew up and possibly killed Brenda, thinking she could find the hiding place of that book with Brenda safely out of the way. They had a huge argument the afternoon of the fire and Brenda taunted her one time too many. But what if Brenda had had the book at her house? Why burn down the house when Shannon didn't really know for sure where the book was? Come to think of it, Shannon might have done something that stupid. Probably a good thing Shannon hadn't hooked up with Sturgis. Now that would be a pair of tempers and stupidity to reckon with. Her alibi was like Swiss cheese. She and her boyfriend were home that night. Again, no physical evidence connecting her solidly to Brenda's death.

Then, TJ thought, there was the actual fire. Whoever set it knew what he (or she) was doing and also was strong enough to knock Brenda out. He would have to know how to arrange the gasoline pours so the house would ignite fast enough to destroy the body. Obviously he hadn't counted on the quick response of the Endurance Fire Department. Brenda's body was meant to be burned beyond recognition. The fire examiners found no means of ignition for the fire, so whoever lit it took away whatever he used to start it. Smart thinking.

As she stared at the whiteboard, willing it to talk to her, a knock on the door disturbed her. Myers stuck his head in and said, "I think you'd better come out here, Sweeney."

She walked out to the front counter and saw Dan Wakeley's wife, Jennifer, pacing up and down. Her red pencil skirt clung to her perfect curves like plastic wrap, but the look in her eyes said she was infuriated.

"Ms. Wakeley. What can I do for you?"

"You can look at this pile of garbage that I found in my husband's tool box in our garage. I knew it! I knew he was cheating on me with some horny little piece of trash, but this really does it."

TJ was shocked. She felt it would be wise

to find a closed door. "Why don't we go over to this room and you can tell me what's happening here."

Jennifer Wakeley followed her back to a conference room and sat down at a long, rectangular table. She crossed her tanned, shapely legs and leaned forward in her chair. TJ closed the door behind them and said, "Now what's the story? Start at the beginning."

Highly agitated, Jennifer Wakeley worked on pulling herself together. Her hands were constantly in motion, tapping fingers on the table, moving them to her lap. She had placed some papers in front of her, folded over in thirds. Then she took a deep breath. "I don't quite know where to start." She stood up again and paced around the table. "I'm so angry I kicked his lying ass out the door and I don't ever want him to come near us again."

"Okay. I assume this is Dan we're talking about?"

"You assume right!" She sat back down. "That lying — angry — I've never been so — oh, I can't believe how he lied to me!" She stood up again, practically knocking the chair over. The arm of the chair hit the wall and she turned and straightened it, setting it down again. "Sorry. You can see I'm just a little . . ."

TJ waited until Ms. Wakeley looked around, sat down, and then TJ repeated, "I can see you're upset. Why don't you let me look at those papers while you think about where to start."

Jennifer Wakeley handed over three sheets of paper, each folded as if it had been in an envelope. While TJ perused the words on each page, Jennifer looked around at the interrogation room, willing herself to stillness. The detective could see her out of the corner of her eye. She checked out the two-way mirrored window, and then she looked toward the door.

TJ had never seen Dan Wakeley's wife when she hadn't been flawlessly coiffed and perfectly composed. When she finished reading the letters, the detective sat back and thought for a few moments in silence.

"I appreciate you bringing these in to me, Ms. Wakeley. We've been running down a whole lot of people Brenda Norris was evidently blackmailing. Looks like your husband was on the list too. Mind telling me how you found these and what your husband said when you confronted him?"

"It's no secret, Detective Sweeney, that Dan and I have had our problems in recent months. I don't know that he says anything when he goes to his shift at the fire station, but I'm sure we have some acquaintances who have figured it out. We've been married for twenty years and our kids are in that teenage period where we don't always agree on what they should or shouldn't do. I believe he comes down much too hard on them, but then he isn't always home to deal with their problems like I am. You know, he does shifts at the fire station where he's there for several days."

"I understand." TJ looked directly at her, wondering once again how Brenda could have been so persuasive with Jennifer's husband. "That leaves a lot of responsibility on your shoulders."

Jennifer opened her purse and pulled out a small package. She took one tissue out and put the rest away, placing her purse back on the table. She started twisting the tissue between her fidgety fingers. "Yes, it does, and he comes home after a couple of days and is often unhappy with how I've handled things." Then her voice became hard. "Well, maybe he should be around more," she said, her voice rising while TJ waited patiently. "Anyway, that's caused some huge arguments."

"I can imagine." TJ reacted. "Is he abusive?"

"Oh, no." She quickly pulled back, moving farther from TJ as her back pushed against the chair. "It's not that. He does have a temper, yes. But I've never been afraid he'd hurt me or the children. Some nights he just leaves the house and is gone for hours. I think he ends up at Tully's and has a few drinks. Then he usually comes home sometime after they close and is much calmer. This, however, has been going on now for five or six months."

"By 'this' you mean?"

"Brenda Norris."

"So it's mostly the kids you fought over until Brenda came into the picture?"

"Yes. But he also acted different for much of that time too, as if he was feeling guilty about something. He'd pull away from me and brood as if he should be telling me something but isn't. I know guilt when I see it. He isn't good at hiding his feelings."

"And then you found these letters. When did you find them?"

"Yesterday. I knew he was worrying about something. He just hasn't been himself. So I searched around the house and figured that if there was anything to find it might be in the garage in his workshop area. The letters were in his toolbox. At first I couldn't believe what I was seeing. An affair? He was having an affair with some little tramp and she was sending him blackmail notes? You notice she only signed her initial. I don't know if he paid her, but I don't always deal with the bills. I suppose he might have found some way to hide making payments to her."

"But eventually you figured out that the initial 'B' might stand for Brenda, right?"

"Right."

"And you're bringing these to me because . . ."

"I came over here with these because I was so angry I just wanted to hurt him. Now I'm not sure. I know Dan didn't have anything to do with Brenda Norris's death. He couldn't. He'd never do anything like that. And I figure she was probably sleeping with more men than I can count. In fact, Dan isn't even going to come near me again until he agrees to have testing done for STDs and HIV. Who knows where that little tramp has been?" More twisting of tissues and hand-wringing. "If I ever get back on an even keel from all this, we will sit down and have a talk. And I mean everything. Where he met her and if he paid her . . ." And suddenly Jennifer Wakeley burst into tears and put her face in her hands.

TJ pulled a box of tissues from a desk

drawer and handed her one, waiting for her to regain her composure.

"I imagine it's accurate to say that your husband was not the only one that was caught up in her blackmail trap. But I have to tell you, Ms. Wakeley, I'll have to question him and also ask about his alibi for that night."

"He's not at home right now. Good riddance. He's probably staying at the fire station, figuring I'll calm down in a few days."

"I need to keep these letters."

"You can have them. I don't want anything that two-bit baggage has touched. I know she's dead and you aren't supposed to speak ill of the dead, but I hope she burns in hell."

"You're not the first person I've heard mention that," TJ replied, standing up and bringing the interview to an end. She handed Jennifer Wakeley a business card and asked her to call if she thought of anything else she'd forgotten.

Ten minutes later, TJ had added Wakeley to her whiteboard lists. The fireman seemed a strong candidate since he was known to have a temper like Sturgis. But he also had firsthand expertise when it came to fire-setting. He could make sure he was never found out. *But I'd think he could be smarter than gasoline pours. Unless he wanted to make it look like he wasn't a pro.* These letters put a new slant on things. Maybe Brenda was pressuring him more and more over the last couple of months. Dan Wakeley was another man with a great deal to lose. *Wonder if he has an alibi for that night?* He was at the Norris's fire with the rest of the department but had been called in because he was off duty. Where had he been before the fire?

A call to the fire station indicated that Wakeley was not on shift at the moment. He also wasn't at home. This would bear some looking into. TJ was about to walk out her office door when it opened unexpectedly and Myers stuck his head in.

"Sweeney, we've got a live one!" He paused, a confused look coming over his face. "I mean, we've got a dead one. Just called in. Dead body out by Shady Meadows Cemetery Road. Looks like a gun wound. Can you imagine? Here in Endurance? Backup is ready to head out there with you." And he disappeared out the door.

Can I imagine? In Endurance? After Brenda Norris, our statistics are already running in the red. The question is how many more of Norris's victims might be out there, and which one was first in line? She grabbed her gun, shield, and car keys and headed out the door. *Why didn't I just get my teaching certificate like Grace?*

As TJ left for the cemetery, across town in a small, second-story apartment, a canine's distressed and bereaved wailing drifted out the windows and into the night.

Chapter Nineteen:
Grace

On Friday morning Grace walked out her back door with an armload of trash bags, some newspapers, and her garden gloves. Dressed in an old mauve shirt and cut-off shorts that she didn't mind getting dirty, she had decided she'd take the morning off from the newspaper and clean out a corner of her garage that had been driving her crazy. Besides, she needed to digest what TJ had told her when she called last night. After that call she hadn't slept very well. This cleaning job was just the thing for stress relief and quiet thought.

Leaning over, she began to move various planters and pots into the center of the garage so she could clean out their dirt and debris and place them in a more organized row, smaller pots nesting in the larger ones. Then she'd stack them up in the back of the garage.

She spread out the newspapers and used

a small hand spade to scrape the old dirt out on the newspapers. All the while she thought about TJ's phone call yesterday.

Ronda Burke had been found in a ditch off the side of the cemetery road. Grace jabbed at the compact dirt, her mouth tightening in a grimace. Ronda — her Ronda with whom she had laughed so many times out at Tully's and, before that, in her high school class. Grace could visualize the scene: police car lights flashing, early-morning darkness, dampness and standing water — it had rained the night before — and the thought of the dead watching them from the little knoll where the grave stones began. Grace had been there often when she ran more regularly. The cemetery had recently refinished the asphalt paths, which made them a smooth running surface. She shivered for a moment, remembering TJ's call, even though it was the last day of June and the temperature was in the low eighties.

She reached over and put three empty pots together, trying to decide whether to rinse them with the garden hose, but she had trouble focusing. Her mind was on the repulsive scene TJ had described at the cemetery. Ronda's body had been rolled off the road into a ditch, face down. When TJ and the coroner turned her over, the blood on her chest had largely washed into the ditch, leaving a bloody pool of water an inch deep. Her face had leaves and debris plastered to it and her eyes were closed. Grace shook her head and her chin trembled. She pulled a tissue out of her pocket and wiped her nose. Then, setting her jaw, she went back to her pots.

TJ said Ronda had looked peaceful. But it was hard to equate that description with the woman Grace knew who had laughed through most of her days and always had a joke to tell or a funny one-liner. *Who had done this? And was it connected to Brenda's murder?* Two unnatural deaths had occurred within two weeks of each other in a town that seldom saw one homicide in thirty years. Normally, TJ didn't describe such horrifying details to Grace, but she had been highly agitated when she called, and Grace knew she was under a lot of stress. Now, with two dead bodies, the chief was calling in even more state help.

TJ told her that Martinez, the coroner, determined that Ronda was murdered between midnight and two a.m. on Wednesday night. No defensive wounds on her hands or face — whoever killed her was facing her and shot her twice in the chest. Death would have happened right away.

Thank goodness for that. She struggled to remember something else. *What was it that TJ found?* Oh, yes, two shell casings were left on the road, and Ronda's car was parked off to the side of the cemetery with the keys still in it. No purse. Ronda was obviously meeting someone, but who and why? And why in the middle of the night? TJ said she'd know more after the postmortem in Woodbury, which was going on this morning. Poor Jake Williams got to go this time, and, according to TJ, he had an uncooperative stomach. She took a deep breath, frowned, and wiped her nose again.

Brenda spent a great deal of time at Tully's. Grace remembered Ronda telling her and Jeff Maitlin that she was fascinated by Brenda's and Tully's conversations in the bar. If Grace were to believe Tully, Brenda practically considered the bar her office, and she drank way too much while she talked to everyone around her. Maybe she told Ronda something that sent her out on the cemetery road. Or maybe Ronda overheard a conversation that concerned whatever Brenda's secret project was about. That was the only connection Grace could devise.

On the other hand, Dan Wakeley could also be involved. TJ had told Grace about his wife's visit to the police station. Grace didn't know Dan Wakeley at all, but she saw Jennifer about town and knew she was quite active in the school PTA for her kids. *I think they have two — a boy and a girl.* Whenever Grace saw Wakeley's wife, she was reminded of a fashion magazine layout — perfect clothes that flattered her figure and hair and nails obviously pampered. Well, it wouldn't be the last time a guy had a roving eye and ended up in the wrong bed. How humiliating it must have been for Jennifer to take those letters in to TJ.

Grace sighed and stared out toward the street. *How can you ever really know what goes on behind closed doors in a marriage? The picture the world sees can sure be very different from reality.* She gathered up the last of the pots and stacked them at the end of the neat row she had created near the back of the garage. As she turned around, she saw TJ pulling into her driveway.

The detective got quickly out of her car, strode over to Grace, and smiled at the dirt smudges on Grace's shirt and shorts. "Is this some new 'dirt look' I hadn't heard about on the fashion pages or are we headed back into grunge?"

"Very funny. I just decided to relieve a little stress."

TJ cackled. "You? Stress? You ought to

come down to the station if you want to see stress. Got any more of that strawberry pie you told me Lettie cooked yesterday, or did you eat it all yourself?"

"No, I have more in the kitchen. Come on in. Got time for some coffee, too?"

Sitting down at the kitchen table, TJ caught Grace up to date on her interrogation of Dan Wakeley.

"Had to turn him loose. No physical evidence connects him to Ronda. He absolutely swears he had nothing to do with her death, or Brenda's, for that matter."

Grace slid a piece of strawberry pie in front of TJ, along with a cup of black coffee and a fork. "How does he stack up with Sturgis? And what's the connection between Brenda and Ronda? Or is there . . . a link?"

"He definitely has a motive — he had an affair with Brenda, his marriage was in a patchy spot, and, in his moment of weakness, she went in for the kill. Blackmailing him, of course, like half the town. A little bit at first and then a lot more later."

"Now you can add him to your cast of thousands of suspects."

"Man, this pie is amazing. Lettie really outdid herself." She wiped her mouth with a paper napkin. "Wakeley has definitely moved to the head of the line. He went to see Brenda the night she died. He needed more time to get some money together without Jennifer finding out. Brenda laughed in his face. But he swears she was alive when he left."

"Did he say how that whole thing — the affair — got started?"

"Yeah. He said he and his wife had hit a 'hard patch' and he'd been drinking quite a bit. Sometimes when he drank he went to Tully's and Brenda was always there. She had a sympathetic ear — you know the drill — and he blabbed it all out for her. One thing led to another and he'd end up at her house. For a while it helped, and then he felt guilty and realized how stupid he was acting. Small town. Wife and two kids. So when he wanted to end it —"

"— she explained she'd need some cash."

"Exactly."

"And where was he during the window of opportunity the night Brenda died?"

TJ laughed and looked right at Grace. "Funniest thing. Says he drove around the countryside trying to cool his temper and figure out what to tell Jennifer when he got home so late. Once he did get home, he says it was only about thirty minutes before he was called out to the fire."

"And did you believe him?"

She laughed and shook her head. "It gets better."

Grace got up and cut a piece of pie for herself. As she sat back down she asked, "Better?"

"Yeah. His three fifty-seven was stolen out of his truck two weeks earlier."

"And the bullets that killed Ronda — let me guess — three fifty-sevens."

"Ah, Grace, I've taught you well. Unfortunately, we don't have the gun and he claims he doesn't either. Without that we don't have any physical evidence to tie him to the case. It's all circumstantial."

"Did he report the gun stolen?"

"Sure did. But if he was planning to kill Ronda, it was most convenient to have it stolen officially."

"So let me get this straight," Grace said, and drank a sip of coffee to wash down her pie. "He has the same caliber of gun that killed Ronda and he's an expert on setting fires. He has no alibi for the night Brenda died, and he'd even seen her before her death. Shift scenes. Where was he when Ronda died?"

"Oh, more and better. He played pitch at the station with a group of the guys — and they agree — but he left about twelve thirty a.m. and drove around — again — only this time he went clear past Woodbury."

"Alone?"

"Alone."

"Boy, that's a lot of anger management. But I don't understand. Why would he have a reason to kill Ronda?"

"He says he doesn't. But Ronda undoubtedly saw him and Brenda making goo-goo eyes at the bar night after night, so put two and two together."

"More blackmail. Man, Endurance sure has no small amount of that going on. I never knew this town had so many secrets to hide."

"He looks like hell. His eyes are red-rimmed, his hair could use a good washing, and his usually clean-shaven face has at least two days' growth. He wasn't quite the Wakeley I normally see. And, believe me, I'd notice. You can tell he lifts weights quite regularly."

Grace laughed. "Ah, TJ. You always look for those muscular shoulders."

"I'm ignoring you." TJ brushed off her hands and pushed her dessert plate aside. "He claims that he never spoke to Ronda except to say hello at Tully's. But I have to tell you, he was sweating bullets when I questioned him. He twisted his hair and bit his lip and cleared his throat. If I was teaching a class on body language he'd be the perfect example for 'hiding something.' Stop and think about it, Grace, he is *the* expert on fires. The state calls him in."

Grace stopped chewing, her fork in midair and her face taking on a thoughtful look. "Why would he do such a crummy job of setting that fire if he were so good? Jeff Maitlin told me multiple pours of accelerants was a sure sign of a set fire. Wouldn't he disguise it somehow so it would look more . . . more accidental?"

"I guess he would if he had had the time. But what if he told the truth about going to see Brenda that night? However, when he left maybe he saw it as an opportunity — not really premeditated?"

"Maybe."

"The next time I have him in I'll use that as a possible scenario. Might get him to open up. And I do think a 'next time' is predictable. I've got McGuire keeping an eye on him in case he decides to bolt."

The strains of "Saturday Night Fever" jarred them both and TJ answered her phone.

"Yeah, Collier. Uh-huh." She looked at Grace and listened intently and a smile slowly came over her face. "All right. Bring it in and we'll go make an arrest." She tapped her phone off, looked at Grace, and said, "Wakeley. They found his gun hidden in some brush farther out from Ronda's murder scene. Registration numbers on the butt of the handle match. It's been fired — twice." She stood up and Grace noticed her lips were pressed tightly together as she pushed in her chair and pulled her car keys out of her pocket. "Time to go pay Dan Wakeley a visit and invite him to spend some time in our jail."

CHAPTER TWENTY

"Tully. I hear you have a special on for my most delicious, favorite of all time drink, margaritas," said Deb O'Hara as she sauntered up to the bar. "Lay a dirty one on me, please, and take orders for my friends here. I'm buying."

"That's what I love to hear," said Tully, chuckling as he reached up over his head for margarita glasses. "Sounds like a good way to celebrate the Fourth. And will you and Grace have the same?" he said to Jill.

"Absolutely."

They sat down on the high stools at a table in the bar and Jill called out, "Oh, and some peanuts too, Bill." He nodded. "Do I have a story for you," said Jill to Grace and Deb.

"Do tell." Deb gazed over at the bar watching Tully fix their drinks.

"I heard this from John Seiver at work. You know, he's also on the city council.

Everyone in town's been watching this, but he had the scoop on the entire set of events and it is hilarious."

"All right already. Get to the story," Grace said, laughing.

"You know that intersection at Main and Adams Street, the one near the Drug Mart store?"

"Sure, the one with the stop signs."

"Right! Remember they decided to no longer make it a two-way stop sign on Adams with the through traffic going north and south on Main. So they put in a four-way stop. All kinds of accidents happened next. People couldn't remember to stop on Main going either north or south because it has never been a four-way stop."

Grace giggled. "It's because of the sixty-five-and-up crowd, you know, like Nub Swensen."

"Right — that and people texting. So after the fiasco of changing the signs that way, Seiver said the city council debated it and thought if they put stop signs in the middle of Main, between the lanes on each side, people would notice them."

"I don't remember that, but I don't drive through that intersection much," said Deb.

"Drivers knocked over and splintered three sets of signs — both going north and south." Grace and Deb laughed and Jill put her hands up and said, "Wait. We have more to the story. Obviously the signs in the middle of the street weren't working, so Seiver said they voted to make it a stop on the Adams side of the intersection, as always, and put signs on Main saying, 'Stop if pedestrians are in the walkway.' "

"Let me guess. People stopped no matter what and were rear-ended," Grace said.

"You got it. Great day for Bert's Collision Shop. And one of the casualties was Mayor Blandford's wife, Polly. She was almost arrested for causing a public disturbance because she got out of her car and marched up to Genevieve Blackburn, who was talking on her cell phone when she rear-ended Polly. McGuire had to pull the two away from each other, and Polly took a swing at him, too."

"Fantastic," said Deb. "I'd love to see His Honor have to go and bail her out." They all laughed at that mental photo. She glanced over at the bar. "This place doesn't seem quite the same without Ronda rolling around." She leaned in and whispered so her voice wouldn't carry. "How awful. I can't imagine anyone hurting her, let alone killing her. What is going on with people?"

Grace glanced over at Tully and then

looked around at the rest of the bar. She shook her head. "I can't believe she's gone. It's only been three days and it seems like forever. Two murders in the past month. People send their kids to Endurance College from Chicago because it's so much safer. Here we are in the middle of corn, beans, and cow pastures, and someone is killing people. It just isn't normal."

Jill, who'd been watching the waitresses at the end of the bar, added, "Looks like he's already replaced her with that cute little blonde over there. She appears to be in charge of the wait staff and she's pushing tables together for that big group."

"Well, you can't blame him. Life has to go on. He has a business to run," Deb murmured.

"Here we go, ladies," Bill Tully said as he set their drinks and a couple bowls of peanuts on the table.

"We're really sorry to hear about Ronda, Bill," said Grace. "I can still remember her in high school. She was so clever and funny and had so many friends. I figured she had quite a future as a stand-up comic, and I know she had plans to pursue that as a career."

"You know, Grace, 'the best laid plans' and all . . ." Tully said. "I still can't believe it either. She was off work that night so I have no idea what happened, other than what I saw in the paper. I just feel terrible. She always brightened the place up and I know she brought in customers. Relied on her like my own sister." His gaze came back to Grace. "I hope Sweeney gets on top of this. If deaths happen in threes, we still have one to go."

"Oh, don't say things like that." Deb shivered.

He smiled at her. "Ah, don't listen to me. I'm just talkin'."

As Tully headed back to the bar, Jill said, "You know he always seems to be in a pretty good mood for all the plates he has in the air. Now he's had to replace Ronda, he's finally finished the renovations, and he deals with so many problems like that idiot, Mike Sturgis. I can't imagine how he can always be so cheerful."

They talked about the centennial celebration and then Deb had to leave for a family outing. Tully came back over to refill Jill's and Grace's drinks.

At the end of the bar Grace saw Bunny Meyer. *Her husband, Jonathan, was such a wheeler-dealer in high school,* she thought. *He stole some funds from the art club cake and cookie sale. Then he grew up and be-*

came a politician for real. Now he's in Wood-bury minimum-security prison making license plates. Politicians never get it, do they? TJ's sometimes right that people don't change very much.

"So, how are the newspaper articles going, Grace? Must be about done since the big fireworks are coming up this weekend. I notice they're already starting to decorate the downtown. Kinda like the little flags that they're hanging from the street lights with the centennial logo on them." Tully abruptly changed topics. "Figured out anything else about those cold cases?" he asked as he slid two more margaritas off a tray.

"I'm wrapping things up, Bill." She reached into her pocket and pulled out the good-luck charm with the raven on it, polished to a shine. "Been carrying this around for a couple of days hoping to get some inspiration." She placed the coin with the raven's head on the table. Tully leaned down and studied it. Then he picked it up and turned it over in his hand.

"Hmm. Not seen anything like this before. Where'd you find it?"

"It's a good-luck piece I found in the box with the Kessler stuff on that fire in 'sixty-eight. I need to take it back and put it with the other things, but I thought I'd carry it around today because it might give me a revelation. I'm going over to the Historical Society tomorrow to look up the old yearbooks on that period of time. Need to see what this Kessler kid looked like, just for the record. He's the suspect in the case. But I think Brenda was working on some other angle."

"Really? What kind of angle?"

"Not sure. But she had a clue in her notes about a Poe short story and I think I've figured that out. So I'm going to keep my nose to the ground and go after some photos from the yearbooks. I'm also thinking about some fire photos."

Tully was silent for a moment. "Well, I don't know anything about all that. Think there's some kind of tie to the story and Brenda's murder? Or Ronda's?"

"Good question. I'm working on that. But TJ's the detective."

"You know, I hear an awful lot around this place with people coming and going. Could be Dan Wakeley's tied to Brenda's death. Maybe she was getting dough from him. Blackmail. They say that Sweeney had him in to interrogate him. I'd put my money on him. He's been in the bar a lot the last few weeks with Brenda Norris. They seemed to be awfully cozy for him being married and all. I wouldn't want to get on the wrong side of his wife either. Seen her in action, and her temper can be just as out of control as her husband's. And, you know, Ronda wasn't stupid. She watched people in the bar, and I wouldn't put it past her to try to get in on that action. Not that I should speak ill of the dead, but, like I said, I see things, and when people drink they tend to blab. Ronda just loved to gossip. Maybe she had some kind of angle to Brenda's murder and it got her killed."

Jill set her glass down. "You might have something there, Tully. Brenda was playing the odds with quite a few guys, from what I hear."

He nodded. "I'm really missing Ronda around here, but, you know, life has to go on. Who knows? Maybe we're all wrong. But I do know that someone out there is killing people. You girls take care of yourselves. Be careful, especially you, Grace. After all, you're checking out the same stuff Brenda was working on. You say you think there might be a new angle to that fire story, but maybe it would be best to leave it alone. That might be what got her in trouble. Sometimes it's best to 'let sleeping dogs lie,' as the preacher said last Sunday. On the other hand, if Brenda died because of her extracurricular activities around town, maybe things will calm down now."

The next morning Grace got up early and bicycled to the Endurance Historical Society. The red brick building that held the town's history had been converted from an old grocery store that went out of business nearly twenty years earlier. Local residents had started a foundation, formed a board, and the town's Historical Society had become a reality. Now Deb O'Hara worked there several mornings a week on a regular schedule among other volunteers.

Grace stopped outside the front window and looked in at the display of pictures and objects that marked the 175th anniversary of the town. Everything was decked out in red, white, and blue, and photos from the town's history were framed and captioned. It wouldn't be long now since the parade was this Saturday — just four days away — and the dinner dance was set for Saturday night. She put her hand up over her eyes to shield the sun's glare and looked at each of the photos. A few were from the time since she'd moved here to marry Roger back in the early 'seventies — photos of parades, earlier celebrations on the centennial year, and then the 150th celebration. It was fun to see how some of the old buildings had been reused for businesses she knew today. She straightened up, parked and locked her bicycle in the rack next to the building, grabbed her laptop and purse from her basket, and walked in the front door.

Today Mildred Dunsworthy, the retired postmistress, was manning the main desk. She was on the phone, so Grace just waved at her and headed back through several rooms.

On one of Grace's earlier trips, Deb had shown her boxes of microfiche that contained old copies of the local newspaper and other cartons that had pages of the Woodbury *Spectator* and the Stark County *Newsletter.* Bookshelves on every wall were filled with city directories, genealogy magazines, census records, and various volumes of the histories of neighboring counties. And, of course, files and folders adorned every shelf with genealogy records.

In a separate room were shelves with old yearbooks from various local schools, many of them donated by area inhabitants, especially when their relatives died. Old yearbooks didn't have much value except as genealogy records.

Grace set her laptop and purse down on a chair and began looking for the Endurance yearbooks. After several dead ends, she spotted them over in the far corner stacked up in neat rows. She saw first the 1971 yearbook, which would have been Brenda's graduating year. Turning her head sideways, she looked for the numbers on the spines of the books. Some of them were out of place. Then she found what she was looking for: the 1968 Endurance High School yearbook. That was the year Brenda would have been a freshman. The Kessler kid was a little older than she was, and Nick Lawler would have been, maybe, a junior that year. Now, more than ever, Grace felt she was on the right track. Brenda knew both of those boys, and she had some kind of insight into that fire story. But what? Did she have some idea of where they might find the Kessler kid — Ted — because she knew him so long ago? Grace pulled the yearbook out and took it over to a table where she'd laid her laptop and notebook. Opening up the yearbook, she started at the beginning.

She was surprised to find a color layout, not black and white, just inside the front cover. It must have been the senior class. They were sitting out on the grass in the park that ran south of the high school. Several had guitars and all were in clothing that shouted late sixties. Instantly amusing.

She opened the first page and saw the school insignia and the name of the yearbook, The Maroon and Gold. Browsing through the class pictures — seniors first — she smiled at all the flipped-up hairstyles on the girls and the dark-framed glasses on everyone.

Grace checked out the freshmen photos and found Brenda right away. She was staring straight at the camera lens with long hair pulled back behind her ears and a mouth that was a straight line across her face. She appeared to be wearing a jumper with a white, high-collared blouse underneath. Pictured up against a brick wall, she was staring straight ahead, a brief glimpse of what she would later become. Grace always felt as if her own students changed so completely in looks from their freshman year to their senior year.

She turned the pages to see if she could find Ted Kessler. There he was. He wore a buttoned-down, collared shirt with some kind of pattern in the material. His hair was really short on the sides and the top had a wave to it. Huge glasses sat on his nose — a little low — and his eyes stared up through the upper part of the lenses. Ears announced themselves prominently on the sides of his head. His mouth smiled in a closed bow that curved symmetrically, and his Adam's apple was really protuberant. He looked very young for a sophomore. *Strange,* thought Grace. *You sure don't look like a killer. Or a football player. But evidently you did play ball. I guess in small towns that happens. The jury is still out on the killer idea, but most people think you did it.* She studied his face, looking for some darker cast to his eyes, some sign of madness. *I guess you can't always see that,* she thought.

She fingered the good-luck charm in her pocket and sat back in the straight-backed wooden chair. *Edgar Allan Poe fits in here somewhere too.* The number in Brenda's notes, 297, referred to the first page of the short story, "The Purloined Letter." It was in the much-thumbed Poe tome in Brenda's office. Grace had taught it a few times when she worked at the high school. It was about the theft of a valuable letter that would have caused a political scandal. It eventually was found hidden in plain sight. No one thought to look for it there. *How did that fit with Ted Kessler? Was he, too, hiding in plain sight?* She concentrated on his photo again, trying to will him to tell her.

Maybe I should check out Nick Lawler, she thought. He would have been a junior or senior, depending on when his birthday fell. She turned the pages back to the front looking in the senior section. He would have been between Lathrop and Lester on page eleven. But no photo. *So,* she thought, *let's try the juniors.* Turning multiple pages, she shifted to the back of the book and looked for Lawler among that class. He should have been between Larimer and Leng, but he wasn't there. *Hmmm . . . Maybe he dropped out or perhaps didn't have a photo taken. Wouldn't surprise me after reading and hearing about his family. They probably didn't care and couldn't afford it.*

She checked the back for an index but didn't find one. Turning to the sports section, she looked for the football team. The team was huge and the photo was taken on bleachers out at the football field. The quality was grainy at best and made it difficult to see individual faces. She traced her finger along the names under the photo — the print was tiny too — and found what she was looking for: Ted Kessler. He looked about as big as the guys sitting beside him, and, with all those shoulder pads on, it was hard to tell much about his development. Grace squinted at the grainy, gray face. Because everything was colorless, she couldn't tell what his hair was like or his complexion. She looked back through the names again and found another familiar one: Nick Lawler. *Ah, I've finally found you.* Counting over in the fourth row of the photo, she saw a boy with dark, curly hair staring at the camera, but again the photo was too small and too grainy to make out his features. *At least he did exist,* she thought.

She set the volume back down, and decided to glance through the rest of the yearbook. Who knew what she might find? Page after page of black, gray, and white photos of long-ago students, most of them into their early sixties by now. Some, like Nick Lawler, dead. Cheerleaders with pompons, saddle shoes, miniskirts, chalk words on actual blackboards, tug-of-war games at the park, class officers, and candid photos. She turned the pages over, looking at candid shots from the school hallways and ball games. Occasionally she saw names and faces of people she knew in town, or sometimes she knew their children or grandchildren. And then she suddenly sat up and pulled the book off the table again. Her mouth fell open and her left hand flew to her chest. There, on page eighty-seven, was a candid shot. Grace leaned forward and stared at two students sitting on the floor outside their lockers. She recognized Brenda Norris and Ted Kessler. *Brenda had known him.* Grace was almost giddy and looked around for someone to tell.

So what did that mean? Were they friends? Could she have known anything about the fires because of her relationship with him? Did she know where he went when he took off that night? He was a grade older than she, but maybe they were more than just casual acquaintances. Brenda had written "The Purloined Letter." Hide in plain sight. Could it be that she knew where Ted Kessler was, and he wasn't so far away?

Frowning, she sat there for several minutes trying to decide how she could find out anything else from this yearbook. *How could she make these pictures speak to her?* Turning the pages backwards, she looked at the football photo again. She'd like to know what the Lawler kid looked like, but it was impossible in this grainy 1968 photo. How could she make that happen?

Then she remembered someone who could: Becca Baxter.

CHAPTER TWENTY-ONE

"Seriously?" TJ said as Grace spread out the voluminous skirt of the dress for her parade attire on Saturday. "Do you plan to use it for a full set of sails on a float?"

Grace smiled and picked a small piece of lint from the skirt. "Got it at the college costume shop and also found ones for Deb and Jill. I figured you'd be on duty 'serving and protecting,' and besides, you don't do costumes."

"Got that right, but I might reconsider for this. Maybe I could wear a long, dark coat, carry a fake, old-fashioned rifle, and stick a handlebar moustache on my face."

Grace hung the long dress up on the back of her bedroom door. "It amazes me that they could put twenty buttons down the back and button and unbutton them just to get it off and on. And, by the way, no corset. I refuse to have my lungs smothered in whale bones. This costume was made more recently so it doesn't have an eighteen-inch waist, thank goodness." Grace sighed. "Jill and Deb are supposed to stop by Friday morning to try theirs on."

TJ followed her downstairs to the kitchen and Grace poured two glasses of white wine. "Sit right there while I cut up vegetables. I'm going to make a pot of split-pea soup." She opened the refrigerator and grabbed a bag of vegetables Lettie had brought from her garden. TJ sat on a kitchen stool next to the island where Grace was busy with a cutting board.

"So," began Grace, "how is your investigation going?"

TJ sipped her wine. "Lots of loose ends to tie up and a decided lack of physical evidence, but we found Wakeley's gun at the scene."

"Does that make him your best suspect? And are these two separate murders, or do you think they're related?"

TJ went over to the pantry, rummaged around, and returned with a box of crackers. She spread a few out on the counter and shared them with Grace. "Right now I'm leaning toward Wakeley for both, but I'm not sure I have a theory yet about how they're tied together."

"Really? You think it was the same person?"

"Would you rather have two murderers loose in Endurance, Grace?"

"Well, got me there." She dropped some chopped carrots into the soup pot. "But the method was totally different: fire and bullets."

"Sturgis is still a prime candidate for Brenda, but I'm not sure I see him tied in with Ronda. I think Ronda played fast and loose with information she heard and tried to hold up the wrong person for money. My guess is she knew something and whoever she was blackmailing killed her. So the question is — how does Wakeley tie in with both murders, assuming they were done by the same killer? Right now that's what I'm working on."

"On the other hand, if Sturgis killed Brenda, then someone else may have killed Ronda."

"That's a possibility, too," TJ said, "unless Sturgis is the one Ronda tried to shake down. Not sure why she'd do that since we have no connection between Sturgis and Brenda other than the lawsuit, and Sturgis doesn't have a licensed gun." She reached over and took a piece of celery from the counter and popped it into her mouth. "But it's easy to get an illegal weapon or maybe steal Wakeley's from his truck. Sturgis could have done that."

"What have you found out about Dan Wakeley that makes you think he's such a good prospect?"

"Got a search warrant for his bank records. Brenda asked for twenty thousand dollars, if I'm to believe Wakeley. That put him between a huge rock and a hard place. How could he take money out of the bank without his wife finding out? His erratic behavior just before Brenda died points to him becoming increasingly panicked over that prospect. She sure had her clutches into him," TJ said, and she took another swallow of wine.

Grace thought for a moment, a puzzled look on her face. "So how does that also put him at Ronda's scene?"

"He doesn't have an alibi for either night when Brenda or Ronda died. Friday night he was out driving around. Seems to do that an awful lot. But we can't get him to admit Ronda saw him with Brenda at the bar, and even though they left separately, they didn't fool Ronda. I think Ronda put the squeeze on him for money. That's why, even after Brenda's death, he took out a sizable amount, thought he'd pay Ronda off, and then he changed his mind. After all, he'd already killed Brenda. Why not also get rid of the one person who was a problem when it came to him sliding back into the good graces of his wife and children?"

"Did you ask him about the money?" Grace said, dropping some celery into the pot.

"Of course. He said he'd decided to take a trip for a week — take some time off he had coming — and let things quiet down a bit at home."

"And what about the gun?"

"He says it was stolen about two weeks back. It's true that he turned in a stolen gun report and it's a registered gun. Then it turns up at Ronda's murder site. But, you know, 'Oh, officer, my gun was stolen,' has a ring of 'Please, I've heard this all before' to it."

"So you are holding Wakeley, right?"

"Can't do it much longer until I have a stronger case that ties him to one or both murders. I can hold him with the gun evidence, but I still need more. Theories and speculation are one thing, but DA Sorensen likes actual physical evidence. Wakeley certainly had the motive to kill Brenda, the lack of an alibi, and the fire knowledge. He's a good suspect for that death, but the case for Ronda's murder is weaker."

"I know people are talking all over town about why no one's been charged and nothing seems to be happening."

"Of course. It doesn't help that your boss, Maitlin, has been reporting on it regularly in the paper. Guess I should be happy the paper only comes out three days a week instead of six."

Grace put the pot on the stove, measured several cups of water, poured them on top of the vegetables, and turned on the burner. "So, I've thought about this constantly, too, as I've worked on the stories for the centennial." She paused and turned around to face the detective. "TJ, what if Brenda's death was not about blackmail? What if Ronda's death was? And what if they were related by something that both women knew? What if a drunken Brenda blabbed something to Ronda at the bar?"

"I'm listening. Like what?"

"Remember when Brenda came up to us weeks ago and talked about some story she was working on that would blow the lid right off this town?"

"Sure, but I figured it was just Brenda, who exaggerated."

"What if she did have a story? And what if it threatened someone? I think, TJ, that Ted

Kessler may not only be alive, but even living somewhere near here under an assumed name. What if Brenda found him? Think about that for a moment. Blow the lid off this town?" Grace cleaned up the last of the vegetable peels, ran them down the disposal, cleaned off the countertop, sat down, and poured more wine into both her glass and TJ's.

TJ was silent for a moment. Then, "Why wouldn't someone recognize Ted Kessler if he were still around?"

"I haven't figured that out yet. But he isn't a teenager anymore."

"And what, pray tell, has led you to these conclusions?"

"I know she was working on some big story. Even Jeff Maitlin says she had something she was keeping under her hat."

"We looked at her research."

"Me, too, and it sent me to the Historical Society. I examined the old newspaper coverage of the fires back in the sixties. And I also checked out the yearbook that had the photos of Brenda and Ted Kessler. She knew him, TJ. In the 'sixty-eight yearbook I found a candid shot of both Brenda and Ted together as they sat on the floor near lockers in the high school. Kessler's also in a photo of the football team. Brenda put a number 'thirty-two' in her notes. I'm curious about whether that might be Kessler's football number. The football team photo is really grainy and it's hard to see faces or numbers. I'm going to have all of those photos blown up and clarified. Maybe that will help me figure out what Brenda was checking. She knew Kessler and she had more information in her head than I do. She didn't need photos clarified or enlarged. She was there. I hope that if I blow up the photos I'll figure out her secret story."

"But what does this have to do with whoever killed her?"

"I'm getting to that. What if Ted Kessler's still alive and she's figured out where? Maybe she also had his photo blown up and aged so you could see what he looks like now." Grace excitedly explained the connection to the Poe story and how Ted Kessler could be hiding in plain sight.

"But why would he come back here?" TJ asked.

Grace's face went from passionate to dismayed. "That's a good question that I haven't figured out yet. But I'm working on it." She turned around and lowered the heat under the soup pot and added a lid. Then, "You know this Kessler kid was a loner and sometimes in trouble. Maybe he set those fires prior to the fire at his parents' house just to get attention. What if his parents found out and he had to do something fast? I've thought a great deal about Jeff Maitlin's description of a similar teenage boy who was a fire-starter. He had a lot in common with this Kessler. And if he were a sociopath, it wouldn't have upset him to kill his parents, especially if they threatened to turn him in."

"So why kill the other kid too, the one who was at their house that night — Lawless? Lawson? —"

"Nick Lawler. I haven't figured that out either."

TJ sat in silence and thought about her friend's ideas.

Grace checked the split pea soup and turned down the burner even lower so it would simmer. She pulled the good-luck charm out of her pocket and set it on the counter. "And then there's this."

TJ picked it up and examined it. "And this is — ?"

"A good-luck charm I took out of the cold-case box from the fire."

"You're carrying around material evidence? I should arrest you."

Grace laughed. "This case is over forty years old. No one really cares. You know I'll put it back. It reminds me to think about the facts. It has a hole through the middle, as if it were used for a necklace or bracelet. Or perhaps it was on a small chain like those old rabbit's foot good-luck pieces when we were kids." She shivered. "Yuck. I can't believe people kept those."

"So how will you use those photos?"

"Well," Grace began, "a good friend in Woodbury named Becca Baxter runs a software company and can do anything with computers. I called her, explained my problem, and asked her how to send these photos. She had me scan them at three hundred percent with a high resolution and send them off to her computer. I scanned the fire photos from the mid-sixties and the yearbook photos of Kessler and Brenda, Kessler's class photo, and a photo of the football team."

"The football team?"

"Kessler was on the team, but so was the kid who died — Nick Lawler. I couldn't find any other photos of him and I just wanted to see what he looked like."

"You have been really busy, Grace. What does your computer guru plan to do?"

"I don't understand all the ins and outs of it, but this is how she explained it. She would put the pictures in her editing program, clean up the dust and scratches, and sharpen them. She's really good at that so I think I'll be able to see faces better. After she gets the pictures clear, she'll burn the files to a jump drive and overnight it to my house."

"And this will tell you — ?"

Grace squirmed a little and poured the last drops of wine into her glass. "I'm not sure. But at least it's part of the puzzle that might help me see a little clearer."

TJ set down her glass, checked her watch, and stood up. "Sounds like an interesting puzzle to me, but I'll still put my money on Wakeley."

"I'll let you know if my information on the pictures can help you any. You may be right and —"

Her cell phone rang, Grace glanced at it, paused a moment, and then hit "ignore."

TJ looked at the screen on the phone. "Maitlin, huh?"

"He can wait." She looked at TJ for a few seconds. "What do you think of him?"

"Think of him?"

"I mean . . . what do you think?"

"Ohhhh . . . that kind of 'What-do-I-think?' Well, I don't know about you, but I'd say go for it."

"He seems like a pleasant person, attractive, intelligent, and it's hard to find someone like that in a small town — at least someone who isn't married. And that's not my style."

TJ scrunched up her eyes and answered, "I usually go for other — attributes."

"We've noticed." Grace smiled and arched her eyebrows. "You know, it's just so hard to meet someone, especially at my age. And those online dating services aren't really my style. I'd prefer to meet someone in person. And, speaking of online dating sites, how do you even know if a stranger tells you things that are true or not?"

"Well —"

"What if these online dating sites have psychopaths and people who lie through their teeth about who they are? You read about that all the time with sexual predators."

"I agree, Grace. After all, I keep telling you you're naive."

"It's just that I don't know anything about Jeff Maitlin, like how come he's single. Has he been married, divorced, or is he a widower? And what was his life like before he came here? If he's still single, at his age, what's the problem?"

"Probably good questions to consider."

"Did you know, TJ, that he knows all

about fires and sociopaths? He said he'd interviewed one at some small paper where he was working when he first started his career. What if it wasn't an interview? What if he knows a lot more about fires than he's letting on?"

"I know I keep telling you you're naive, Grace, but now you're becoming suspicious of everyone."

"Don't you find it coincidental that he came to town just before these murders occurred? We know nothing about him and we don't even know if his past — as he tells it — is true. Has anyone thought to check him out?"

"Why?"

"Maybe he's moved around a lot. Maybe he has a reason to do that — like fires?"

"Why don't you just ask him? Gotta go," and TJ headed out the back door. " 'Dear Abby' I'm not!"

Grace walked back to the stove and checked to see if the soup was simmering. Then she turned and watched as TJ crossed the street to her own house. Changing her thoughts, she shook her head gently back and forth. She picked up her wine glass and the good-luck piece on her counter and thought about her afternoon. She had only a few touches to put on her centennial stories and then she'd give them to Jeff. Her eyes narrowed. Maybe she should get on her computer and do some detecting herself — check out his background and see if he's been at other newspapers. After the parade on Saturday and the big dinner/dance on Saturday night, she'd be able to settle back and write her book reviews. She sighed. Somehow that prospect sounded bleak.

Chapter Twenty-Two

"Nice hair, Grace," Bill Tully said as he gazed at her newly arranged 1800s hairstyle.

"Lettie did that. We tried to figure out how to fix it to go with the dress for the parade. I haven't had the courage to pull it apart yet."

To change the subject, he remarked, with a smirk on his face, "Told you it was Wakeley all along."

It was Thursday afternoon and she had stopped by his sports bar for a cup of coffee and a piece of apple pie after turning in her stories for the centennial edition on Saturday.

"I wouldn't be too sure, Bill," she said, and stirred some cream into her coffee. "He's innocent until proven guilty, you know."

Tully shook his head. "Small town, Grace. Lots of talk, talk, talk. I heard, for instance that they found a gun that was registered to him out by the cemetery road."

"How do these things get out?"

"You'd be surprised what people talk about. We have a regular coffee group here in the morning that plays cards and they know everything that goes on in town. Don't know where they hear it. Must be a leak at the police department."

She took a sizable bite of apple pie and chewed it thoughtfully. "He definitely would have the knowledge to start a fire, but somehow I can't imagine a fireman doing that."

"Ah, Grace. They're just people like everybody else. When pushed against the wall they react like other humans. And I hear tell that sometimes firemen start fires because they're bored and want to have something to do."

"Really? That's crazy."

"Maybe so, but it's a crazy world out there." He put down the glasses he was inspecting and leaned over the bar. "You wanna know my theory?"

"Sure. Hit me with it."

"My theory is that Wakeley tried to break it off with Brenda when he decided to stay with his wife. They were hot and heavy — him and Brenda — in here on several occasions. I know Ronda noticed it. She saw an opportunity to make a little money and threatened to tell his wife. Other people in town were aware of him and Brenda here at the bar, but some folks just let people mind their own business. I can't believe no one else told Jennifer Wakeley." Grace noticed his eyes narrow and his face take on a darker look. "Maybe Ronda had other ideas. I know you like — liked — Ronda, but I gotta tell you, I've seen her when she's out for herself. And I've heard her opinions about people — not exactly kind. So if Dan Wakeley set that fire to kill Brenda — and he certainly knew how to do that — then maybe Ronda was his unfinished business. 'Loose ends,' as you often say. Anyway, that's my theory and I'm sticking to it."

He cleared some glasses and bottles and pulled them behind the bar, starting a steady stream of water running into a sink. While Grace ate her pie in silence, she thought about how his ideas could be plausible.

Then Tully moved toward her again and changed the subject with, "So, get your stories done for the paper?"

"Sure did. That's why I'm celebrating with your famous pie. My stories are in to Jeff Maitlin and the big centennial issue comes out on Saturday morning."

276

"Guess that means you can really feel retired now, Grace."

"I suppose." Her face fell visibly and she took another sip of coffee. "Somehow that doesn't feel like such an interesting idea. I wondered about what I'd do if I retired. Of course, I hadn't planned to step into Brenda's job because I didn't imagine that she'd die. To follow her research and write centennial stories has filled a void, since I didn't know exactly what I'd do when I stopped teaching." She sighed. "But even things you fall into have to end eventually." She looked at her coffee and poured a bit more from a carafe on the counter. "I still wonder a lot about that fire story."

"Fire story?"

"Yes, the one I talked to you about the other day — the Kessler fire."

"That's been so long ago, even before I got here. Seems like a lot of fuss for something no one much remembers."

"I hate to have loose ends — as you remind me. Know what I mean? I still think Brenda had some clandestine knowledge about that fire story. But I guess we'll never know." She started to say something about the photos she'd sent off to Becca but dropped the idea with a deep sigh.

Tully glanced at Grace's hand again as

she laid down her fork.

"So would this be a good time to tell me about that scar on your hand? I know I mentioned it before but we were both too busy that evening to talk much."

Grace looked down at her hand and held up the scar so Tully could see it. "I got it in college. A fire. I lived in an off-campus house and a fire broke out in the middle of the night. Both my roommates died, but I was rescued by the firemen. I look at this scar often and think about them — Gail and Robin — my roommates."

"I wondered about it but didn't realize it was a reminder of such a terrible event. Fires are sure strange creatures. They're so beautiful and yet so destructive."

She rubbed the scar on her hand. "I don't like to think much about fires. They frighten me."

"Makes sense," he replied. Then he turned and went back to his work while Grace took a few more swallows of coffee.

Tully washed glasses and cleared off items on the counter beneath the bar. Grace could hear him whistling a song she remembered from high school. After a few minutes he came back over to Grace and said, "You know, I asked somebody the other night about the Kessler farm — where it used to be and all. Jack Maddox. He's old enough to have been around back then. After you mentioned that story, I was curious about where it happened. He said the house is gone, of course, but the old barn still exists. Isn't much to look at but the walls are still intact. He said it never burned."

Grace was shocked. "Really? Who owns the land now? I had the impression the Kesslers didn't have relatives left."

Tully shook his head. "No clue."

Grace pulled out her phone and opened it to the notations app. "So where is it? Maybe I could still get a picture." She looked out the window and saw with dismay that it was already late afternoon. "Oh, looks like it will have to wait a bit. So what did Jack say about the site?"

"Well . . ." Tully looked up and thought about it for a moment. "He said you have to drive out on the old highway west of town, and if you count from Miller's Corner it's seven miles exactly and you hit a four-way stop. You get off on the right — a gravel road — and go another three-quarters of a mile. Watch for an old mailbox on the left and you drive in on the lane past that. The road takes you to what used to be the house, and the barn is maybe, oh, fifty yards away. He said you'd have to walk at that point 'cause you won't find a road from the house location to the barn anymore."

She looked at Tully and shook her head. "You'll have to repeat that so I can get it all down."

"I can do better'n that. I wrote it down as he told me." He pulled a small notebook from the shelf under the counter and tore out a page of paper. "Here it is. I can't swear that the directions are right — you know Jack Maddox — but they might get you there."

"Oh, Tully, you are a savior!" she exclaimed, re-energized from her funk about the end of her journalism career. "I had no idea that any building associated with the Kesslers still remains. I could get a picture of this before the story actually goes to press tomorrow afternoon. You are the best!"

He smiled at her childish enthusiasm. "All in the line of duty, Grace."

She glanced at her watch. "I still have time to stop at home, change clothes, and maybe drive over there to find the place. Then I could go back tomorrow and take some pictures. I'd be able to get them in the story before it goes to press late tomorrow afternoon. Oh, Tully, thank you, thank you. This will work out well to update the story."

"Sure, Grace. Good luck."

■ ■ ■ ■

Grace drove to Sweetbriar Court, thankful not to encounter too many Nub Swensens on the road. On the way home she considered what to take with her. Maybe she should call Deb and Jill to remind them about dress try-ons tomorrow morning. No. She needed to get out in the country before it began to get dark. She'd take care of that when she came back. Her camera? Should she take it? She thought about it as she ran up to the front door. No — too dark soon. She'd take it tomorrow to get the photos. Grace was a planner. She needed to find out where this place was. Even though she'd lived in Endurance for years, she didn't know the countryside or the farm roads well. She raced up the stairs to change clothes, grabbed a flashlight from the kitchen counter just in case, and tore back out the front door.

She set Tully's directions on her car seat and drove west through town toward the highway. All the while she thought about a brief write-up for the paper tomorrow that would bring the readers up to date on what the Kessler land looked like now. *This will be perfect,* she thought. *I can figure out the angles of the shots tonight and then get them in the daylight tomorrow before the newspaper goes to print.* She picked up Tully's notes and looked at the first direction about where to count the miles: Miller's Corner — Count seven miles.

By the time she reached the mailbox where she was to go on a path toward the site of the Kessler house, she noticed the light was already beginning to fade. She almost missed the turnoff because the gathering shadows covered landmarks. She turned left past the mailbox on a simple dirt pathway almost covered at times by vegetation that had grown over the path. She was surprised to see tire tracks in the dirt that formed a trail for her to follow. *Might be hunters at this time of year,* she thought.

She drove carefully over the tracks until they came to a halt in a clearing. Then she stopped the car and reached for her flashlight and cell phone.

"Ah, I can't believe I've done that again," she scowled. Her car had bucket seats and a console in the middle, and every so often she dropped her cell between the two. It was impossible to get her hand in the narrow space and she'd have to get out of the car, push her seat completely forward, and stick her arm under the seat and, if she were lucky, she'd find the phone. She sighed at the prospect and got out of her car, dropping her keys in her pants pocket. All around her Grace noticed how the shadows of dusk had crept in without her notice. The sunshine on the highway had given way to deep shade and she was glad she'd brought her flashlight. She started to retrieve her phone but decided, "Oh, I'll get it later. I'm running out of daylight."

She pushed the lock on the car door and began to consider which way to walk. Off to her left was a vast grove of thick trees, whose shadows crisscrossed on the ground. She saw what appeared to be an opening and thought it might have been a long-ago path toward the barn. "I'll try that way," she said to herself, as if she thought that talking out loud would make her less nervous. Night was closing in and maybe she should have waited until tomorrow. She could hear crickets chirp constantly and occasionally the trees rustled. *Wind or some animal?* She wondered. *Oh, this is silly. Come on you scaredy-cat.*

She silently trudged toward the break in the dark copse of trees. Watching the ground with her flashlight beam a few feet in front of her, she could see dirt spots where the grass had worn away. Shining her beam on the trees on either side of the path she could just make out as she went along, Grace hummed, hoping to give herself some courage. She thought about the lion in *The Wizard of Oz. Courage,* she thought to herself. *I will find this barn and then I'll come back tomorrow. It will be brighter in the daytime and I can get some great shots.*

She almost stumbled over a good-sized stone and heard what she identified as an owl hoot. *I hope this place doesn't have bats,* she thought as she glanced up nervously at the tree tops. Grace walked as carefully as she could and made good time. She considered the weekend plans to keep her mind off the sounds in the trees and the darkness. Jill and Deb would be over tomorrow morning to try on dresses, and then she'd come back out here and get the snapshots and take them to the newspaper as fast as possible. Jeff wouldn't send it to press until midafternoon, so she should be able to make his deadline. She looked down as she hiked and tried not to trip over any of the clumps of weeds and grass that had grown up in the makeshift path. The sun had gone down and now it was almost completely dark. *Maybe this wasn't such a good idea,* she thought. But just as she formed that idea, she came into an open area and saw a huge, dark structure that loomed in the shadows.

She shined her flashlight ahead of her and spied an ancient barn, crumbling but still standing. It was exactly like she imagined old barns to be — boards nailed together in various lengths, some rotting a little more than others. The roof was barely visible because trees had grown up, around, and practically enveloped the entire structure. The barn must have been red at some point because she could see flecks of paint still visible on a few of the pieces of wood that covered the front.

She hiked closer and discovered a piece of cement at an angle on the ground that probably led into the barn long ago. The barn door was a double door, closed with a two-by-four that sat on brackets. It didn't connect to anything now, and Grace decided that time and weather had moved it to this lopsided angle. Several feet to the left of the door was a miniature window in the wall and up high near the roof. *It must have been used to let air in to the animals,* Grace thought. Walking over to the small window, she shone her light through and up toward the inside ceiling of the barn. She could see the narrow boards, some splintered with age, which held up the underlying roof boards. Weathered and water-marked, they had deteriorated over years and years of neglect. *At least I don't see bats,* she thought. Hanging from some of the foundation boards were old wagon wheels and some farm tools that Grace had seen in museums but couldn't name.

Wow. This is like a museum in itself, she thought. She walked around toward one of the side walls, which showed through a hole in the overgrown trees and bushes, and she saw another window much lower than the one on the front of the barn. Shining her flashlight into that opening, she could clearly see piles of boards and pieces of metal from who knew what. All the barn contents looked as if they hadn't been disturbed in years.

She shined the flashlight around from corner to corner and saw an additional wall that must house a room in one corner. *Maybe it held tackle for horses and farm supplies,* she thought. Moving the light still farther to the left of that room, she noticed some objects that were out of place — red, modern-day gasoline cans, several piles of rags, and paper grocery sacks filled with something she couldn't see. *Those shouldn't be there,* she whispered to herself. So intent was Grace as she looked at the objects and tried to rationalize their presence with the dilapidated tools in the barn that she didn't hear the soft footsteps that stole up behind her. Suddenly, she felt a sharp pain in her head and all went to blackness.

CHAPTER TWENTY-THREE

A surge of smoke washed over Grace in the darkness, and it felt like a layer of smothering waves. *Not to panic. Calm. Don't get flustered. Feel your way.* But her blood rushed to her head, and she was covered in sweat, and her heart pounded. *This is so hard.* She covered her mouth to ward off the smoke.

She realized her eyes were closed. She opened them only to tiny slits. Still darkness. *Am I dreaming? My eyes are open. Why can't I see anything?* She moved her hands out from a blanket that covered her. She was on a hard floor. But she wasn't back in college. This wasn't college. *What? Where am I?*

She moved her head a little and groaned. "Ahhhh. Oh, my head," she moaned out loud. Her hands touched the light blanket and, exploring the blanket and floor, she realized she had a pillow under her head. *But where? Where was she?* The floor was hard, maybe dirt. The air was in-your-bones cold and the darkness was total. *This is no fire dream.* Her head pounded, and she thought if she moved it the pain would be worse. Gingerly, she placed her hand on her cheek and moved it cautiously around, over her ear, and toward the pain near the bobby pins Lettie had put in her hair. Grace felt a sticky, wet place and a clump of moist hair where the ache began. *Ahhhh,* she thought. *I must have had an accident. I hit my head?* She could feel her shoulders and neck ache too, infinitely painful as she moved each part of her upper body.

Pushing the blanket off carefully, Grace moved first her right leg and then her left. Something cold and hard touched her left ankle. She bent over from her waist, still lying on the floor, and moved her hand down her left leg. Trying to ignore the ache in her head and shoulders, she touched something solid, ice-cold. It felt like a circle, hard, metallic, cold, like the handcuffs TJ wore on her belt. She investigated it with her fingers and found a place where it latched. It was one of a set of handcuffs. But it was around her ankle. She reached farther down her foot and discovered that the cuff was attached to a chain of some sort, its mate dangling in the air. *What? What happened? Why am I tethered here in some dark place? Where is this?* She pulled tentatively on the chain and discovered that it had quite a bit of give. She inched it toward her, moving ever so slowly, and listened to it slither across the floor. Finally, it stopped. It was caught on something.

Shivering, she pulled the blanket back up over her and tried to think. *She was at Tully's bar having . . . coffee and pie. When was that? Hours ago? It must be dark now. Then what? She ate pie and talked to Bill and then she left to do . . . what?* Ahhh, her head kept up the dull, rhythmic pain.

She lifted her head gently, despite the pounding, and peered into the darkness. Her eyes started to adjust to her surroundings and she looked up — *oh, God, that hurt* — and saw a bit of light that came through some opening way up high.

"A barn. But how did I get in here? I was looking for Kessler's barn. I remember walking through the trees at dusk and I had a flashlight . . . where did it go?" she said out loud. She felt around on the floor but didn't find any objects near her. "My car. Somebody should see my car when it gets light. I just have to wait." And then she remembered the chain attached to her leg.

"I was walking toward the barn door and something hit me on the head. That's why the blood. Someone hit me. I've got to get up, got to try to find a way out. Whoever it was will come back."

She pushed off the blanket and used her hands to press up from the dirt floor. A wave of dizziness hit her and she stopped and took some deep breaths. Slowly she pushed against the ground again, untangled her legs, and got up to her knees. Another rush of light-headedness stopped her and she waited until it subsided. *I need to figure out this space if I can move far enough,* she thought. She could smell the mustiness of the barn, its dampness because it had been closed up for so long. She remembered looking in through a window and she thought she saw a room near the back with a door that had a piece of lumber across it, sitting on brackets. *That must be where I am,* she thought. She listened for sounds. It was totally quiet except for crickets. Then she heard an owl outside and realized that she could hear because the window up high was open. Maybe that was her way out.

Putting one foot on the ground, she pushed up from her other knee and suddenly felt wooziness in her stomach. She waited for the nausea to taper off and then pulled her other leg up, the left one with the cuff and chain. Now she could see the window up high — it had no glass — and it was open to the night. The light source was a full moon whose edge she could barely detect on one side of the squared opening. The pale light was just enough that, as her eyes got used to the darkness, she could make out black shapes in the room.

"Time to explore," she said to herself. "Let's hope nothing but me moves."

Going in the direction of the chain, Grace followed it with her foot and then barely caught herself as she almost fell over something on the ground. She knelt, put her hands out, and discovered the chain was attached to a ring shaped like an "O" that rose up from a small slab of concrete into which it had evidently been sunk. She placed her hand on the metal ring and pushed. It was immovable. Sitting down next to it on the dirt floor, she tried to move the metal "O" but it wouldn't budge. Suddenly, the impossibility of escape hit her like a blow to her chest. She felt a rush of anxiety and her breath came out in gasps. *Calm,* she thought, panting. *I have to stay calm. Breathe. Breathe. Slowly. More deeply.* Her breathing evened out a little and she waited, motionless.

Once she reached a degree of composure, she stood again — this time a bit more easily — and began to edge toward the nearest wall. She placed her hands on it and felt the wooden boards. Then, slowly, she crept along the wall, probing each board, and occasionally she wiped a cobweb off on her pants. Her foot touched something solid and she reached down, seeing the shadow in the dim light from the window. It was a pile of small boards stacked up against the wall. Inching past them, she once again situated her hands on the wallboards and edged a few feet until she felt the corner of the room. Pausing for a second, she followed the wall past the corner, moving her feet slowly sideways to make sure she didn't fall over any unseen objects. Her foot touched something solid and she reached down tentatively and discovered a wooden crate, open at the top, and propped up sideways against the wall. It was empty. The owl hooted again somewhere outside the barn, and she could hear the trees rustle in the wind.

Grace moved past the crate and touched her way down the wall. Suddenly, she felt a bit of give in the surface. She pushed on it. It must be the door. She moved her hands along the surface and found hinges. Pushing on it again, she could feel a little give, but it must be locked on the other side. Then she remembered that she saw the piece of wood across the brackets inside the barn. She sidestepped over and felt her way around the edge of the door from the top and down the side. No doorknob. No handle. No nothing. It was perfectly smooth, so you could only open it if you took the wooden piece off the brackets on the other side.

Until now she thought she might find a way, despite the chain, to get out. But now the desperateness of her situation caught up with her and she slid her back down the wall and dropped to the floor. Tears formed in her eyes and her chest began to heave in deep sobs. "Ahhh." She winced as she realized it hurt her head more to cry, but her misery outweighed her pain and she wept until eventually she had no more tears — only pain and throbbing and darkness and the dejection that came with the impossibility of escape.

It was totally quiet now, except for the sighing of the trees outside and the occasional hooting of what she began to think of as her friend, the owl. *I'm going to die here alone,* she thought. *Whoever hit me will come back.*

And then it was still and shadowy all around her.

She straightened her sore shoulders and aching head and thought to herself, *I won't let them defeat me. I need to stop feeling sorry for myself and find a way out of this.*

TJ. What would she be doing now? Why wasn't she looking for me? They should miss her by now. Of course, she didn't even know what day it was. Maybe it was still the same night that she came to the barn. Or maybe it was Friday night. TJ and Deb and Jill and Lettie. They'd know she was missing. Why, they might even have a search party out for her already. She felt for her phone in her pocket. *What had she done with it? Left it at home? In the car?* Then she remembered that it had fallen down between the seat and the console in her car.

No, I'm through crying, she thought. Maybe someone was in the area. She could yell. Maybe someone would hear her. She stood up and moved over toward the wall with the window. Then she looked up, put her hands around her mouth, and screamed, "Help! Someone help me. I'm stuck in the barn. Help!" and she repeated it three times for good measure. Her head hurt so badly, and she felt so dizzy after the gargantuan effort that she had to sit down again before she passed out.

Silence. Only the crickets and the owl listened. *But people will know I'm missing,* she thought. *They'll look for me. I need to be ready when they come.* And she began to massage her shoulders and neck with a gentle, circular motion. Now she could hear a new sound: her stomach growling. *How long was it since she had eaten?*

"Ah, I guess that depends on what day it is, or what night," she muttered.

So, we can check off screaming. What's next? She pulled on the chain and found it to be strong and unbreakable. *Can I find some solid rock or something I can use to smash this chain?* The only items she could touch or see in the room were wooden boards and that crate. So that left the handcuff around her ankle. She felt it and found the tiny keyhole that kept it latched. No use thinking about that.

Why would someone do this? And who knew she was out here? Not Lettie — she'd been too rushed to leave a note. And if I ever get out of here I'll hear about that from Lettie. She laughed.

Why, oh why, didn't I wait until daylight when I could get those pictures? She tried to come up with what she had told people over the past week. Again and again her mind returned to the Kessler fire and the good-luck charm and her assumption that Ted Kessler was still alive. She tried to think about how old Ted Kessler was. *The fire happened in 1968. Ted Kessler would have been about fifteen. That would make him fifty-eight today. Come to think of it, everyone in town knew I was working on this story. Endurance has a lot of fifty-eight-year-olds. Tully must be that age and he sent me out here.*

But why did he put me in here? Why would Bill Tully do this to me? He's always so friendly. Why not just kill me? And how could he pass all this time when he's really Ted Kessler? Wouldn't someone have known him? And when will he come back? If it's still Thursday night, everyone will be out at the fireworks tomorrow night. I have to think about how I can get this chain off, she thought.

So far nothing came to mind. If she could get the chain off, maybe she could find a way to get out of the barn without using the door. She walked over to the far wall again and presumed that the door was on the inside wall of the barn opposite this wall. Getting down on her knees, she felt near the barn's foundation. The wall came down solidly on the dirt floor. She moved along the bottom of the wall boards and felt for a place where the wall and ground didn't meet, perhaps an opening she could enlarge. Moving a few inches at a time, she came to a spot — her fingers could feel a space between the wall and floor. *I could use the corner of one of those boards to dig out some of that dirt, and possibly create a space where I could crawl out. Well, I could crawl out if I could figure out how to get the chain off.* "One problem at a time," she could hear her mother's voice in her head. "Yes, Mother." Then she wondered if she was becoming delusional from lack of food and water and a large knot on her head. *Perhaps,* she thought, *but it's a plan.*

She wobbled cautiously back to the corner of the room and used her hands to feel the ends of the boards in the stacked pile. "Ouch!" she said out loud as she felt a splinter go into her finger. She put the board down and tried to feel the end of the splinter to pull it out, but it broke off in her fingers. "Great. One more pain." She moved several boards over to the area where she planned to dig and thought that if anyone came back she could cover up the opening with the other boards. She'd have to feel it, however, since it was still really dark. Using the corner of a board, she pushed it into the dirt as hard as she could. The dirt was solid but not impossible to move. *This may take all night,* she thought. *Well, what's time?*

Grace worked at the escape hole and then took a break when her shoulders and arms got tired. She began to see a little more light in the room. She looked down at her wrist to check the time and then remembered she didn't wear her watch anymore. *Now that was a stupid decision, Grace.* It must be near morning. At least with light she wouldn't feel as isolated as she did in the dark. She worked steadily and listened to the voices in her head.

Grace under pressure, said Hemingway. She almost laughed out loud at the play on words. *Trust thyself: every heart vibrates to that iron string,* from her old friend, Emerson. *It's not the size of the dog in the fight, it's the size of the fight in the dog,* Twain wrote. And her mother's voice said, "You're stronger than you think, Grace. Believe in yourself."

By the time the light was brighter and she could see her surroundings, Grace had a decent, wide — although not very deep — hole near the wall. She quit digging and put the boards in front of the hole in case Tully came back. She'd work on it more in the daylight once she'd rested for a while.

Exhausted, she sat down again, her back supported by the wall. Her head still pounded, but it didn't feel quite as bad as before. She thought about what she had seen when she approached the barn with her flashlight. It might help to remember what the barn looked like when she tried to make her escape.

Escape? Who am I kidding? She thought. She pulled on the chain again and now in the daylight she could see that it was solidly attached to the ring in the floor. She examined the cuff around her ankle and pulled on it, but her effort produced nothing but scrapes on her skin. Collapsing against the wall again, she examined her memories about the barn. *Huge double door, wagon wheels, farm implements, a door in the back . . .*

And then her anxiety came back . . . *Gasoline cans and rags.*

CHAPTER TWENTY-FOUR:
TJ

TJ relaxed in her squad car at the corner of Main Street and Lincoln Avenue. On her way to a meeting of the murder task force, she had time to drive around the main part of town and look at the burgeoning decorations.

Everywhere people had attached signs, streamers, and red, white, and blue bunting. Banners hung from the street lights on both sides of Main Street. On the corner, the Penny Saved Shoe Store had plastered their windows with colorful drawings of shoes worn at the time of the town's founding and colored by one of the elementary school classes. Across the street the Clip 'n Curl Hair Salon had arranged dummies in the window with various hairstyles from the early 1800s. The Senior Center, First National Bank of Endurance, and Maloney's Law Offices had bunting hanging over their windows and balconies, and Mildred's

Boutique had window dummies dressed in fashions from the 1800s, probably borrowed from the college costume department.

As she drove into the next block, TJ blinked twice before she realized it was only a realistic mannequin of a woman who held a book in her hands outside Harlow's Bookstore. The book was a copy of a simplified Endurance history written for elementary schoolchildren by the librarian and printed by Stafford's Printing Company, a local business. Everywhere she looked TJ saw red, white, and blue, along with signs, banners, and pictures of the town's earlier days. All of Endurance wanted to get in on the centennial celebration. *How surreal this seems,* she thought, *when we're in the middle of two murder investigations.*

She took a sip of her coffee and listened to a dispatcher's message over the radio. Driving past Tully's she saw the usual cars of retirees who played cards at the bar each morning. Otherwise, all was quiet there. She saw Patrick Gilmour walking out of the restaurant, a black satchel in his hand. *Grace probably had him in school, too. Slipped outside the back door during gym class and smoked pot. And sold it. Now he's selling legal drugs for a drug company. Who says high school doesn't get you ready for the real world?*

TJ knew what was normal for the area during the morning hours and nothing unusual stood out. No unusual behavior, no one running except the familiar joggers. Farther up the street near the Endurance Grain and Dryer and The Feed Service she noticed the carnival people had just pulled into town to set up a Ferris wheel and rides for the kids. *An extraordinary Friday morning in Endurance is on the horizon,* she thought, *and I'm working on two murders.*

Turning the corner at North Pine Street, she drove to the police station, glanced at her dashboard clock, and pulled into her parking spot at 7:55.

As she unlocked her office door, TJ glanced up at her whiteboard, or, as she called it, her rogue's gallery. Wakeley was now at the top of her suspect list and cooling his heels in the jail downstairs. So far he'd admitted nothing and his lawyer, Frank Becker, was in to see him as soon as they booked him. He had no priors, unlike Mike Sturgis who had a list a mile long. So far Wakeley's wife hadn't been in to see him.

"Sweeney," Chief Lomax barked as he stuck his head in her door. "Meeting now in the conference room. Rafferty's here, along with two other detectives they could spare from Woodbury."

"On my way, Chief." She left her gun and badge in her desk drawer and locked the door, following him to a room filled with men and one woman. Collier and Williams sat at a conference table, and Corey Rafferty stood with two other men she didn't know. The only other woman was the district attorney. Lomax did the introductions and all sat down with papers and reports in front of them. Ten minutes into the discussion of evidence to pin Wakeley to both the murders, TJ's phone vibrated. Pulling the cell phone out of her pocket, she glanced at the text message as she held the phone under the table. It was from Jill Cunningham. "Grace not home for dress fitting. Know where she is?"

She probably just forgot, thought TJ. She quietly texted Jill back with "No, in a meeting." Then she double-checked to make sure she had turned off all sound. The discussion continued, Corey Rafferty concluding that they had ample evidence to hold Wakeley and the district attorney, Sharon Sorensen, mentioning a bond hearing the following day. "Unlikely the judge will let him out when his gun was found at the scene of Ronda's murder," said DA Sorensen.

304

"Does anyone find it unusual that Wakeley is too good a candidate for these murders?" TJ spoke up in the silence.

Rafferty's head yanked up from the table in TJ's direction, disapproval on his features. "What do you mean?"

"Well, I mean his gun is found near the scene, he gets a blackmail note from the first victim, he has no alibi that is rock solid, he knows about fires, and he just happened to report his gun missing a week or so earlier," TJ said.

The chief looked at her in amazement. "I thought you told me you had him nailed to the wall yesterday. Why, now, have you changed your mind? He's the perfect suspect."

"I know Dan Wakeley and I've watched him in action at fires. He isn't stupid. Sure, he knows how to start fires since he's had a lot of training. And sure, he and his wife went through a tough stretch, which Brenda Norris took advantage of, but somehow he doesn't appear to be your typical sociopath or pathological liar or just plain killer. And if he killed either or both of them in a fit of passion, he doesn't appear to be sweating from a guilty conscience. My gut tells me this could possibly be a setup."

Corey Rafferty dropped his pen and said,

"That's crazy, TJ. We've got this guy dead to rights. Of course, he turned in a stolen gun report because he planned to use the gun on Ronda Burke. And he had every reason to kill Brenda Norris because she planned to take away everything he had: his wife, kids, reputation, job, you name it. I think I'm a bit more objective since I don't actually know these people. This is an open and shut case."

"You may be right about objectivity, Corey, but to know these people and their personalities and history isn't always a disadvantage. We have to explore what ties the two victims together. Ronda met someone she planned to blackmail." She paused and said very distinctly, "We don't know — nor have we proof — it was Wakeley who planned to meet Ronda. We have to ask if Ronda's murder was separate from Brenda's murder — something Ronda knew that had nothing to do with Brenda — or did Ronda find out about Brenda's murderer and decide to blackmail that person? I think that gets to the heart of the issue and we don't have that piece of the puzzle. We still have a line of people who were angry with Brenda. If it isn't Wakeley, if he's being set up, we still have a murderer on the loose in Endurance. Or possibly two murderers."

Chief Lomax broke in to their debate. "At this point our best evidence points to Wakeley. But if you want to pursue other lines of thought, you're free to do that, TJ. Corey and Sharon can continue to build the case against Wakeley. I'll have Corey interview Wakeley, with his attorney, this afternoon."

"Works for me," TJ said as she eyed Corey Rafferty across the table.

The meeting broke up and TJ looked at her watch. She had about thirty minutes before another roundtable the purpose of which was to lay out everyone's responsibilities for the centennial celebration this weekend. She went to her office and put in a call to Jill.

"Jill, what's up with Grace? Are you sure she didn't have somewhere to go this morning and she forgot?"

"You may be right, TJ, but she seemed so excited about these costumes. Her house is locked up and her car is gone."

"I'll give Jeff Maitlin a call. Maybe she's at the newspaper office."

"I already did. He hasn't seen her since yesterday. She told Rick Enslow she was going to have some coffee at Tully's yesterday afternoon to celebrate the finish of her stories. You might check with Bill."

"Right. I can do that. I'll check with him

after I'm done here. Thanks, Jill."

At the department meeting, TJ discovered she would be on duty for the parade the next day and the shootout reenactment at the bank Saturday afternoon. In a small-town police department she wasn't just a detective. Sometimes she pulled patrol duty, too. But Collier and McGuire had the fireworks tonight. Satisfied, she drove over to Tully's.

She walked in, sat down at the bar, and ordered lunch from Eva Sandoval.

"Tully around?"

"No, TJ, he's gone for the day. His truck had a major repair problem and he had to have it towed to Woodbury. Rod Simpson did the towing and Bill said he was going with him. Probably get back tonight or tomorrow morning. He was so mad — we expect a lot of business because of the centennial."

"You haven't seen Grace Kimball in this morning, have you?"

"Grace? No. She was here yesterday afternoon, but I haven't seen her today."

TJ finished her pulled pork sandwich and drank the last of her diet soda.

After paying her bill she walked out of the bar and glanced at the photos of the town's history on the wall. Her eyes stopped at one

in particular — the fire photo at the Kesslers' house back in the late sixties. She
turned and walked back to the fire photo
and studied the details. The faces were
impossible to make out, although she recognized the deputy fire chief, Richard White.
The entire two-story house was in flames
and the firemen with their high-powered
hoses fought voraciously, but they grappled
with a losing battle. The ample crowd that
watched must have heard of it by word-of-
mouth. TJ was impressed by the number of
spectators in the middle of the night. But
the quality of the picture was too poor to
make out individuals. *Grace was sure that
Kessler kid was still alive.*

TJ glanced silently at the photo one more
time and then strolled out the front door.

CHAPTER TWENTY-FIVE

"I'm telling you, TJ, Grace is missing. You need to get over here right away." Lettie's frantic voice pounded through the phone.

"I'm on my way," TJ responded. She put on her badge, holstered her gun, and was out her office door in three minutes. *Where in the world could Grace be?* She thought. *This makes no sense.*

It took her five minutes to drive to Grace's house, and as she went in the front door, Lettie was immediately on her.

"Oh, TJ, thank God you're here. I can't find her anywhere. Car's not in the garage. Clothes from yesterday are in a heap on her bed. Obviously, she didn't sleep in her bed and that's not like Grace. Not like her at all," Lettie sputtered. She marched from the living room to the kitchen, talking non-stop.

TJ followed her. "Take a breath, Lettie, a deep breath. Now, sit down a minute and go back to wherever this starts."

Lettie moved toward the kitchen counter, poured two cups of coffee, and sat down in a chair. TJ followed her lead, glancing at the clock on the wall. It was almost six o'clock. The fireworks would start in a few hours.

"I got here mid-morning, as always, picked up dishes and odds and ends in the kitchen. I put some chicken out to defrost and noticed I didn't have any carrots to —"

"Whoa," TJ put up a hand. "Cut to the Grace part."

"Well, I was getting to that. Just hold your horses." She stood up from the chair, started walking around the kitchen, and continued. "The problem is, I didn't go upstairs. Didn't even think about it. Or look in the garage. Why would I? Figured she was down at the newspaper office. So by the time I got the stuff for the chicken and made some dishes for dinner I realized it was awful quiet around here."

"Grace would usually be home during that time?"

"Well, of course. She's been spending lunch out and staying at the newspaper until late afternoon, almost supper time. You know, her stories had to be finished. And today she was supposed to be done with those stories, so I figured she'd be home

311

early. Where could she be, TJ?"

"Good question. You went upstairs?"

"Yes, and, like I said, her clothes from yesterday are in a heap on the bed. That's not like her at all. She must have left in a hurry. What can I do, TJ? She's never done this before. This isn't good. I just know this isn't good."

"Is anything else missing? Was anything out of place when you came in this morning?"

"Nothing was out of place. Her purse is gone and her cell phone." She glanced around the kitchen and immediately her eyes locked on the counter behind TJ. "And a big flashlight. She always kept it there on the counter near the back door. It's gone."

"Anything else?"

"Not that I can think of. Suppose she's been kidnapped?"

"Highly unlikely."

"What explanation is there?"

TJ thought a moment. "Someone might have come along and invited her out somewhere."

"And she took a flashlight with her in case she needed to bash them over the head?"

"Hardly."

"So what are you gonna do about it?"

"I can put an APB out on her car and see

if anyone has seen it."

"A what?"

"An All Points Bulletin," TJ answered. "I'll have Myers pull up her license plate and get that on the scanner."

"What else?"

"Are you sure her cell phone is gone?"

"I haven't seen it anywhere."

"Let me try to call her." TJ pushed the speed button for Grace's cell phone and waited. Lettie watched her, hoping that Grace would pick up. "Nope, it went right to voice mail."

"What do you want me to do?" Lettie asked.

"You might go upstairs and see if you can figure out what clothes she's wearing. I don't know if you can, but if you know what she wears, you might notice something missing. It would help if I had a description."

"Sure." Lettie marched up the back staircase, headed to Grace's bedroom.

TJ walked around the downstairs. Nothing was out of place. *That was a good sign,* she thought. She strolled through the dining room to the office and saw Grace's briefcase. Opening it, TJ found several papers with research about the centennial stories. Again, nothing seemed out of place or torn or unusual. She walked over to an end table and looked at the photographs. Several were of Grace's three children — Roger, Katherine, and James — and a few were of Jill and the rest of their group. Grace's favorite photo of Roger was always in the same place. Behind a couple of the frames sat a photo of TJ when she graduated from high school in her cap and gown, and Grace was next to her with an arm around her. She picked it up and studied it.

I owe you my life, Grace Kimball, and if you're missing — which means you're also in trouble — I will find you. Please let it be in time.

Lettie came into the room. "Looks to me like a pair of denim capris, canvas shoes, a brown T-shirt, and — let me check the coat closet — ah, yes, a light jacket that's beige. I call it beige and she calls it tan." She sniffed. "Of course, I'm right."

"Okay, Lettie. Thanks. I'll find her. You might stick around in case she comes back on her own. Call me if that happens. Meanwhile, I'll get on it."

Before the detective could get out the front door, Lettie grabbed her arm and forcibly turned her around. "TJ, she's gonna be okay, isn't she? You'll find her, won't you?"

"Absolutely, Lettie," and she was out the door and into her car.

CHAPTER TWENTY-SIX:
GRACE

Grace stopped digging and assessed her progress. She could probably get her head, arms, and legs through that hole, but she definitely needed it deeper if she was going to get her middle through without getting stuck. *Winnie the Pooh and the Honey Pot,* she thought, remembering the story she used to read to Elizabeth. Time to take a break for a few minutes and then go at it again. Of course, the hole wouldn't do her any good if she couldn't get this chain off her ankle. She'd have to think about that problem, too.

It was still light out and she decided it must be Friday. She hadn't heard any fireworks during the darkness last night so it must have been Thursday. If tonight were the centennial fireworks, everyone would be there, but Deb and Jill would have found her gone this morning when they were supposed to be trying on dresses. *Who else would figure it out? Does TJ even know where the Kessler barn is? They have to be looking for me by now.* Her mind raced, searching for answers.

She was thirsty, tired, and her ankle was bleeding a little where the handcuff chaffed. Her stomach had stopped rumbling hours ago. She thought about Lettie at her house. *I didn't leave her a note telling her where I was going. She's probably angry. I'll have to tell her she's right about that one when I get out of here. If I get out of here.* She looked around at her little world and decided it was time to start digging again. Swallowing hard, she tried to loosen tense muscles.

Grace crawled over to the wood pile and found her "shovel." All the while she thought about how she could get the cuff off her ankle. She worked steadily, making the hole deeper and pushing the soil through to the outside. It was getting more difficult because the dirt was harder and rockier the deeper she went.

She heard a sound and stopped digging to make sure she wasn't hearing things. Cocking her head to the side, she listened, her senses heightened. No, it was a noise like the doors opening at the other end of the barn. She actively strained to hear any other sounds and turned cautiously, searching for

317

potential weapons. Her wood — she'd need to move it quickly. She quietly stacked all the wood pieces in front of the hole as fast as she could. Then she pulled herself over to the far corner, waiting to see what happened. The piece of wood holding the door closed made a sliding noise as if someone were pulling it out of the brackets. Grace bit her lip and her pulse raced. Then the door slowly opened and Bill Tully stepped in, carrying a couple of plastic sacks.

"Grace. Hope you slept okay last night. Sorry I had to hit your head but it seemed like the simplest way to get you where I wanted you. Brought you a bottle of water and a sandwich. I would have come sooner only the bar was pretty busy what with the celebration going on and all."

Grace relaxed her tense muscles and her eyes narrowed. She looked at him and said, "Tully? Why are you doing this? Why are you bringing me food?"

"I tried to warn you to let that fire story go. You're too persistent. And when you talked about that good-luck charm, I realized you'd have to be disposed of. You're just too smart for your own good, Grace."

Speechless, Grace shuddered and heard her heartbeat pounding in her ears. *How could he talk in such a matter-of-fact voice about disposing of me?*

Sensing her confusion, he said, "Oh, don't worry. It's all right. You're going to go down in history. That should make you feel really special." He looked at his watch. "It's about seven-thirty and the sun will be down soon since it's July and it stays light. But not long from now it will be dark and the fireworks will start. Everyone will be there and won't really be thinking about anything else. Endurance will get another glorious fire, far better than the one at Brenda's. I'm sorry you won't be here long to see it but think of your immortality. You'll become part of the town's history just like the Kesslers."

Tully sat down on the crate and handed her the bottled water and sandwich wrapped in waxed paper. *I should keep him talking as long as I can,* she thought. *Don't make him angry. I'll need as much strength as I can muster so eating isn't a bad idea.*

She reached for the sandwich and then stopped. "How do I know you haven't drugged this or something?"

"You shouldn't do drugs. As a teacher you should know that. I consider you a friend. We've known each other for a long time. Here, take it. You need to keep your strength up."

Grace tried not to look at him strangely.

319

What world was he living in? Keep my strength up? She used careful words, hesitating and clearing her throat. "I thought you considered Brenda your friend, too. That didn't seem to keep you from killing her." *Get him talking — keep him talking,* she thought. She took the sandwich and bottle of water.

He chuckled. "Brenda." He shook his head. "She was too smart for her own good, too. Just like you. She had to snoop and try to figure out that fire story. Fortunately, like so many other folks, she drank too much, and that meant she talked too much. You'd be surprised how many people do that with bartenders. I knew when she didn't recognize me that I'd done a perfect job. Dyed my hair black and my contacts changed my eyes from blue to brown. Of course, it had been about forty years since she'd seen me. I've become broader and a lot older. But I knew her immediately. What a job I did of hiding my old mannerisms and acting like someone named Bill Tully. I'd had years to perfect that. Even hid the scars from the Kessler fire. My beard covers most of them and a little shoe dye helps the spots where a scar kept my beard from growing."

Grace balled up the piece of waxed paper and put it on the dirt floor. Then she drank deeply from the bottle of water. The cap was still tight so she assumed he hadn't doctored it either.

"Brenda had a spectacular funeral pyre. The secret is taking away the starter. It 'hinders the investigation,' as the fire chief would say. Too bad the fire department got there so quick. I was hoping that wouldn't happen. If I hadn't killed her she would have eventually figured it out and bled me poor with her little blackmail schemes. She told me about those, too, you see."

"How could you do that when you were such good friends in high school?"

"Friends?" he scowled. "Brenda and I were never friends. It was Ted Kessler she ran around with."

Grace stared at him, trying not to gasp. "Ted Kessler?"

His darkness turned to laughter. "That Judas? He's long dead, Grace. See, that's one of the things I learned at the Kesslers — about Judas, the betrayer."

She cleared her throat and said in a soft voice, her breath catching, "Nick Lawler. So your friend Ted is buried in your grave."

"And a very fine resting place it is, Grace — better than he deserves — looking out over the meadow and wild flowers."

"Was the coin with the raven on it his?"

Nick Lawler's face darkened. "That damn,

stupid thing. He wore it around his neck. He was always talking about it. Some author he liked wrote a poem about a raven and Ted was always quoting lines from it."

That must be how Brenda figured it out, thought Grace.

Lawler swiveled to the side on the wooden crate and reached into the other plastic sack. "And now, Grace, something special. You're going to see something only Ronda Burke has seen. Well, and me, of course. After all, I am the designer. This is special. I look at it a lot." He pulled out what looked like a scrapbook to Grace. Opening the cover, he held it up so she could look at it, as if she were an eager child and he was reading a book to her.

"See, here are the fire stories from the early fires Ted and I set. I'd never really had a friend before, Grace. He loved to watch fires as much as I did once I showed him how to set them and how beautiful they were as they burned. Here's the barn we set, our very first production. Pretty, huh? Course in black and white you can't see all the incredible colors. And there we are on the civilian lines watching the firemen put it out. But they didn't save much. We were too good. No one even guessed."

"What about Ronda? How did she see it?"

He snapped the book shut and stood up, menace on his face. "I'm showing you these masterpieces and that's all you can talk about? That piece of crap, Ronda?" He took a step toward her and she shrank back in the corner trying frantically to think about what she could do to calm him. Her legs were weak and she looked down and calmed her trembling hands.

"No, Bill, er, Nick. I'm interested. Sit down again. Show me."

He stopped moving toward her and frowned. "I thought you would like these photos, Grace."

"Oh, I do, Bill, I do. Show me more."

He sat back down and turned some more pages, describing the fire that burned most of the downtown, barely escaping when a policeman was checking doors on his regular rounds. His voice rose and his face became animated. "This was practically a whole block, Grace. A clothing store, doctor's office, shoe store, pharmacy, and even the bank. It was the best fire we set and people were talking about it for weeks and weeks."

"That is a beautiful fire, Bill."

"You can call me Nick, you know, if you want. Only you know about my name now and I know you won't tell. It's been years since anyone's called me that."

She stared at him, especially his mad eyes and crooked smile, and figured it would be best if she went along with his self-indulgent story. Her mind fumbled, searching for something to say. "I'm so used to calling you Bill, it's hard for me to think of you as someone else."

"That's all right, Grace. You can call me Bill. You know, no one else has seen this but Ronda, and that wasn't because I showed it to her. That sneaky, lying bitch. She figured it out from Brenda's stories at the bar. When I was gone one day, she got into my apartment and found this under a lot of stuff in my desk drawer. She wanted fifty thousand dollars. What else could I do?"

"I agree. People aren't supposed to get into your private things. That was so wrong of Ronda. You must be right about her. But she was killed with Dan Wakeley's gun, Bill. How?"

"Oh, that's the good part. She thought she was so smart. But she wasn't as smart as me. You should have seen her face when I met her out at the cemetery and pulled out that gun. She had a purse with her but couldn't get to it fast enough. When I looked in it and got rid of it I found a little handgun that would hardly have killed a flea. Clever, ha! The only bad thing is that no one else could find out how much more clever I was. Only you, Grace."

"The gun? Dan's?"

"Oh. Well, the night he got drunk in the bar and the cops came in and took him home, I found his handgun in the truck's glove compartment. I'm good at picking locks — it came in handy, especially in Tennessee. The police had Wakeley at the top of their list. It was a thought I had about using it down the road if I needed it. I've got a gun but it isn't registered."

"That was very clever. Even Sweeney wasn't sure that Dan was innocent. You're right. He's been her top prospect for Ronda's killer. Pretty slick, Bill. Quite ingenious."

His eyes narrowed and he pulled out a knife from a case attached to his belt. "Don't patronize me, Grace. I know I'm clever. The police haven't caught me yet and they never will." He moved over toward the pile of wood in front of Grace's hole. Her breath caught and she almost forgot to breathe. Shocked, she watched as he picked up a small stick and went back to the crate. Sitting down, he began whittling on the stick. She let out her breath. Then she looked down at her hands and realized she had dug her fingernails into the palm of her hand.

"So how come you burned down the Kesslers' house? And why were you living with them in the first place?"

"Well, I wasn't. Not exactly. I just stayed there sometimes. Remember you asked me about my past and I told you it was a long story? Well, I have time now." He looked up toward the window. "Isn't dark yet."

"So how did that happen?" Grace sat back, trying to look like she was comfortable and he didn't scare the hell out of her. Softening her features, Grace loosened the death grip on her hand. She felt the area of the sore spot on her head where she had been hit. The blood was dried. She also felt something else — Lettie's bobby pins — and that made her remember Roy Trotter.

CHAPTER TWENTY-SEVEN

Grace thought it still looked light in the barn, but it was definitely less light than a while ago. She hoped that by now someone had missed her back home and TJ was figuring out where she was. What was taking her so long? Her only chance was to keep Tully talking so that TJ would have time to find her. Watching his beady eyes, she knew that she needed to keep him focused on talking about his cleverness so he wouldn't go over to the wood pile and see the hole she had dug out. Her mind racing, she fumbled for something to ask him.

"So, the Kesslers?"

"That takes a bit of explaining. Hmm — we've got time. You see, I was actually born in Washington State. It was right after the war, 1950, and my old man and mom had four kids already. He also had a disability that kept him out of the war. Them times during the war were good, according to my brothers. Odd jobs kept them in food, but once the soldiers came back, work was hard to find."

"I can imagine," Grace said. She tried to sound empathetic, forcing her voice to remain calm. "So what's your earliest memory?"

He looked down at the piece of wood he was carving. *It must be a nervous habit,* thought Grace. *Something to keep his hands busy.*

"My earliest memory?" He looked up and pursed his lips. "Hmm . . . probably being hit so hard I flew across the room. My old man. Don't remember what I'd done. Maybe cried too much. Must have been four or five. Mostly I followed my older brothers, but they didn't want me hanging around with them. So they'd spit on me and occasionally hit me and tell me to go home. Left me with my mom. I was too young to know that she couldn't keep off the sauce. Alcohol — her drug of choice. Figured that out later. But when I was little she mostly drank cheap stuff and slept a lot of the day. So I just kinda figured out how to entertain myself. Guess that's where I learned about being alone."

Grace hesitated, her mind racing, and she renewed her cautious words. "How did you end up in Endurance when you grew up in Washington?"

"My old man heard about a construction job back in Illinois. Some guy just passing through. By the mid-fifties construction was doing pretty good since a lot of tract houses were being built once the soldiers were back. He managed to get us there somehow. Don't remember much about that." He looked up from his whittling and pushed the pile of wood shavings around with his foot. "Got a job building houses. One day he was working on a roof and he fell. Claimed he was hit with a two-by-four from another worker who didn't like him. Might be. He could be an ugly son of a bitch when he wanted to be. He landed on his back and it was broke. Between surgery and rehabilitation, he got hooked on painkillers. Never worked again that I can remember."

"Didn't your brothers work?"

"Oh, some. But they were mostly out of the house by then. I haven't seen them in, oh, twenty, twenty-five years."

Grace shifted her leg and rubbed the area where the handcuff had scraped off some skin. She kept trying to think of questions — anything to keep him talking. "So how did you get to Endurance?"

"I was fourteen when that happened, but

I was pretty scrawny. My old man could still put some pain on me. One of the guys my dad worked with was moving to this little town he'd heard of, and we weren't doing much good in Rockford, so I guess my parents decided to hitch a ride. We had to steal to get enough to eat and get clothes, and I got good at stealing and picking locks. I went to school but not exactly all the time. I was used to getting hit by then. But eventually I got big enough my old man couldn't beat me anymore. I'm sure I was a forgettable kid at school. My mom drank steadily and my old man collected his check and bought more painkillers, legal or not."

Grace forced herself to look at him and said, "You seem to have done pretty well for yourself despite the sporadic days in school."

"Well, Grace, I learned. I was pretty good-looking in high school. Course my hair was brown and my eyes were blue, not like now. But I could mostly charm the teachers and talk the girls into just about anything. I finally figured out if I was friendly and helpful, I could get what I wanted. Stealing came naturally since my parents taught me young. But you know, I looked around, especially at them, and thought maybe I was born for better than this. I just knew I could do better than they had. Maybe I was destined for great things. I just couldn't figure out how."

Grace looked at his face as he talked. *Jill had been right,* she thought. *He did come off as charming and earnest even when he was planning to kill you.* She took a deep breath, willing her hands to unclench.

He must have noticed her hand movement. "You know, when I look at that scar on your hand, I kinda figure it's destiny that we're friends and that you understand me."

Grace put her best "understanding" face on, but all the while she was thinking about what a despicable person he was and how he had, indeed, fooled everyone. *But not Brenda,* she thought. *And not Ronda.*

He was still scraping wood off the stick he'd picked up and talking along as if he were explaining his entire life to her. She acted like she was listening and cocked her head to one side. But behind her careful attention to detail, Grace was thinking about Lettie's bobby pins.

"Didn't want to kill the Kesslers. They kinda took me in, you know. I met their kid, Ted, on the football team. Coach talked me into it. Guess he thought I was big enough to play ball. But I didn't have money for shoes and he said he'd take care of it. It wasn't as if he felt sorry for me. He was just kinda matter-of-fact about it. Ted Kessler played on the team and we started talking. I'd always been alone before. He didn't care about my folks — where I came from. Anyway, they'd had a fire at a shed on their farm and William — that's his dad — called the fire department because he was afraid it would spread too fast and get some other buildings. Changed my life."

"What do you mean?"

"I can still see it. Those flames going up to the sky. They were beautiful, all orange and shadowy and it almost seemed as if they were going up to heaven." Grace watched the rapture on his face as if he were seeing the flames just yards and years away. "And then the firemen arrived — nothing exciting ever happened in my life till then. I watched them the whole time they were there, looking at their uniforms and equipment and seeing how . . . how they were thanked by everyone that came by to watch. Like nothing I'd ever seen before. And as I thought about it, I realized I could make that happen. It was powerful stuff."

Grace watched his face transform into a smile and an almost trance-like state. *I've got to get out of here,* she kept thinking. *He's insane.* She wrapped her arms around herself, willing her legs to be stronger.

"The only thing bad about the Kesslers was that they kept after me about going to church and becoming a Christian and being kind to people. I went once. That was enough. They wanted to change me into something I didn't know nothing about. I listened, kind of going along with them for a while. Ted was there too but, despite all their goody, goody words, he'd climb out the drainpipe near his window at night and we'd go out and set fires.

"But the Kesslers would talk about it at dinner at night, about all the farmers who'd lost livestock in the fires. They said some of the fires were wiping people out. And Ted began to change, to feel guilty, like what we were doing wasn't right, wasn't 'Christian,' he'd say. And he began to talk about confessing what we done. I couldn't have him do that, could I? So I waited and thought about what I'd do." Grace noted his feverish eyes and determined tone.

"William and Terry — those were their names — let me stay at their house, even overnight in their guest room. They called it that — 'the guest room.' Of course they didn't know Ted and I slipped out a lot. So I stopped by my parents' and stole some of my old man's pain pills. He'd never miss them, and she was always so drunk she wouldn't know what was going on. And I crushed them up and doctored their milk that night. They slept like babies. And I moved Ted to the guest room and used gasoline all over the first floor. By the time it hit the upstairs they'd never know. Worked perfectly." He hesitated, then smiled at Grace and added, "Fire trucks came out and it was the best fire — by far — I'd ever set."

Grace shivered again and thought about how she could get out. The longer he talked, the crazier he sounded. He appeared to be enjoying himself, as he explained with such pride things he'd probably never been able to tell anyone. And now it was getting dark outside. She could barely see the front of the barn through the door he'd left open. Adrenaline rushed through her body and her breathing quickened. She would have to be ready the moment he left.

"I watched the Kessler fire from some trees back of the house. After it took the house to the ground, I headed out of town figuring no one would miss me and they'd all think I died in the fire. Sure enough, everyone thought it was me that died and Ted who set it. After that I worked in a lot of places, mostly washing dishes or cleaning bars. Every so often the fire bug would hit me and I'd set a place and leave again. Mostly traveled through Tennessee, keeping out of trouble."

"So why'd you decide to come back here?"

"Well, this is home, at least the only home I'd ever stayed at for more than a few years. I found I could pass as Bill Tully. I'd saved a bit of money for a down payment on a broken-down bar, and I talked some people into loaning me the money to fix it up. I could always do that, you know. I became a 'respectable' community member and no one knew. No one suspected. I fooled them all. Here I was, a seventeen-year-old high school dropout, and I owned my own place. And it would have stayed that way if Brenda hadn't come snooping around. But I took care of her and Ronda, too. And after tonight, no one can tie me to any of this."

"I have a feeling TJ will figure it out."

"Nah. I'm too smart, Grace. No one's caught me yet. Not Sweeney, not anyone in town, and, after tonight, not you."

"Someone will see my car, Bill." *And I'm hoping the battery in my cell phone hasn't run down.* She uncrossed her knees and pushed up her sleeves. A fluttery feeling in her chest told her the time was close.

"Don't think so, Grace. Moved it back in

the trees. Even a helicopter couldn't find it. I'll get rid of it once I set the fire. Shouldn't be hard."

Grace thought, her jaw firmly set, *I don't think so, Tully. I think I'm smarter than you.*

"We're friends, Grace. But I can't let you tell people about me. Don't worry. It won't take long. And you're used to fires; you said yourself that you'd already been in one. Maybe you were supposed to die in that one. That's what I thought about when you showed me that scar on your hand. You cheated death that time. A death is owed. Now here you are again with an imminent fire. See, I'm just making things right."

He laughed as he stood up to leave. "Just think, you'll have a ringside seat to my most beautiful creation."

Tully moved over to the door and reached for something Grace couldn't see. As he came back she could tell he was carrying a gasoline can. Her eyes widened, her breath caught, and she could feel her legs starting to shake. All the strength she had gathered drained out of her like air leaving a pinpricked balloon. *He can't mean this. It can't be happening again. But this time I can't get out. This time I'll have no one to rescue me.* She pushed herself back to the corner, clutched her arms to her chest and pulled herself in, willing her body to curl up in a ball.

"I'm just going to let this soak in for a while before it gets dark," he said. He moved around the edges of the room pouring gasoline on the lower parts of the wall, covering the box he'd been sitting on and the pile of sticks she'd so carefully piled up against the wall. Then he came over to her and poured the last few ounces down her back and legs.

"Ahhhh," she screamed as the cold liquid went down her back. She couldn't breathe and her chest tingled. Her whole body shook with chills.

"There. That'll make sure it goes up fast. I'll get the front part of the barn next. It's starting to get dark and the fireworks are probably about to start. Guess this is good-bye, Grace."

The fumes from the gasoline were overwhelming and her heart pounded as she thought about what he had done. Cowering in the corner, she couldn't look at him as he walked out the door. She could hear him splashing gasoline around the main part of the barn. It was getting dark and she didn't have much time. He'd left the door open so the fire could get back to her faster. Grace couldn't quite see what he was doing out at the front of the barn, but she figured it would only be a short time before she would start smelling smoke. She thought about her children and TJ, Deb, and Jill. She thought about Lettie. She could see Robin and Gail's faces and the house they'd lived in. Her memory roamed over every inch of that house and the night the fire had started. She pressed her lips together, pulled her shoulders back and thrust out her legs. A gathering feeling, a sense of purpose and calm, a shrugging off of terror washed over her.

"I may have given up before," she said to no one but herself, "but this time I'm going to get out. See if I don't."

CHAPTER TWENTY-EIGHT:
TJ

TJ drove back to the station from Grace's house and on the way she called the desk. "I want you to look up Grace Kimball's license, car make, and model, and put out an APB on her car."

"Got it. What's the problem?"

TJ explained the situation and said she'd do a cursory pass around the spots where Grace might be. After driving down Main Street and the public square, she turned and headed east toward Tully's. She even checked around the back but found no Kimball car. Then she drove over to the Historical Society, thinking Deb might have left it open late. Nothing. It was as if Grace had disappeared off the face of the earth. She glanced out her window. It was starting to get dark, enough that the street signs were hard to see. She was just about to go back to the station when she had another call from Lettie.

"TJ, come back. You gotta see this."

"What? Is Grace back?"

"No. But I got a package for her that was just delivered — by a special courier. Must be something important. Should I open it?"

"Yes, and tell me what's in it." She heard the strip being torn off the package and the rustling of paper. Then it was quiet for a moment.

"It's one of those oblong computer things — jump drives, I think Grace calls them. And there's a note."

"What's the note say?" TJ asked with amazing patience.

"It's from somebody named Becca Baxter. I think that's a friend of Grace's. She says she got the photos as clear as she could get them and she hopes they will tell Grace what she wants to know. Hmmm . . . wonder what that could be about."

"I know what it's about. Grace had her blow up some pictures and make them clearer. I'll be right over."

TJ could hear Lettie begin to cry, her voice quivering in an uncharacteristic way for Lettie. "I don't like this, TJ. She must be in trouble."

"I'm working on it. Just hang on till I get there."

She made it to Sweetbriar in record time

and raced in the front door. Lettie met her, red-eyed, and TJ gave her some quick assurance and left for the police station, jump drive in her pocket.

In minutes she rushed in the door and asked Myers which officers were on shift that night.

He looked up from his computer screen. "Collier was put on the fireworks. Jake Williams is around — back in the break room."

"Good. Taking Williams with me. We've got a missing person — Grace Kimball — and she's in trouble. I need Jake for backup since everyone else is on the centennial stuff. Call Jake up to my office," and she took off running down the hallway to boot up her computer.

Jake came a few minutes later, and TJ explained Grace's newspaper research, the Kessler fire, and the photo blowups as she brought up her computer program and stuck the tiny oblong in the port. He stood behind her, peering over her shoulder. The drive appeared to have three photos on it. One was labeled "football," one said "two teenagers," and the third said "young boy."

The first picture was the one of Brenda and Ted Kessler sitting in the hallway outside their lockers. TJ scanned the photo, checking for any detail that would give her a clue about what Grace suspected. Brenda Norris stared at her from the screen but TJ couldn't see anything unique or unusual about the teenage Brenda. Her eyes moved over to Kessler, who was in a short-sleeved shirt, jeans, and boots of some sort. She moved in, magnifying the photo, and could see that he had a chain around his neck. "Oh, shit," she said out loud as she saw the edge of something attached to the chain. "That explains a lot. Let's bring up the 'young boy' photo."

She pulled up the second photo of Ted Kessler. It was his school picture and Grace's friend had enlarged it considerably so it was much clearer and larger than it had been. TJ immediately checked out his neck and saw the chain once again. But this time the charm attached to it was clear — a circular disk with a raven in the middle. "Unbelievable. They got the wrong guy."

"What are you talking about?" Jake asked.

"I'll explain it to you when we get in the car. But for now I have to check out the football team picture. I think I already know what I'm going to find."

She pulled up the photo of the Endurance High School football team. TJ could now see the faces clearly. She scanned the jerseys and came to the number thirty-two. Then she looked at the names identifying the players and realized what had happened. "Nick Lawler, number thirty-two. But we know him by a different name, don't we, Jake?"

He leaned over TJ's shoulder. "He looks really familiar to me but I can't quite place him."

"You can't recognize him because he was only seventeen back then. Today he's in his late fifties and owns the sports bar downtown."

"Bill Tully."

"Jake, do you know how to work the software program to trace a cell phone with GPS?"

"Yes, but we can call the cell phone company and have them triangulate it. That would be faster."

She wrote a number on a piece of paper. "Good. Go out to Myers, get that done ASAP, and have them find Grace Kimball's cell phone. Here's the number. And below it is my cell number. Have the phone company pinpoint the location for me. Tell them it's an emergency — we're in a hurry."

"Gotcha." He started out of the room as she added, "And Jake, bring extra ammo for your gun."

She checked her gun and then pulled an

extra magazine from her cabinet. Then she holstered her gun on the right side of her belt and the magazine in a carrier with her handcuffs on her left side. She thought she knew where Tully had Grace and, with any luck, they could get the location quickly and verify her guess. She just hoped that Grace's cell phone was on and the battery wasn't dead.

She said to herself as she went out the door, "I think I know where she is, even without the cell phone, but better have that as a backup." She met Jake at her car and they headed west out of town.

"That phone company had better be as fast as you say. If I'm wrong about where Grace is we may be too late." TJ's fingers clenched on the steering wheel, her knuckles white with strain.

"Way I understand it, the technology's so accurate these days a wireless carrier can let you know a phone's position within about three hundred feet," Jake replied.

"Keep talking. Helps my nerves to listen. How does it do that?"

"Her phone has a software app running in the background. She isn't even aware of it. Because the app uses GPS positioning, the provider can send us pinpoint accurate information. And that's not even the best part —"

"And that's — ?"

"You don't need a warrant anymore to check the location. So we're —"

TJ's cell phone went off and she handed it to Williams.

"Williams here." He was silent, listening intently. "Okay. Thanks." He turned to TJ and said, "Sounds like a pasture up ahead. How did you know?"

The red emergency lights flashed eerily onto the trees and Jake felt the car speed up. "The old Kessler place. I believe there's still a barn left standing." She gripped the steering wheel tighter and stared into the night, watching every movement of the lights on the road. When she saw the mailbox she was looking for, she turned onto a dirt pathway and shut off the emergency lights.

Through clenched teeth, she hissed, "Pray to God we're not too late."

CHAPTER TWENTY-NINE: GRACE

The sandwich and water Tully had brought gave Grace a second wind. She could think much better than she could when he first came into the barn. Shivering from the gasoline that felt colder and colder on her legs and back, she kept calm and ratcheted up her resolve. "I know I can do this, but I have to keep my head," she whispered to herself so if Tully were nearby he wouldn't hear.

She scooted over to the cement where the chain was connected to the ring in the ground. Feeling with her fingers through the darkness, she found the key lock on the handcuff. *There it is. Now if I can only manage to do this by feeling what I need to do.* She pulled one of Lettie's bobby pins out of her hair, stretching it out until it was one long piece of wire. Then she stuck the edge of the pin under her shoe so she bent it up. It was shaped like an "L." *There has to be a way to trip the spring, a way to get it to come open by applying some pressure to the key-hole.*

Silently she thanked her former student, Roy Trotter. Her last assignment before retiring was to have her seniors do demonstration speeches. He'd brought in a pair of handcuffs and, surprised, she asked him where he'd gotten them. He'd found them in one of his parents' bedroom drawers, he explained with a pained look on his blushing face. It was all Grace could do to keep from laughing. Roy said he'd slip them back before they found out. Then he demonstrated to the class how to open handcuffs using a bobby pin. *Bless you, Roy Trotter,* she thought. *And if this works I'm going to find you and hug you . . . and maybe your adventurous parents, too.*

Using her left hand to feel her way to the keyhole, she stuck the bent end of the bobby pin into the lock. She applied some outward tension and twisted down. Nothing. No spring came open.

Then she smelled what she had dreaded ever since she felt the gasoline dribble down her legs: smoke. Tully had evidently lit the fire out near the front of the barn. She could see the beginning of flames moving quickly across the barn floor outside her room. *Hold yourself together, Grace, and do it again,* she told herself, trying not to let her hands shake. She put the bobby pin into the keyhole a second time. *Concentrate.* This time she went in at a slight upward angle. She applied tension outward the way Roy had shown her and twisted it down. Suddenly, she felt the spring open and her ankle was free. *Amazing what an English teacher can learn when she listens to her students.*

She moved over near the opening and tried to look out without sticking her head clear out the door. Everywhere she could see orange flames — the whole front of the barn was on fire and the flames were almost to the room she was in. She clutched her throat, her hands trembling. Adrenaline kicked in and she woke from her motionless state and tried to close the doors into the barn but they wouldn't budge.

I need to check and see if I got that hole big enough. She kicked all the wood pieces away from the wall and threw them behind her, thinking the fire might get to them first, lick its chops, and gobble up the wood before thinking about moving forward for a few seconds. She stuck her head and arms through the hole easily and then started crawling out into the grass. *Ahh . . . fresh air,* she thought, breathing in deep gulps. She'd almost cleared the barn when her back caught on the wood at the bottom of the wall. She tried to move more slowly, feeling the wood scrape into her back. Inching forward, she winced as pain hit her in waves. But she knew she had to get out and scrapes and abrasions were a small price to pay.

Suddenly, a voice shouted loudly, "Ms. Kimball, hang on and let me help you!"

Looking up, she saw Jake Williams, a wonderful sight that she would memorize and remember forever. He clawed at the boards above her and she could hear splintering. Then she felt some of the splinters hit her back, but she was, thankfully, released, and she half-crawled, half-slid out with Jake's help. She turned over on her sore back, winced, and stretched out her arms.

But her languor wasn't to last. Jake helped her up to her feet and said, "We need to get out of here. Tully's still on the loose. TJ had him cornered up at the front of the barn while I checked out the back. Come with me and stay close."

Grace could see he had a gun drawn, and he took her over to the cover of some trees as they circled around to the front of the barn. The trees were like silent sentinels, tall poplars, dark on one side and lighted on the other by the flames from the barn.

She followed Jake, wobbling slowly, looking around in every direction. Every foot seemed like a mile and, with weak knees, she stuttered across the grass. Now it looked like daylight, the flames leaping up to the sky, soot falling, and smoke cascading out the front of the barn. *This must be what Brenda's house looked like,* she thought, tilting her head to the top of the barn. Then, turning, she could see TJ's squad car and she could also hear sirens in the night. Someone must have called the fire department.

Jake suddenly stopped and motioned to her to look up in front of them. She could see TJ behind the open door of her squad car in a silent and focused tableau. Her rifle was balanced on the car door and aimed up high at the window of the barn, her face a study in concentration. Grace and Jake circled wide and rounded the front of the barn but at a wide angle so they could see the flames and the doors and TJ. As Grace looked back up at the window, she saw a solitary figure in a challenging posture, standing and looking down.

Bill Tully had gone back into the barn, climbed a ladder to what was left of the hayloft, and was standing in the window. He had a gun in his hands, and the next thing Grace knew, he'd fired it twice toward TJ's car. Sweeney took a shot and Grace saw Tully jerk back as if she had winged him on an arm. Suddenly, Grace's terrified eyes saw the entire loft fall inward and down into the flames with Tully trapped in the middle of it. She screamed and covered her eyes.

And then TJ was there, her arms wrapped around Grace, hugging her. The detective pulled back and asked, "Good God, Grace, why do you smell like gasoline? Are you trying to kill yourself?"

And Grace, ignoring her question, stammered something about a "Roy Trotter."

Then she collapsed.

CHAPTER THIRTY

Grace glanced around the faces in her hospital room — the hospital had insisted on keeping her overnight for observation. *Seems kind of strange to me, since they usually rush you out the door before they've even examined you,* thought Grace. "Observation" meant they wanted to patch her back and put her on an IV to help with dehydration. She had been in shock when TJ brought her in. Now she was feeling relaxed, her hands loosely clasped in her lap. For some reason she cried easily. That just wasn't like her.

TJ had already chastised her for making them both miss the fireworks. Grace had called and talked to her children in Arizona. She was a bit teary with them, but she kept saying she needed to talk to them and loved them. TJ explained that when a terrible shock happens, it makes you feel better to talk with people you love, even if it is long-distance. She promised Roger, Jr., she would fill him in on her near-death experience soon when she felt more like talking about it. For now it was just enough to hear their voices and tell them she was alive.

Deb and Jill came and went. They brought a beautiful vase of pink and white flowers — roses, baby's breath, carnations, and lilies. Deb explained that they were so worried when she didn't show up for the dress fitting on Friday morning.

"And to think you were in another fire and escaped again!" Deb wailed, putting her arms around Grace and hugging her until Grace had to loosen her arms from her painful back. Jill declared, with her usual perfunctory air, that they were going to have to keep a closer eye on her in the future. After consoling each other about Grace's narrow escape, the two women left to go to the parade, promising to send her lots of photos.

Then there was Lettie. She brought in five copies of the morning newspaper so Grace could read her stories, presumably five times. Lettie had heard the story of the hairpins that helped Grace get out of her shackles — "And to think I put those pins in your hair and they saved your life! Wait till Mildred and Gladys hear about this!"

Lettie gasped.

"You are my hero, Lettie," Grace commented, trying to keep the humor out of her voice.

"Now, Gracie, I've moved some of my things in to stay with you for a couple of days so I can take care of you just like the old days," Lettie said, patting Grace's arm.

TJ looked over Lettie's head and winked with amusement at Grace, who smiled and took the bad news with stoicism.

Lettie sniffed, adding, "And I hear Dan Wakeley's moved home with his wife during a fragile truce. We'll see what happens there. Gladys said that Mike Sturgis was at Patsy's Pub, drunk as a skunk, and declaring he'd sue the police department for false arrest."

"That should be interesting," said TJ, "since we didn't arrest him."

"Well," Lettie said, "you know that Mike Sturgis doesn't have the brains of a snail. I knew he couldn't kill anybody because he'd probably shoot himself in the foot or set his pants on fire."

Grace laughed and then groaned because laughing hurt her back.

"Oh, that reporter, Kelsey Karnes, called and wants an interview. I told her to leave you alone until you felt better," Lettie reported.

"I'm sure that went over well," said Grace.

"I'm off to see what needs to be done at the house before the parade. You'll be home sometime this afternoon and I will be all ready to nurse you back to health. Got soup simmering on the stove already. See you later." And Lettie was out the door.

"Oh, TJ, please save me from this fate," Grace said as she stretched her beseeching arms.

"Sorry, Grace. You're the one who gets yourself in these messes. Now you have to pay your dues. By the way, we recovered Tully's gun from the ashes and debris. No registration, of course, and no serial numbers. Seems ironic that he died in a fire of his own setting."

"He told me he loved the flames." After a pause she added, "How did you find me, TJ?"

"Ah, that's magic, Grace. Just good detective work. We like to keep the inner workings of our investigations on the down-low."

"Can I join in this conversation?" asked Jeff Maitlin, sticking his head in the door and bringing Grace a bouquet of daisies.

"Hi, boss. Those daisies are just beautiful. Thank you."

"Looks like you have some other admirers, too," he said, and pointed to three other flower arrangements.

"Better that I get them in the hospital rather than the funeral home," she said soberly. "We were just talking about Bill Tully."

"I hear he admitted killing a lot of people," Jeff said, looking over at TJ.

"He told Grace he killed the Kesslers because Ted was going to turn himself in for those fires years ago. And he killed both Brenda and Ronda to keep his secret."

Grace added, "So perhaps old Ben Franklin was right. Three can keep a secret if two of them are dead. Unfortunately for Tully, other people figured it out. He was an unhappy man, abused and neglected when he was young, and able to lie with ease as an adult. I felt a little sorry for him."

"Grace!" TJ walked over to her bed. "He was a cold-blooded sociopath who didn't care about anybody, and he could tell the truth as easily as lies. It didn't matter who stood in his way and their lives meant nothing to him. He doesn't deserve your sympathy. He tortured you with the idea of fire. He'd have killed you in a horrifying way if you hadn't outsmarted him."

"I'll second that," Jeff said. All three of them were silent for a moment.

"What I don't understand," said Jeff, "is

how they could have been so wrong on the identification of the Lawler kid — Tully — in the first place."

"I can help you with that," Grace said. "I've thought about it a lot. When I talked to Deputy Chief White he said that they didn't have any dental records on the Lawler kid or Ted Kessler. The parents, yes. And back then they wouldn't have had fingerprints on file unless Kessler or Lawler had been arrested. It wasn't like today when parents routinely have their children finger-printed in case some ugly event happens down the road. No DNA either in 1968. So the fire chief simply used the location of the body — the extra bedroom — to identify it as Lawler's. Tully, er Lawler, was counting on that so he could just disappear and start a new life."

TJ glanced out the window and then turned back to Grace. "I did some checking on the background he gave you about Ten-nessee and Kentucky. At least two depart-ments were uneasy about him. He seemed to turn up at fires. He was questioned at least a couple of times about suspicious fires and they had his fingerprints on file as Tully. The departments faxed fire photos from three different towns and there he was — watching right on the front lines. They didn't have enough information on him to hold him, and since he never left any kind of starter material, they didn't have an MO to try to match a pattern. He just favored gasoline, and heaven help the person who got in his way."

"I'd agree, Grace. No sympathy," Jeff seconded and glanced at his watch. "And I need to change the subject for a moment. I fired Shannon Shiveley. Hate having sniveling, lying employees, so she's gone. That means I'm short on news reporters. Thought you might be willing to help a bit from time to time if you think your future novel can spare you."

Grace was silent.

"Nothing? No reaction?"

"I was already thinking about how retirement is going to seem a bit tame compared to the last week. But despite the excitement, I'd rather not live through that last week any other time in my life." Her cell phone began playing "Nine to Five" and she hit the decline button. "It's Jill. I'll call her back."

Jeff laughed. "Do I have a ringtone?"

"Sure. You want to hear it?"

He nodded. She pushed the buttons and the mellow sounds of "New York State of Mind" started playing.

Jeff smiled. "Perfect. So if you continue to work for the paper, it doesn't mean you need to dig up any more murderers. But I do want you to put in a story about Tully and explain the facts about the Kessler fire. It's about time Ted Kessler had some peace."

"I'd be glad to do that."

"And consider further employment?"

"Yes," Grace said, a wide grin on her face.

Jeff let out a deep sigh. "So when are you blowing this joint?"

"Probably as soon as the doctor comes in and releases me."

"I hear Lettie has the sickroom set up at your house."

"Oh." Grace put her head back and looked up at the ceiling. "This may be more than I can bear." She gave TJ a martyred look.

"I have a suggestion," Jeff said. "Of course, it depends on how you're feeling."

"And what might that be?" Grace asked, her features softening.

He walked over closer to the bed where Grace was sitting up on the edge, her legs dangling over the floor. "If you're feeling up to it, let's go to the dinner and dance tonight. At least you'll get to see a little of the celebration. You've already missed most of it."

She looked at Jeff with a bemused smile. "Sounds like a great plan to me. Of course, Lettie will probably have a curfew for me."

"Ah, I can take care of Lettie," he smiled. "Pick you up around six p.m. Don't know about the dance part. You're still pretty sore and tired, I'd imagine. We could always watch the dance part."

"Thanks, Jeff. My back is still pretty sore."

"Well, off to the parade." He turned, waved to TJ, and left. Grace looked at TJ and said, "You know, he has the most beautiful periwinkle blue eyes." Then she sighed.

TJ lifted one eyebrow quizzically. "Well, I just have one question before I go."

"Yes? How did I get out of that barn? How did I manage to leave my cell phone on so you could find me? How did I happen to dig a hole under the wall? How did I keep Tully from killing me before he set the barn on fire? Fire away! Well, maybe that wasn't the best way to put it."

TJ gave her a quizzical look. "Who is Roy Trotter?"

"Ah," she said, lying back on the bed. "Ow. Darn back." She sat up again. "That is a secret, my dear TJ, that you will not hear from my lips. I have to keep some of my secrets to myself."

"Hmmm." TJ walked over to Grace and added, "I'm glad you're still with us."

For a moment Grace was silent. Then her eyes filled with tears and she said, "I'm glad you found me. Thank you, TJ. You are the best of friends, and I owe you my life."

The detective smiled and gently shook her head. "Seems to me you've been amazingly lucky so far. I think maybe you should stay away from fires. Three might be a charm."

After TJ left, a nurse came into the room with a thermometer and blood pressure cuff. The nurse said, "All right, Ms. Kimball. We just need one last reading and you can check out. I think your sister-in-law has been called to come pick you up."

Grace let out a deep breath. She looked at the nurse and thought to herself, *Clarissa Durdle, one of the good ones. She did her term paper on Florence Nightingale and it was superb.*

EPILOGUE

Saturday, October 1, 2011

Grace glanced at the yellow, gold, orange, and red leaves adorning the trees in a perfect Midwest fall tableau. *This is why I don't live in Arizona,* she mused. She glanced at her three children and granddaughter, hoping they couldn't read her thoughts. She could imagine what they probably texted to each other after she'd called them from the hospital a few weeks ago — M call U 2? Did she cry this time? Think we should go home and C her?

A gentle breeze blew some of the leaves on the ground and they rustled, brushing up against each other and swishing across the grass. Soon the green blades would be dying and the cold November chill would start to set the stage for winter. But for now it was enough — the beauty of the fall and the sun shining down on the groups of people standing nearby.

After Grace's stories appeared about the misidentification of Ted Kessler and the details leading up to the fire at his house, Jeff Maitlin spearheaded a drive to amend a terrible wrong. The funeral home donated flowers and the townspeople gave generously, hoping to put a closing chapter on this miscarriage of justice. Jeff had even twisted Mike Sturgis's arm and gotten some money out of him. Grace smiled when she remembered she'd been suspicious of Jeff.

The minister was just finishing the short graveside service. No longer was there a small stone moved off yards away from William and Terry Kessler. Now the couple was joined by a grave and a coffin that had been exhumed and moved. She looked at the newly carved gravestone and read the words:

"Theodore Austin Kessler, Beloved Son, 1952–1968."

Grace looked at the faces of her townspeople as she listened to the words of the Reverend Ellis Groves. Most of her neighbors had turned out, and she saw faces of people she had met when she first moved to Endurance and faces of their children whom she had taught. "This is where I belong," she whispered, her lips barely moving.

As she stood next to Ted Kessler's grave, she sorted out the conflicting thoughts she'd considered as she occasionally rested on the sofa surrounded by her books in the aftermath of the murders. No more fire nightmares since the death of Nick Lawler. It was as if a burden had been lifted, an understanding that she was stronger than she knew. *Thank you, Mother.* And then she considered the retirement issues. Teacher Grace had been feeling used up, sad, unhappy about no longer being in a classroom. That feeling was balanced by her realization that she'd accomplished some good. Every time she turned around she saw another former student who had become part of her memory — some more than others.

She smiled and almost laughed, but TJ's elbow jabbed her side, reminding her where she was.

Grace looked across the grave at the faces of her friends — Deb, Jill, and Lettie — and she thought about how she had cheated death twice. Perhaps she was being given more time for a reason. Maybe she was supposed to stick around.

She decided she had more stories to write, more wrongs to right. Maybe a novel set in her little town could be entertaining. Lord knew Mayor Blandford and his wife Polly were great material, and so were the eccentric characters she saw every day. The town's history could use more research, and putting it on paper would be a perfect project. Who knew what she might dig up — another old murder or two?

The service ended and people began to turn and leave the cemetery in small groups. She crossed over to her children and hugged each of them. Then she explained that she had something to do and she'd be home shortly. She turned to Jeff Maitlin and they both walked over to his car. He opened the trunk and they picked up two bouquets of flowers. They crossed the road and walked up a path where they put one bouquet on each of two new graves — one for Brenda Norris and the other for Ronda Burke.

"After all," Grace told him, "I knew them a long time and loved their better qualities. Even now I could name them for you." She said a brief prayer over each grave. Then she said to Jeff, "I need to do one more thing before we leave. Please go ahead and wait for me at the car. I'll be right there."

She turned and marched back over to Ted Kessler's grave. Leaning over, she pulled a shiny object out of her coat pocket, a small metal circle with a raven's head, and laid it on top of the coffin. Then she turned and motioned to a man from the funeral home who was waiting to remove the chairs and green carpet. She had recognized him earlier when they walked into the cemetery for the service.

"James Trotter, I just knew that was you." A young man — probably in his mid-twenties — with long brown hair hanging into his eyes, turned and smiled as he recognized her. She was thinking, *I remember he was suspended for making a peephole into the girl's locker room his junior year.* She sighed. *I guess it is my teacher's fate to remember these silly things forever.*

She smiled back at him and said, "James, I need to get hold of your brother, Roy. Do you have his college address?"

ABOUT THE AUTHOR

Susan Van Kirk, was educated at Knox College and the University of Illinois. After college, she taught high school English in the small town of Monmouth, Illinois [pop. 10,000]. Some of Grace's fictional memories are based on that experience.

Van Kirk taught an additional ten years at Monmouth College, where she also began writing. Her short story, "War and Remembrance," became one of the chapters in her creative nonfiction memoir, *The Education of a Teacher (Including Dirty Books and Pointed Looks). Three May Keep a Secret* is her first Grace Kimball Endurance mystery. She divides her time between Monmouth, Illinois, and Phoenix, Arizona, where her three children and nine grandchildren live. Currently, she and Grace are headed for another adventure.

The employees of Thorndike Press hope you have enjoyed this Large Print book. All our Thorndike, Wheeler, and Kennebec Large Print titles are designed for easy reading, and all our books are made to last. Other Thorndike Press Large Print books are available at your library, through selected bookstores, or directly from us.

For information about titles, please call:
  (800) 223-1244

or visit our Web site at:
  http://gale.cengage.com/thorndike

To share your comments, please write:
Publisher
Thorndike Press
10 Water St., Suite 310
Waterville, ME 04901